LINSENBIGLER

THE BEAR

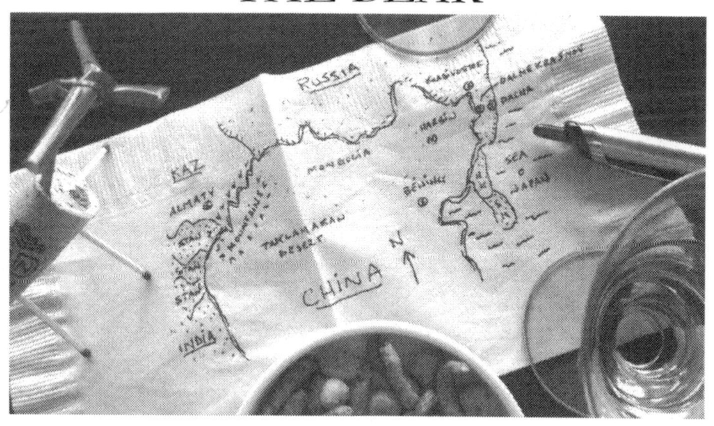

BRIAN M. WIPRUD

Cover, editing and interior design by Conglomerated Publishing, a subsidiary of Conglomerated Beverages, purveyors of fine cocktail ingredients world-wide.

Cover Insert Graphic: "The RMS Queen Mary" Interboro News Co. (Postcard) 1940. Rear Cover Background Graphic (Excerpt): "1799 Clement Cruttwell Map of the Russian Empire." Cover formatting and layout by Jamey Jackson and Skip Baker.

ISBN-13: 978-1974210534

DEDICATION

For Joanne, as ever and always.

ACKNOWLEDGMENTS

Many, many thanks to Helen Hills, Joanne Murdock,
Messrs. Jackson and Baker
and others for providing editorial assistance.

CHAPTER 1

I WAS THRUST INTO HYSTERICAL FAME after I escaped death at the hands of a drug lord.

Those are words I certainly never imagined putting to paper, or thought remotely possible. I had enjoyed a slice of renown prior to that unfortunate episode, but that slice had become an entire pie.

Alas, ours is a media-driven world, and my employer Conglomerated Beverages trumpets my famous brand of cocktail amenities at every turn. My publicist, Terry Orbach, created a media frenzy over my death, my surprise survival, my escape and the video of my sword fight on an ocean precipice. Doubling down on that exploit, it was a mere six months later that an axe-wielding escaped convict attacked me in a restaurant. I fended him off with a chair. Surveillance film at eleven.

They make me out to be a swashbuckling, cocktailing, adventuring hero. They have even trademarked my dashing whiskers.

In truth, I am merely a survivor.

Christmas had just passed, and I returned to New York from the Bahamian axe incident to find that my Boone Linsenbigler brand had reached epic levels of popularity.

On New Year's Eve in Times Square, Conglomerated Beverages pulled out all the stops. A veritable shrine to yours truly had been erected on the traffic island at 44th Street in the shape of a ship: *SS Linsenbigler.* It had a crew of busty girls in buccaneer costumes brandishing plastic swords. Times Square's mega signs surrounded the ship, a canyon of light flashing with my likeness twenty feet tall. There I was in lights, a fine figure of a man on a windswept promontory, my magnificent whiskers flowing, and a bottle of my famous "Boone Linsenbigler's Plain and Fancy Cocktail Bitters" held out in one hand for all to admire. A pirate maiden led me to a stage on the poop deck, and the assembled throng of revelers on the streets of New York City surged on all sides chanting my name: *"LINSENBIGLER, LINSENBIGLER, LINSENBIGLER…"*

Awaiting me on stage was the state's pompous Governor flanked by a patrician senator, his silver hair sparkling with camera flash.

The governor introduced me: "Ladies and gentlemen and citizens of the great State of New York – and beyond – I introduce to you an indomitable man who is a true American hero, a man who at all odds defeats his foe and comes out on top, which – by almighty God – should be the manifest destiny of this great nation!"

The crowd roared at such a decibel that I thought my skull would crack. Kaleidoscopic flashing lights and my own likeness swirled all around me – it was as if I had been slipped a powerful narcotic. As the governor continued his polemic, the senator next to me leaned in and shouted into my ear: "What are your affiliations, son?"

Now, my exploits up to that point hardly needed any more documentation as they had been trumpeted far and wide to market cocktail ingredients that – according to a subliminal logic – will magically transform you into a rumbustious hero.

The pretense of marketing does not make my exploits any less harrowing, even though some skeptics on the internet have claimed the adventures were a hoax. The fact of the matter is that I am an ordinary person by almost any standard, one that has been placed in harm's way and saved his own skin. By sheer cunning, a penchant for cocktailing and a deep desire not to be killed, I had managed to survive. Oh, and I was luckier than a shit-house rat, to boot.

Yet as someone who has stood with his back to a cliff, sword in hand, fighting for his life – as terrifying as that was – that moment in Times Square was a close second.

I know my place as Conglomerated's poster boy and can play the part, but I try to keep my feet on the ground and resist my publicist's attempts to turn me into a complete phony.

What was terrifying about Times Square was not only the excessive adulation, the deluge of flashing lights and deafening, undeserved admiration. It was: *What are your affiliations, son?*

If that doesn't put a chill up your back, only a submarine firing a giant machine gun at you will. (Which happened to me and I think 'the hero' wet himself.)

They wanted me to be a politician.

We could make this guy President!

Regrettably, we live in a nation that repeatedly mistakes fame with quality, expertise and competence. My ambitions lie completely within the confines of traveling to exotic fly fishing destinations and my next happy hour. I'm the fool who travels the world to chase fish. I'm the exultant tippler there at the end of the bar with tall tales and a deft bar trick for the ladies. Through dumb luck, I created a cocktail bitter that went viral, and as a result I have become a somewhat reluctant but well-paid shill for a booze company.

I'm not political if for no other reason than it's all a horrendous bore and is all about arguing and being angry at other people.

I make no time for that.

I shouted back in the senator's ear: "My party, sir, is the cocktail party, and none other."

He pulled away, eyeing me shrewdly, but his grey eyes twinkled beneath the shimmering silver coif. That look told me that the senator, and those he represented, wouldn't take a simple no for an answer.

Terry had of course neglected to mention that my appearance would be a part of a de facto stump speech by the Governor and a vetting by the senior senator. He had set me up once again and charted my course into the Sargasso Sea of party politics, likely in the name of making sure my brand didn't "stagnate." Surely, the fevered pitch achieved that New Year's Eve could not be maintained.

The ball dropped and I was able to dismount the stage and enter a celebrity lounge where I was finally united with a bourbon and soda. That reverie lasted all of five minutes before Terry scuttled into the room. I say 'scuttled' because he has the shape and motions of a large beetle, and has a long rubbery proboscis like that of a weevil. He packaged me into a limo and hustled me to a raucous after-party at a rooftop restaurant, views of the city and beautiful girls all around me.

You might think that I was enjoying at least part of this extravaganza, but I cannot dispel that notion too forcefully. Having pumped-up B-list women throw themselves at you is actually rather revolting. Indeed, you might imagine a fine romp, but their real intent was finding a spot in the gossip columns. I could not help but reflect on Tanya, the DEA agent I had left back in Nassau a mere week before. None of these showgirls could hold a candle to that firebrand.

Terry sidled next to me, his proboscis quivering with glee at his handiwork. "Boone, don't just pick any girl, we need you to take home one that will make a splash in the tabloids. There will be photographers outside your building in the morning."

Ah, to what lowly fathoms the hungry whale of fame can take you if you dare harpoon it.

I put a hand on his shoulder. "Brilliant, Terry. Should there be a sex tape? You know, one that mysteriously finds its way to TMZ?"

His eyes widened. "Could you manage it?"

Patting him on the back, I said: "You underestimate me, sir. Look, you go find the right woman, and I'm going to go to the men's room and freshen up, how's that?"

"Super!" Terry crawled into the crowd as I backed away to the coat check and elevator.

Our limo was still downstairs but I thumbed off my phone and ducked around the corner into a subway. I punched out the lenses of my Ray-Bans and wore them like they were glasses to help keep from being recognized. I also raked down my fancy whiskers so that they draped over my mouth, my overcoat pulled close around me. My trip home to Brooklyn by subway was uncharacteristically brief and uneventful, the trains still well attended due to the city-wide celebrations.

My doorman Frank didn't recognize me at first. "Oh, it's you Mister Linsenbigler. I saw you on TV. Brother, there were a lotta babes on that stage, how come you don't got one?"

I marched past him, headed for the elevators, and quipped: "Frank, believe it or not, most of them were transsexuals."

"No shit!"

"Frank, you know what to do if Terry shows up here?"

He flashed a thumbs up: "Not home!"

Once inside my penthouse, the door secured behind me, I leaned against it just to enjoy the feel of a barrier between me and the pulsating frenzy. My eyes closed, I could still see the flashing lights and hear the roar of Times Square.

Good Lord, Boonie, this is just too, too much. We've only been back a week but we have to escape.

When I finally caught my breath, I tossed my overcoat over a bannister and strode into my living room and up to my bar.

My bar. Home sweet home.

As you would expect, I had used my new-found wealth and fame to good effect in decorating my penthouse duplex in all manner of fishing trophies and vintage tackle. The living room was boxed on two sides by floor to ceiling glass walls that overlooked the magnificent arch at Grand Army Plaza and Manhattan beyond. My bar was a vintage rattan "J' shaped affair – you might say it was a tiki bar except there was no ticky-tacky thatch roof to it nor any South Seas décor, just a large rattan-framed mirror behind it and lava lamp sconces at either end. The underside of the bar and sconces lit up with the flick of a switch and in a matter of moments I had in hand a proper cocktail befitting the rigors of the evening: Havana Club 7 year Añejo, neat. After a sip, I dropped a lime wedge into it for some tang.

My furniture was also vintage rattan, and I flopped onto the flowery cushions of the couch and gazed out across the lights of the city. My heart pounded. I was having a mild anxiety attack. *Relax, Boonie, relax!*

Did they really think they could drag me kicking and screaming into public office?

My phone was digging into my hip so I fished it out of my trousers and out of habit thumbed it on.

Naturally, there were many messages from Terry that I did not bother to inspect or listen to.

I did note that I had an email on my private account. Taking a deep sip of rum, I checked in to see who was mailing.

On this mail account I exchange pleasantries, fishing yarns and cocktail recipes with friends and acquaintances, mostly from before I was famous. As such, from time to time, I receive invitations to round out a fishing party, and this email was from just such an acquaintance by the name of Willard Dacksman III. I had never met him but he was a friend of a friend and an ardent angler, by all accounts. Fishing is like a brotherhood of people hell-bent on pestering our poor finny friends. As such, an angler will often drop everything to join a relative stranger in this pursuit.

The subject line read merely "Russia's Far East." It seemed 'Dax' had a trip laid out to the remotest far east of Russia to angle the frozen landscape for an obscure type of fish called Romanoff Char – in brief, a fish like a salmon or trout that migrates rivers to spawn. The river was fed by hot springs, so unlike other rivers out there, this one would be free-flowing and not frozen solid. This was a new lodge that had just opened in an area that had not been fished much, which is music to the ears of any angler. Dax said he could obtain me a visa, which would be waiting for me at the Russian embassy in Paris.

The note contained the usual apologies for how last-minute the entreaty was as someone had to cancel last-minute. The trip was for ten days beginning in a little more than a week's time, jumping off from Paris to Moscow. Oh, and for me, the world-famous angler Boone Linsenbigler, the trip would be all-expenses paid if

I would assist in promoting the lodge, have my picture in their brochures holding up big fat char.

"Dearest Dax: See you in Paris."

The next morning, as I exited my building for a cab, the paparazzi's camera flashes accompanied my escape. I was caught not with a B-list girl but my rod cases and luggage.

Of course, I later learned that Terry managed to have one of those photos published on the cover of The Post with the caption: *BOONE JILTS STARLET.*

CHAPTER 2

I DID NOT NEED TO BE IN PARIS until the following week. Yet if I stayed in New York, Terry would initiate the next round of promotional tours or pimping me out to starlets.

By the same token, I knew from past experience that the intrepid Orbach would seek me out in Paris and follow me to the wilds of the Russian far east. He would do this to try to turn whatever I was doing into a promotional event.

Having accepted Dax's invitation, I sat in the glow of my bar and tried to think of how I might make the trip in a way that my publicist could not join me, and I dismissed out of hand hiding in Paris for a week looking over my shoulder.

My father was a man possessed with nonsensical sayings, and one of them came to mind: *A man in a canoe with galoshes is his own island.* This might have made some sort of sense had he said it in a relevant context other than when he was poised to carve the Thanksgiving turkey.

As I am able to apply this nostrum appropriately, I poked around on the internet and found that the Queen Mary II was to set sail for England on New Year's day. It would arrive in seven days, leaving me an entire day to transfer to Paris, meet up with Dax at the airport, and snag my flight to Khabivostok.

Brilliant, if I do say so. On an ocean liner, I would be safe from any intrusions by Terry.

My choice of staterooms was limited to the upper tier due to the lateness of my reservation, but as long as all expenses were to be paid, who cared the cost? Well, even if they balked, I didn't mind so much, I could afford it, and when – by God – would I ever have the impetus to travel a classic ocean liner again? I could all the while make mild inroads toward publicity on my own by tweeting from the Queen Mary II, the trappings of which were assured to be admirably elegant and timeless enough that they would be in keeping with the caliber of the intrepid gentleman drunk, yours truly, Boone Linsenbigler.

It took me the rest of the night to pack gear, so I was utterly sleepless by the time I went up the priority gangplank and was met by my sleepy-looking butler, who showed me to my stateroom on an upper deck, forward. It was not larger than a normal hotel room, but this wheat was separated from the chaff by fine linens, drapes and appointments, not the least of which was a bottle of chilled champagne.

You heard correctly: my room came with a butler. He wasn't dedicated to me exclusively, mind you, but don't you just love the sound of that? *My butler.* That's almost as good as *my bar*. I was also to have a pillow concierge provide me with a selection of duvet and pillows that matched my whims. Fresh flowers and fruit would be delivered to my room each morning, and most importantly, I had a fully stocked bar. *First rate!*

And so it was that I was quick to change into a plush terry robe, make myself a breakfast martini (gin, vermouth, splash OJ), toss myself onto a deck chair on my private balcony, and watch Manhattan's glittering pile begin to slowly recede, the Verrazano Bridge soon passing overhead. It was about that time that I realized the ambient temperature on New Year's Day in New York Harbor was a bit too brisk for cocktailing al fresco in a robe. I repaired to my room and dove under the plush red covers of the king-size bed and fell fast into slumber's coddling arms, serene with the knowledge that my publicist and the hoi polloi were beyond the moat.

Slowly coming awake, I found myself thinking of Tanya back in Nassau, and then trying not to. We had our time together, but down deep she was a soldier, whereas I am a lover, angler and cocktailer. Past forty, I am experienced enough to know the difference between animal attraction, friendship and love, much less life-partnering, and as such I think we were both resigned that there was no future for us as a pair. Ah well – there I was shipboard steaming the Atlantic for seven days, fancy free, whiskers in top form. Likely as not I might happen upon some companionship if I kept a keen eye. But if not, I would have little difficulty keeping myself amused with the amenities on board.

There were at least ten bars aboard ship.

I bounced out of bed and looked out the slider: mainland had vanished. I could only hope that Terry Orbach would not appear on deck via helicopter, parachute or jet pack. You may assume I jest, but I had learned not to underestimate the lengths to which Terry would go to strap the leash and muzzle on me.

Ready to enjoy my lack of supervision, I was up for a shower and some mischief, but I was distracted by a red and gold envelope peeking from under the cabin door. Upon examination, it proved to be an invitation from the ship's captain to dine with him that evening at his table. I should have guessed that my inane fame would catch up to me. Believe it or not, from time to time, I simply forget that my name and appearance are well-recognized.

There was a knock at my door, and a dour voice came from without: "Mr. Linsenbigler? It is I, Beamish, your butler. Am I disturbing you?"

I snugged my robe and opened the door. "Not at all, Beamish, I just awoke from a nap."

Beamish was half a foot down from my six feet, with a swarthy complexion and a dark wedge of thick black hair. He had large, sleepy eyes, beak-like nose, and wore pinstripe pants, vest and paisley cravat. His shirt was snow white.

"Excellent, sir. I wanted to drop by to mention that dinners are formal attire in this class, and wanted to spare you any inconvenience should you not be prepared. Did you bring a tuxedo?"

I snapped my fingers and winced. "Damn."

"Fear not, Mr. Linsenbigler. I noted that you booked

your stateroom as recently as last night and therefore may not have come prepared. We will be able to provide you with the proper attire, if you wish. Otherwise, you will have to dine on the lower levels. I understand there is a pub below decks."

"By all means, Beamish, by all means, suit me up."

From the pocket of his vest Beamish produced a cloth measuring tapc that he let it roll out down to his knees. "May I take your measurements, sir?"

"Sure, yes."

He circled me, studiously stretching the tape across my shoulders, around my waist and neck, and down my leg. Clearly, he had done this many times.

I asked: "Would you like paper and a pen to write down the measurements?"

Beamish wheeled around in front of me, rolling the tape deftly back into a spool. "I have it memorized. Do you have any special requests?"

"Requests?"

He nodded deeply. "Vest or cummerbund?"

"Hm, vest!"

"Studs or buttons?"

"Buttons."

"Favorite color for the accessories? Or classic black?"

I tapped a finger to my lips, squinting at the ceiling. "Beamish, are you familiar with who I am, seen me in the media?"

He suppressed a smile. "It is hard to imagine anyone who has not."

I laughed inwardly at that remark – if I was not mistaken, he was suggesting that he was as tired of my relentless celebrity as I was.

"You seem to be quite expert in formal wear, Beamish, and you know my reputation. Can I leave it to you to set me up with whatever you feel best for the dashing adventurer Boone Linsenbigler?"

He rocked on his heels, avoiding my eyes. "Consider it done, Mr. Linsenbigler." He turned and began collecting my martini glass and empty miniatures. "It is three-thirty now, and I can have your formal wear here at five. Shall I bring you pre-dinner canapés at six? Or will you repair to the bar? I believe the latter – knowing your proclivities – may be more to your liking."

"Beamish, you're spot on."

His smile loosened as he wheeled out the door, closing it behind him: "Thank you, sir."

He was back promptly at five.

I was showered, trimmed and shaved and ready for my fitting.

Beamish's choice of formal wear was not an option I realized was available when I entrusted him to assemble it. In fact, his choice was one I had not considered at all.

I stood before the mirror. Waist up I was in a smartly cut military-style formal jacket with epaulets and heather buttons. Under the jacket was a matching vest and white tux shirt with slim black bow tie.

Waist down was another matter.

My lower half was draped in a red MacGregor tartan kilt.

A kilt with a small leather purse on a chain around my waist. It hung in front of my crotch. Below the kilt I wore black knee socks, garters and red flashers, one of which Beamish had fit with a small bejeweled dagger.

Beamish sensed reassurances were in order.

"If I may, sir, the 'purse' as you call it is a traditional highland *sporran*, and the dagger is likewise de rigueur and called a *"skeen-doo."*

I raised an eyebrow at him in the mirror. "And you say my mother was Clan Gregor so that makes this costume less ridiculous?"

"If Wikipedia indicates correctly, her maiden name was MacGregor. Which means that you could surmise that Rob Roy is your direct ancestor."

"Like the drink?"

"The drink, sir, was named after the famous highland adventurer named Rob Roy MacGregor. If I might be so bold, you appear to have some of his traits for survival under duress. As such, I thought that this clan formal dress was entirely appropriate for one of your lineage, and that it would further provide fodder for conversation along the lines of your famous relative Rob Roy."

I eyed Beamish suspiciously as he darted around me tugging at this and that to make sure all my lines were straight. "We don't know that to be true."

He glanced up at me in the mirror and smiled. "We don't know it to be untrue, do we? At worst, it is an embellishment."

"Is Beamish your real name?"

He cleared his throat, and stood at attention, his primping complete. "If you would prefer to call me Papdapakoulopis, that is your privilege. I find Beamish more commodious. Now, I would encourage you to take in what you see there in the mirror and own it. You will be – pleasantly so – surprised at the positive reaction that this highland formal dress will afford you."

I scoffed. "Would James Bond wear this?"

"Indeed, George Lazenby, as James Bond, wore highland formal in the 1969 movie 'On Her Majesty's Secret Service.' If it makes a difference, with this attire you will receive ample attentions of the ladies aboard ship. They will want to know what you wear under your kilt."

"Really?"

"Absolutely"

"What do I say?"

"That depends on the lady and your level of interest in her."

"Beamish, are you serious?"

He patted me on the shoulder. "Mr. Linsenbigler, you were bold enough to trust me, and with good reason, I am a butler of the first order. If for some reason you regret this choice, by all means come back to the room, ring me, and I will suit you up in an ordinary tuxedo."

I had not gotten ten feet from my door on my way to the bar when an elderly woman exiting her room gave me the once over and said "Hoo-wee – what do you wear under your kilt?"

"Socks and shoes," I quipped, still uneasy with being gussied up. Yet I trusted Beamish, somehow. He seemed to understand my *modus operandi.* So like the ocean liner excursion itself, when else would I have a chance to venture forth in the trappings of Rob Roy? As my Greek butler suggested, I just had to 'own it.' So I strode into the elegant, subdued bar with purpose and authority, heads turning to follow my progress.

"Good evening, sir." The barmaid was Indian with large almond-shaped eyes and maple complexion. She had a long black braid, and she didn't bat an eye at my attire. Sliding a napkin in front of me on the bar, she asked: "May I make you a cocktail?"

Imagine ordering anything *other* than a Rob Roy?

"Indeed, what's your oldest Macallan?"

"We have the eighteen year."

"And your oldest Port?"

"We have Taylor Twenty."

"I'd like a Rob Roy made from those, easy on the port, stirred on the rocks, and with a lemon twist."

She nodded and went about her business.

Carefully, I began to survey my immediate surroundings, beginning with those folks at the bar left and right. To my right were two older couples, the women decked out in sequins and the men in vintage tuxedos. They politely raised their glasses to me when I looked at them, and I bowed my head in return.

To the other side was a brace of older gals in their sixties who looked as if they had maybe been recently widowed or divorced and had teamed up to take on Europe. They were draped in satin, and when I looked their way they averted their gaze, though one of them caught my eye briefly and returned a fetching blink.

The barmaid was before me again, stirring my Rob Roy in a large snifter. She promptly poured the cocktail with a flourish into a cut crystal double old-fashioned glass. Her slender fingers tweaked the lemon twist and wedged it into the pile of ice.

I took the drink directly from her with a nod of thanks and gave it a sip. Just as I had remembered it, a truly superb Rob Roy, and I told her so.

Her cheeks flushed, and the courtly domestic veneer cracked. "Excuse me for saying so, Mr. Linsenbigler, but as a bartender it is an honor to serve you a cocktail."

As I have suggested, I'm not so full of myself (yet) that I disdain mixing it up with my fans. Especially when they can distract me from the fact that I'm wearing a skirt in public. I pulled out my phone. "Well, then, how about a selfie, for my Twitter feed? Shall we?"

She beamed with excitement and I snapped the photo of me in the foreground with my cocktail and she leaning in over the bar with a smile and cleavage that had the camera's autofocus confused for some moments. "What's your name?" I asked.

"Khushi."

I wrote: *Aboard the Queen Mary Two, being served the best Rob Roy ever by Khushi, the best bartender on the high seas!*

She thanked me and bottled her enthusiasm so that she could tend to the older couples down the bar.

"So how many best bartenders have you met on the high seas?" came from behind me to my left.

I turned to behold a woman likely a little older than I, with lazy, bounteous auburn curls and emerald eyes set in a pale round face. She wore a slinky black dress and had a necklace of green stones that matched her eyes. In her hand was her phone, and it was open to my Twitter feed, the selfie I just posted on her screen.

I smiled politely. "I firmly believe that at any time any bartender can be the best, if even only temporarily."

Those emerald eyes looked at me quizzically, the small red lips below toying with whether to be amused. She glanced down at the phone again. "I suppose being the best bartender – temporarily – might include having great tits?" She spoke slowly, and with a slightly smoky drawl.

I toasted the air with my drink. "And why not?"

"Is it OK if I join you or are you otherwise occupied?" She titled her head toward Khushi.

"A sterling rule of mine is never to hit on the bartender." I gave a half bow and waved my palm at the space and barstool on my left: "By all means."

She slid next to me, but not close. "Even if I'm not a fan?"

"Well, I would hope you are at least neutral. I can't say I cotton to drinking with the enemy."

Plopping her sequined clutch on the bar, she waved over Khushi. "I'll have what he's having." Then she turned to me, slowly raising a hand. "We don't know each other well enough to be enemies – yet. I'm Hailey."

I gave her paw a gentle shake and squeeze. "Boone."

Hailey's eyes darted about the room. "I'm surprised you don't come with an entourage of some sort."

"Well if you must know, I escaped captivity to make this voyage. Sometimes I need a little breathing room."

"Got kinda cramped in Times Square, did it?"

I rolled my eyes. "Indeed it did. So I arranged all this last moment."

"Headed to London?"

"Paris, then Khabivostok. You?"

Her drink arrived, and she held it up to the light to

admire its color. "I'm not sure where I'm headed."

I held out my glass. "I'll drink to that!" We clinked glasses and sipped.

"Boone, that's a hell of a Rob Roy. I guess it would have to be if you dress in a kilt for the occasion. Is that a house mix or one of yours?"

"One of mine, and it literally saved my life once."

"You won't find these ingredients where you're headed. So what's in Khabivostok?"

"Angling for char."

"After all that business you went through in the tropics with smugglers, aren't you a little shy of traveling to some place like Russia?"

I shrugged. "My impression is that the Russian government has a firm grip on everything that goes on in that country."

She bit her lip and squinted. "Likely so."

"What is it that you do, say, for a living, or are you a jet setter?"

She poked at her ice cubes, took a sip, and without looking at me said: "What if I told you I'm with the CIA, or something like that?"

"A spy or a chef?"

Her eyes met mine, and she drawled softly. "Espionage."

"Or something like that? Well, if you said you were a spy I would ask you to prove it."

Hailey sidled in a little closer, her voice low and intent. "Did you ever think, Linsenbigler, that there might be people out there, governments that are interested in who you are and what you do?"

Now I am quite sure that many of you have engaged the opposite sex in bar talk that was meant to be provocative, and while I could not recall a similar such diversion as pretending to be a spy, it was not what I would consider out of the realm of coy verbal foreplay. In fact, as I had become famous, it wasn't unusual for people I met to try to impress me with what they did even if to slightly fictionalize their circumstance. So if she wanted to pretend to be a spy, so be it. Especially if this was indeed foreplay. Hailey was one of those odd women who are as sexy in what they say and how they act as in how they look. Though in my calculus at the moment, I must say that I was rather of the mind to make sure I had surveyed the other ladies on board before throwing in with the first one that happened along.

To be perfectly honest, I was a little unsure if she was actually interested in making a play for my affections or just toying as a cat does with a fur mouse. Some women are like that. Perhaps some men are as well. I don't know.

So I replied to her question about governments interested in yours truly.

"Should anybody other than my venerable employer Conglomerated Beverages have designs on Boone Linsenbigler, they will have to go mano-y-mano in a cage match with my intrepid publicist, Terry, and good luck to them!"

A waiter approached and stopped at my elbow. "Mr. Linsenbigler, the Captain would like me to escort you to his table."

"Capital," I said to the young man. And to Hailey: "It was a pleasure." I bowed and followed the waiter away from the bar and the redhead. I might have felt as if I passed on an opportunity, but something told me I had dodged a bullet with that one.

CHAPTER 3

DINING AT THE CAPTAIN'S TABLE may sound like the bee's knees but it turned out to be unconscionably dull. For starters, the captain was quite taken with the fact that he had whiskers similar to mine, and like some other conversationalists I've run into, the ship's commander was eager to demonstrate that his stories from his years at sea were a match for my heroics. I'm more than willing to concede that others can be and are more interesting than I, but in this instance, that wasn't the case. The captain seemed to have innumerable stories from when he was a young officer on a destroyer. Each tale was more of a laundry list of procedures and ended when the ship made port. Apparently, his ship never engaged an enemy and he was never in harm's way unless you count the time he had a mild case of botulism or some such from tinned turkey and giblets.

You might likewise imagine that those assembled at his table were some sort of social luminaries when in fact, for all I could make out, they were just regular customers, ossified gentry stuffed into tuxedoes who boasted about how this was their tenth, twentieth or thirtieth crossing of the Atlantic by sea. I was by far the youngest person at the table.

And not a one asked what I wore under my kilt, or said anything at all about the way I was dressed, so I did not have the opportunity to even float the yarn about Rob Roy being my ancestor.

So it was with some relief that the baked Alaska was wheeled away and I begged the table's indulgence that I might retire to the deck for a cheroot.

That was not as easy as it might sound, for all the while I was being summarily bored to death at the Captain's table the rest of the dining room – and the ladies in particular – had been eyeing yours truly for the favor of a selfie. I had to pass through a veritable gauntlet of fans with their phones – which as a celebrity I realize is my lot to endure. There's a reason they pay you a lot of money, so suck it up, I say.

I emerged like a butterfly from its chrysalis when I finally made the doors to the foredeck, the January sea air as refreshing as an ice pop on an August afternoon. You might think I felt that same sea air beneath my kilt, but the skirt was surprisingly warm. As it was made of layered wool, little wonder, and since heat rises I surmised that the heat was more or less trapped there.

At the railing, I took in the sight of open ocean, the horizon defined deftly by starlight, and the rest dimly illuminated by a crescent moon. The seas were relatively calm, and the ship sliced and surged decisively east toward Southampton. As I fired up my cigar, my mind wandered to the unsettling conversation with the redhead, focusing not so much on what she said but the seedling of fear that she had carefully embedded into my brain: *Good Lord, you don't imagine that this trip will somehow turn into a nightmare like the Caribbean?*

Gazing over the twinkly dark waters and at the stars flickering overhead, it was hard to imagine that such a thing could happen more than once, or that the odds of such a thing were even remotely possible. I supposed I had to be thankful that the Queen Mary was not following the same route as the Titanic and was sailing well south of the route. Just the same, I trained a keen eye all around just to be sure. No icebergs.

That I could see.

Foreign governments interested in me? Hogwash. I did not feel particularly adventuresome that evening, not to the extent that I felt like seeking out women to ask what was worn under my kilt. As such, I wandered my way back inside and to my cabin nearby.

Just as I was keying the lock, Beamish hailed me from the end of the corridor, and approached. "Can I bring you anything, Mr. Linsenbigler? A nightcap?"

"Thank you, Beamish. What did you have in mind?"

"A Drambuie?"

I flashed him a thumbs up and he strode off.

Prying myself out of my highland formal, I was unsure of exactly how one was supposed to hang a kilt, which is really a rather heavy affair that will torture any but the stoutest hanger, so I draped it over a chair for Beamish to deal with. Snug in my robe, I heard a knock at the door, and it was Beamish bearing a snifter of Drambuie with a ball of ice cream floating in it. He explained: "It's a small ball of cinnamon ginger ice cream."

I took a sip. "I'll have to remember that recipe. Damned good, Beamish."

"And I take it the highland formal was to your liking?" He took to wrestling my kilt onto a hanger.

"People said surprising little about it. Of course, I wasn't at the most interesting table. Any way I can get out of sitting with the Captain the rest of the voyage?"

"I'll see what I can do, sir."

"And I had a drink with a peculiar redhead at the bar, named Hailey. Any idea who she might be?"

He shook his head, but answered: "I will find out."

"She seemed to think she was a spy or some such, role playing I suppose."

"Yes, it is not unusual for women in particular to embellish when they are at sea. I suppose they feel that this is quite the adventure and that they need to live up to it." My clothes all tucked away, Beamish stepped to the cabin door and turned: "Anything else?"

"Ever see any icebergs on this voyage?"

He smirked dismissively, pivoted and left.

Dimming the lights, I opened the slider to my balcony and stepped out into the chill.

"I thought you'd never come."

In the dim light cast from my cabin was the form of a woman in a fur coat reclined on a chaise lounge.

Staggering with surprise, I said: "Good heavens, how on earth did you get out here?"

"My name is Katya and I climbed from around the side." Her words slithered in a Slavic accent.

I gulped audibly. "You climbed? Over the open ocean, where to fall would mean certain death?"

"Darling, in life you just have to make sure you don't fall. But I've fallen for you."

"Why on earth are you here? You likely startled a few years from my existence!"

"When we did that selfie together in the dining room, I think we both knew we were meant to be together, darling."

I didn't remember Katya from all the others in the crowd worth a hoot. Building my resolve, I downed half my drink. "Look, Katya, you seem like a nice person…"

Don't you like it when people say 'you seem like a nice person?' Clearly and almost unequivocally, it means 'you are insane.' That was my meaning. I digress:

"…but this is an intrusion, and I must ask that you depart with all due dispatch."

She rose slowly, tucking her full-length coat around her, and backed toward the railing.

"Good Lord, woman, not that way, not out over the ocean again, I'll let you out to go your way through the cabin."

If I had to guess at this late stage, this was her intent all along, to get access to my chambers.

I guided her through my slider into my room. She was wearing a white fur coat and tennis shoes. Katya had long, silky copper hair draped around her shoulders. Her eyes were small and brown on either side of a stately nose. I led her to the door, whereupon she turned and opened her coat, and fixed those little gimlet eyes on me from under a forelock.

On her chest were two nipples red as wild strawberries atop large scoops of ice cream. Below that was ship shapely, an alabaster vessel yaw as could be. Her lower mizzen was as copper as her foresail.

She gasped: "Can't I seduce you Boone? Just once?"

Men are base creatures, I no less than others. That doesn't mean that none of us – from time to time – manages to assert some discretion.

I straightened my robe. "Look, Missy, you might have seduced me had you not crawled across the outside of the ship over the icy waters of the open sea at night in just a fur coat and sneakers." I gently closed her coat. "As such, I am not accepting your generous offer, and wish you a good night and the help of a psychiatrist."

I reached around her, opened the door, and smoothly shooed her out into the hallway.

She pouted, bundling her coat around her.

"Boone, we could have made fucking all night long. Maybe I'll see you later."

With that, she wiggled her way down the corridor and vanished around the corner.

I snugged my door closed and leaned against it, not too unlike after I got home from New Year's Eve. It seemed that my level of fame invited this sort of episode. Were I to give into one like that I'd have a serial stalker on my hands in the snap of the fingers. As such, I made sure my balcony slider was locked and crawled into bed, promising myself that were I to enter into some sort of liaison on this ship I would have to be damned careful whom I chose. For example, someone who wasn't intent on having my baby. You could be damned sure that I was going to pilot well clear of redheads of any hue.

So it was that the next day I proceeded in a leisurely, reserved and measured way. There were a few hours wiled away in the fore library reading up on Russia's Far East. I was eager to understand where I was going and the lay of the land.

Lunch at the bar in the Commodore Club – where I regaled some fellow passengers with the bar trick where I make an orange disappear. Afternoon tea was held in the Queens Room and I imposed myself into a group of older women and charmed them to death, all the while people taking selfies and likely posting them to the internet. As such, it came as no surprise that a waiter approached me with a dispatch from the ship's radio room:

"I'll see you in Southampton. Send photos. Terry."

As I tramped about the ship, I kept a keen eye out for any approaching redheads and enacted evasive maneuvers as required.

On the second night, there was a Latin dance held in the Queens Room, complete with lessons, followed by an open dance floor. I had the good fortune while captive on that drug lord's island to have been partnered with a lovely girl who taught me to samba and mambo, so I skipped the lesson part and made my appearance not in a kilt but in a trim and dashing tuxedo.

I took a turn or two with the inexperienced, before the swarthy dance instructor approached. Not a red hair on her raven head, Miranda was shapely and spirited, and as we danced, she let me take complete command of her in a way that is remarkably seductive. I rose to the occasion, if I do say so, and we stole the dance floor, many sidelining themselves just to watch us cut the rug.

Miranda was not in awe of Boone Linsenbigler. She was taking me as a visceral, sexual being, but fully in charge of her own, if that makes sense. Plainly, this woman was her own person and not wanting anyone's baby.

That said, when the evening was done, I merely asked if she'd care to join me for lunch the next day. She looked up at me uncertainly, and said: "I should not. I am not to socialize with the passengers."

I smiled: "But will you?"

She did, and I sought her out the next night for a dance class in ballroom dancing. Things heated up from there, and I found myself arising from her bunk in the bowels of the ship where the staff lived. Utterly worn out from an abundance of lust and in need of further rest in my own quarters, I did my best to elude the staff as I made my way to the upper decks. I was becoming an ardent fan of women who were adept at dancing – I think this is because they are keenly aware of how to move their bodies in a sensual way for their own pleasure as well of that of their partner, starting on the dance floor.

The trip trailed on nicely enough in that vein, with Miranda having to work evenings as dance instructor and not be seen on intimate terms with a passenger. I would show up late to the Queens Room once she had finished dance instructions, join for a few last dances, and then have some cocktails with others before we split up as if we were going our separate ways. No doubt, some of the staff knew what was afoot, but we managed to keep our assignation largely on the QT and not develop into any sort of onboard sensation. The affair was discreet, and more importantly, balanced, neither of us expecting or wanting more than our secret liaisons together.

As the end of the trip drew near, the urgency of eluding Terry in Southampton began to weigh on me, and I sought out the advice of Beamish in that regard. He had been quite discreet with my comings and goings from below deck and had provided me with a sneaky route back from Miranda's cabin to my own that helped avoid scrutiny. I had even told him of the horrendous apparition that was Katya, and he kept me informed of her general whereabouts when he knew them so that I could take evasive actions if necessary. It seemed she was ill in her cabin much of the time.

The morning prior to docking in Southampton, Beamish stopped by my stateroom with my flowers and late breakfast, as had become the custom.

"Mr. Linsenbigler, I do believe I have devised a plan whereby Mr. Orbach can be diverted. Do you object to me using Katya in this plan?"

I cocked an eyebrow at him in response, and he continued:

"My idea is to tell her you wished to revive your tryst once off ship, and as such direct her to seek out Mr. Orbach once ashore to that end. The intent is to keep Mr. Orbach at the passenger debarkation gantry whilst you depart through the employee gangway down below. I trust the eager Katya will keep him there waiting for you to emerge. There are customs agents at both portals, so there will be delays, but generally speaking the employee portal is far less congested and you should be on your way with all due dispatch – we have afforded other celebrities seeking to avoid the press this courtesy. I suggest that if you stay below decks this evening, that you depart directly from there and not return to your room. Bring a change of clothes for traveling, and have Miranda return your formal wear to the rental shop once you have gone. I will affix your luggage tickets this evening once you are packed and ensure that they are directed to the correct point of entry. I suggest you leave promptly once the gantry opens to secure a cab to the train station. Your train to London leaves at 10:30, and your further instructions on to Paris by train are here."

Beamish handed me a discreet list of departure instructions.

"Top notch, Beamish. If you ever get tired of butlering the high seas, look me up."

He smiled and bowed. "That would indeed be an honor, sir."

I spent the day mostly in my cabin and balcony, and by evening had my baggage and fly rod cases lined up next to the door, an envelope on top with a thousand dollars in it for Beamish. It was hard to figure out how much to give him, but he was clearly worth every penny of that as long as I could afford it. Besides, I was serious when I said I wanted him to come work for me. Can you imagine? I could!

Dressed in a tuxedo with an especially fancy brocade vest, a small duffel with my travel clothes in hand, I set out on the town, as it were, livening up the crowd in the Commodore Club, and cocktailing and eating my way toward my final assignation with Miranda. As soon as she saw me, that raven Latin beauty put aside the lessons. We waltzed and fox trotted late into the night, bottle after bottle of champagne tipped on its head in the ice bucket. I shouldn't wonder that we should have blindfolded the band! So much for keeping our attraction on the QT.

Exhausted by the time the maestro's baton finally found rest, we strolled on the deck and did some good old-fashioned necking in a shadowy nook.

That's where we parted. The week had been lusty and intimate and finally just a glorious night of dancing, so we decided to say goodbye on that note rather than a sleepy, rumpled one the next morning.

Which worked out fine because I needed to attain what little sleep the rest of the night had to offer.

My baggage was gone when I got to my room, and that left me feeling a little melancholy, a mood that waned as soon as my head hit the pillow, my dreams filled with the strains of Strauss waltzes.

CHAPTER 4

THE NEXT MORNING went according to plan. Mostly.

At the appointed morning hour, I donned my traveling clothes: khakis, pullover blue wool sweater, London Fog windbreaker and running shoes. I half expected Beamish to pop in, but he did not show. So I skulked down the corridor to the service elevator and down through the kitchen to the employee's gangway – very much the way I used to come from Miranda's but in reverse.

As Beamish had suggested, the exit was only lightly occupied and my bags were there for me to move through customs.

My eyes darted this way and that searching for Terry's approach but did not find it. Much less the lunatic red head, Katya.

Passing through customs, I followed signs through the white-arched terminal to the taxi stand where a line of little white foreign-looking cabs awaited under cool, overcast skies.

Yet before I could approach the head of the line, a black Mercedes limo slid in front of them. The back door opened, and out stepped Hailey in a black pant suit and looking very business minded. She waved and shouted: "Linsenbigler! This way."

I hesitantly approached, and stopped in front of her as the trunk opened of its own. Some cabbies began shouting at her about blocking them, and she ignored them.

"Hailey! What the devil is this?"

"I'm giving you a ride to St. Pancras Station and the Eurostar train to Paris. Come on, throw the luggage in back and get in. This way you'll be sure not to miss the train."

While this was peculiar, I could not imagine that such a favor posed any kind of specific danger. I shrugged, hefted my baggage and rods in the trunk, and got in beside Hailey. We slid away from the ship terminal, cabbies still shouting at us.

The driver was behind tinted glass, the leather seats cushy and the interior amazingly hushed. The usual trappings of waterfront slid by: piers, container facilities, and shipyards. Inside, Hailey's perfume or shampoo delicately tickled my nose with gardenias. I turned sideways toward her.

"This was unexpected. I had not seen you the entire crossing."

"There was no need for you to see me, Linsenbigler. What was important was that I saw you."

I raised an eyebrow at her and she continued. "I'll try to explain it again. You are an enormously popular person, a celebrity, and people listen to what you have to say and follow your every move. The entire crossing created yet another sensation on the internet because people on board were posting photos and taking video."

A light sweat broke on my brow. "Video?" *Good Lord, please don't tell me Miranda issued a sex tape!*

"Yes, in particular of you and Miranda."

My sweat turned cold, and she continued.

"That dance number last night got the entire web wanting to know who she was, whether you were a couple."

I cleared my throat. "So the video, this video was of me dancing?"

Her brow wrinkled, and she shot me an eye as if I was an idiot. "Yes."

I practically melted into a puddle of relief onto the floor of the limo, but composed myself: "Look here, Hailey, why precisely are you making any of this your business?"

She smirked, but not at me, toward the passing traffic. "Let's say I'm your guardian angel. Do you recall what I told you at the bar in the Commodore Club last week?"

I sighed.

"Some nonsense about foreign governments caring about me."

"What did the senator ask you on New Year's Eve, on stage behind the governor?"

I scoffed: "Oh, nothing really, I can't recall…"

She rolled her eyes. "I can refresh your memory. He asked what your affiliation was."

"How do you know what he said?"

"Look, don't you get it, Linsenbigler? We hear everything. We read everything. We know almost everything that people do or say. Including you. How? A million ways you can't even imagine. Let's start with the fact that people carry their own tracking device and listening device. It's called a smart phone. Only it's smart in both directions."

"So for whom do you work? You mentioned the CIA…"

She flashed an identification badge with her picture on it, and I read aloud: "National Institute of Standards and Technology, Weights and Measures Department."

She rolled her eyes again, seemingly exasperated with my ignorance. "Satisfied?"

"But…"

"Linsenbigler, we never say who we really work for and even if I put a name to it, you probably would never have heard of us. Look, you are more influential than you may think. Certain people are talking about moving you into politics. Yes, I know, you're line is that the only party you're interested in is the cocktail party. Ever heard the line about power? The corrupting influence of power?"

"Certainly, but…"

She snorted. "Better men than you have caved. The point is, if other governments believe that this is where you are going they want in on the ground floor. Or they want you compromised."

"Compromised?" My head was spinning. Could all this be true? Boonie is just a barfly, a nice enough fellow when he has to be, an angler with fancy whiskers. How could this be happening to little old me? As my father likely would have said: *Sailing is all in the footwork.*

She eyed me for a few moments, sort of taking stock of me. "Had Miranda been a risk, I would have stepped in. Better that we knew where you were sleeping every night than not — especially away from your own room. That was a close call with Katya."

I practically gagged: "You know about that?"

"You think she was just an insane rabid fan, don't you?"

"She wasn't?"

"No, she wasn't, but she spent most of the rest of the trip in bed with a stomach virus, thanks to me."

"And Miranda?"

"She's clean, and there is no sex tape. That could have been a way to compromise you. They could offer you women, gifts, sweetheart deals, all of which could look bad later when you're in the Senate and have a vote to make. A vote that concerns them. You can vote one way and none of the dirt becomes known. Or you could vote the other way and deal with the consequences. So I suggest going forward that you keep it zipped up and your head on straight – your guardian angel won't be along to protect you beyond Moscow."

Not knowing what to say or do, I closed my eyes and focused on the muffled rumble of the tires and the sway of the Mercedes chassis, hoping that I was somehow dreaming.

Without opening my eyes, I finally asked: "How do I know you're with the good guys, Hailey?"

"You don't."

Opening my eyes, I peered at her serene, knowing smile. "Then why should I listen to you?"

"Because it sounds true?" She squinted at me. "What other purpose would I have in following you around?"

I squinted back. "That's a very good question. In today's world what sounds true often isn't, or it is some version of the truth."

Nodding, she said: "That's a very healthy attitude – I suggest you keep it."

"Why aren't you asking me to cancel going to Russia?"

She thought about that a moment. "We want to see what happens, if anything."

"Ah!" I leaned in. "So you intend to let me go there so I can report back what happens and see if the Russians are interested in me. In effect, you want me to be your spy!"

"Don't you want to catch some Romanov char, enjoy the hot springs, drink iced vodka and eat caviar? Don't you want to escape your publicist and have fun with your pal Dax? If I had not shown up, you would have gone in any case. So go. Just like the rest of your life, there's nothing keeping us from watching what happens. Though I think overall you should be a little thankful that you know what's going on and with any luck won't have some sort of scandal ruin your relationship with Conglomerated. Remember making your own cocktail bitters in that basement apartment in Elizabeth, New Jersey? Eating mac and cheese out of a box? You've got it good now. Don't blow it."

That sounded like a threat, and I was tempted to say

so. Was she suggesting that if I didn't 'play ball' that whatever agency she worked for had the ability to ruin me? Based on our conversation, I had to assume that this is what she was suggesting.

I stared out the window, trying to think clearly. Should I cut and run? Maybe she was trying to frighten me off for some other purpose?

What precisely could happen on a fishing trip in the snowy nether regions of Russia? Suppose someone there tried to do precisely what she said? All I had to do was not compromise myself. I had been on plenty of fishing trips where not once did I hop in the sack with the ladies, and I think I had the wherewithal to avoid accepting any bribes or involving myself in any investment schemes. So what precisely did I have to fear chasing Romanov char?

The more I thought about it, the more the clouds parted. It seemed to me that Hailey and her 'agency' – if there was one – were being a tad melodramatic. Feh, it all sounded like bunk, to be honest. Fine, she can drive me to the train station; follow me to Moscow, her dime. Made never-no-mind to old Boonie. Should she come snooping around when I return home and ask about what happened I can tell her I caught lots of char, sat in hot spring, drank vodka and ate caviar. Though according to her they know everything that happens so that would not even happen.

In sum total, I was getting a free limo ride to the train station. So what? All of her talk was none of my problem because I wasn't going into politics anyway. And Terry wanted a sex tape!

I cleared my throat. "I don't suppose there's any ice

in this limousine?"

She raised an eyebrow at me: "Ice?"

"Fear not." I reached into my pack and retrieved what appeared to be one of those clear plastic pencil cases that contain shampoo bottles and are standard for passing toiletries through TSA security. I unzipped the pouch and procured two three-ounce shampoo bottles filled with amber liquid. From my pocket, I produced two silver discs – folding cups – that I extended into cocktail vessels. Folding down the armrest between us, I nested my cups in the cup holders and poured half of each shampoo bottle into each. Next, I pulled a thermal mug from my bag and added ice to the cups. Naturally, I had cherries and bitters in my kit as well.

She watched me with interest. "You know, it's barely past nine in the morning."

I grinned. "In New York, the afternoon is about to broadside cocktail hour. My internal clock never lies."

I held the two collapsing cups at arm's length and swirled them for thirty seconds. Then I extended one to Hailey: "Manhattan?"

She laughed lightly and took the cup. "Really? Not a gin martini here in Jolly Old England?"

"Cheers!" We clinked, and sipped.

I felt better having taking command of the situation in classic Linsenbigler style. I'm the master of my own destiny, damn it, as well as my cocktails.

We spent the better part of the ride to the station in relative silence, she scrolling her phone while I watched the British traffic swirl around me in the wrong direction. This was the first time I had been in England, and soon it would be my first excursion to Europe. I admit to being somewhat of a Philistine in regards to my neglect of culture. If fishing isn't involved I'm not much interested in looking at castles, and I find European history a rather plodding treatise on the futility of governance. This of course says more about me than Europe. I was unmoved by the novelty of my surroundings, which was only a place to pass through on my way fishing. That said, when we pulled up to the train station, I marveled at the towering Victorian red brick building, which sported a gigantic clock tower. This was not the type of train station one finds in the states. The limo pulled into a drop off lane and came to a stop. Hailey turned to me.

"I hope you take what I said seriously, Linsenbigler."

I collapsed our empty Manhattan cups and slid them back into my nap sack. "Message received, Hailey, though I would hope that my message was received as well. I am not interested in politics and have no craving for power, no matter the circumstance, so I believe I am immune to corruption or being compromised."

She smirked and opened her car door. "Noted. There will be a limo like this one to get you to the Russian Embassy for your Visa, transfer to the airport, and flight to Moscow."

I collected my gear from the trunk as she checked her phone again. I said: "Just the same, I appreciate the heads up."

She looked up from her phone as I retreated toward the station entrance.

"Catch a big one."

CHAPTER 5

WERE I TO REGALE YOU with too many particulars of the train trip to Paris and my subsequent transfer to the Russian Embassy and airport, I fear tedium might prevail. Or as my dad might have said: *Toothpicks have no place in meatloaf.*

I slept on the train to Paris, flanked by people muttering mostly French.

The Paris limo took me through wide boulevards packed notably different from New York mainly by the lack of SUV's, preponderance of small sedans, and abundance of people on scooters. The cabs were not yellow, and the surrounding buildings were primarily pale stone. I was disappointed that I did not hear many high-pitched car horns or any of the honk-bray police sirens or any accordions blaring from cafés. There was a light drizzle, it was cool and the many trees were skeletal and had no leaves. Oh, and we passed by that big arch. So in London it seemed sort of the same but with more red brick buildings and they drive on the left. Fascinating! Feh, all mundane if you ask me – where's the fishing? None, you say? Onward!

The embassy was a large pale building, but modern with square disjointed colonnades. It was barricaded behind a fence and surrounded by grass and bushes. When I entered, a long line of people was waiting under a sign marked 'VISAS' and so I got in queue. It was only a few moments before a stout man with a severe widow's peak and round specs tapped my shoulder.

"Mr Linsenbigler?" His accent was growling Russian.

"Yes?"

"Please come with me, I will issue your Visa."

They must have been watching their security cameras for my entrance. I was certainly getting the royal treatment from all sides!

So it was that I was whisked into a small drab office with a wall festooned with the county's red coat of arms featuring a double-headed eagle. The man inspected my passport quickly and stapled my Visa into it. I couldn't have been in the embassy for more than five minutes.

The airport was the usual fascinating grind and devoid of any royal treatment, but I soldiered on to my gate in due course, the occasional traveler recognizing me with a double take.

Willard Dacksman III was a man I had never met. He was quite active on some of the fishing chat rooms, particularly those in which the more exotic fishing destinations were discussed. It was clear that he lived for a time in Nairobi and fished the Aberdares for brown trout with some regularity. He also apparently found himself in Papua New Guinea where he pursued enormous barramundi in jungle rivers. My fishing adventures – the previous one notwithstanding – had been tame affairs by comparison. Just the same, I read Dax's dispatches with great interest, hoping one day to get a chance to go somewhere more exotic.

As I intimated before, it might seem odd to throw in with a stranger to travel to the other side of the globe, but my experience had been that serious anglers constitute a fellowship.

I had been exchanging the stray text with him over the past week to alert him of my progress. That morning he'd texted me that – as luck would have it – there was a brasserie directly next to our gate for the Moscow flight. I was to meet him there.

It used to be that I would make every effort to carry my rods and essential gear onto flights rather than check them. The theory was that even if my checked luggage was lost in transport I could still fish with what I had in hand. Unfortunately, the rod cases sometimes exceeded some sort of criteria for carry on, and as such I was forever battling flight crews. Eventually, having never had my check-in luggage misdirected, I relented and began checking all my bags except a light carry on with the essentials. I mention all this parenthetically because when I used to enter an airport bar, I was burdened with all manner of awkward rod cases that inevitably smacked into other patrons as I walked by or clattered to the floor when I tried to secure them next to me. There's the bull in the china shop, and then there is the traveling angler in the crowded bar. So I entered the brasserie with a certain sense of relief that I was not burdened with rod cases.

At the far end of the dark wood and brass-trimmed bar, Dax caught my eye. He was the only one at the bar wearing a fuzzy lambs-wool Cossack hat. It was dirty blonde and looked like a drum-shaped afro on his head. Below this enormous hat was a wiry man with a heavy brow and compactly curled mustache. To my eye he looked like an orphan from a barbershop quartet. An enormous smile spouted when he saw me, and he jumped to his feet and blurted something in Russian. When I drew near he flung himself on me like the long lost brother I never had.

"Boone! Come, have a drink! This is going to be an adventure you will never forget!"

His enthusiasm caught me a little off guard, as you might imagine, for someone I'd never met. The exclamation 'adventure you will never forget' gave me an odd sense of foreboding.

There was no seat next to him at the bar so he took it upon himself to rearrange the other patrons so that I could sit next to him. Maybe it was the curly hat or his energy level, but one got the impression that in a previous life Dax had been a wire fox terrier.

Before I could direct the barman as to my beverage of choice, Dax injected. "A chilled vodka for my friend."

I interjected, waving the slouching barman closer: "Actually, I'd rather have a 1789, not too sweet, on ice with a wedge of fruit of your choice."

The barman came to attention, clearly up to this challenge, and clearly weary of dishing out Kir Royals and French 75's.

"But you must drink vodka!" Dax was aghast. "We are headed for Khabivostok, and must drink vodka!"

I raised an amused eyebrow at the fox terrier. "Lookee here, Dax. I'm all game for this fishing trip, and for the vodka, too, once we get there. Be that as it may, I'm rather certain we won't see any proper cocktails or much of anything but vodka or brandy the entire time we're in Russia, so I'd rather drink a French cocktail while in Paris."

He smacked himself in the head. "You're right, Boone, I apologize, sometimes I get overenthusiastic. Barman, I'll have what he's having. What are we having?"

"1789 is the year of the storming of the Bastille, and the drink by that name is made variously with aperitif white wine, lillet and whiskey. These French don't have many booze-forward drinks, but this is a good one. I noted your greeting: do you speak Russian, Dax?"

"*Konesho.* Of course!"

"Why of course?"

"I'm a diplomat, and when I was up and coming you had to speak Russian to have a shot at the State Department."

"I see. So where are you stationed?"

"I'm between assignments. I used to be in Nairobi and then Port Mosby, and then briefly Sudan."

"Sudan? I can't imagine there's much fly fishing there."

His eyes were alight with eagerness. I could see by the amassed wrinkles around them that he was older than he first appeared, and had spent his share of time outdoors in harsh environments. "*Au contraire!* You just need a little help from our little friends."

Our drinks arrived, garnished with pineapple. The bartender eyed me, waiting for a sign of approval. I gave it a sip, savored, and then flashed him a thumbs up. He gave a brisk nod of thanks. The pineapple was an inspired garnish, a perfect layer in the drink's flavor profile. I adjusted my gaze to my companion, curiously. "Little friends?"

"Our little friends are what we refer to as attack helicopters."

I gulped and paused; he sensed my trepidation. Dax waved a hand in the air and continued: "It's not that big a deal. See, the British imperialists left trout everywhere across Africa, including the mountains of South Sudan. Nobody had fished those trout in maybe sixty or seventy years. Problem is that, well, the Imatong Mountains still have pockets of SPLA."

"I don't pretend to be up on all the latest doings in Africa, Dax. So there are rebel groups near the trout streams?"

He beamed. "You are sharp! Exactly. To get in there to fish we needed some little friends to go soften up the opposition. You know, lay down a little ground fire, and chase them out of there."

I cocked an eye at him, wondering how much of this was true. "Why would the South Sudanese government lend you their military for trout fishing?"

"Quid pro quo, right?" He laughed and rolled his eyes. "We give them aid. If I ask a favor, it's hard to say no, especially when they love any excuse to shoot up the bushes. Fishing was outstanding – here, look." He held out his phone and scrolled through innumerable fish photos until he stopped on one. It was of him holding what appeared to be a two-foot brown trout in his arms. Next to him stood what appeared to be a South Sudanese officer with a sly grin. Behind them in the air was a helicopter, and I could see smoke drifting across the hills in the background.

"Good Lord. You're serious, aren't you?"

Dax looked pleased with himself, and smoothed his little mustache. "Boone, I take my fishing very seriously, I never lie about it, even like the time I was skunked fishing border waters of North Korea."

I took a deep sip of my drink and let all that sink in. Then I asked: "You don't expect any particular danger on this trip, do you?'

"You, Boone Linsenbigler, afraid of a little trouble?" He looked askance at me, like I was kidding. "After what you went through down there in Central America?"

I raised an eyebrow and leaned in. "I like to fish, Dax, not get killed."

"Pshaw! This trip is pure bunny slope, my friend. Russians have everything under control. There are no rebels, and no insurgencies to mess up your back cast. I mean, as you probably know, there are tigers in this area, but our guides carry Kalashnikovs, purely as a precaution."

I nodded, trying to reassure myself that nothing was amiss. "And the rest of our retinue? Are they meeting us here?"

"Nope!" Dax smiled and leaned in. "We got the last two spots in a Russian group that will be the first to fish in there. We're the only two Americanos. Think of it, Boone – you may well end up being the only person you know other than me that has bagged a Romanov Char."

"What's the lodge like?"

"Boone, its classic Russia. The lodge is a dacha that was Khrushchev's exclusive hunting camp. There's a *banya* and everything."

"Banya? That's a steam bath, they have those in Brooklyn."

"I'm sure that this is a little more authentic than what they have in Brooklyn. It's a low log cabin, and in the better ones, there are stout women who thrash you lightly with birch branches while you sweat – *vanick*. When it gets too hot, you jump outside into the snow, then go back in, drink a warm beer, start over."

I sipped my drink, thinking to myself that if the women were stout, that Hailey's worries about my seduction for blackmail were unlikely. "Egad, how long does this *banya* go on?"

"We fish from like 8:00 or 9:00 until 2:30 or 3:00 or until we're tired of catching char or too cold or both. Then come in to the lodge for a bowl of soup and a hot mead, then *banya* until its dinnertime. You'll sleep like the dead, and then do it again the next day. It's possible we may take a side trip by helicopter to fish another river."

"So do you know any of these Russians that we'll be fishing with?"

"Only on the chat rooms, and once to Boris by phone. But I speak Russian, so I can communicate everything. I know this is a straight deal, Boone, we're going to have a great time."

I finished my drink more quickly than I had anticipated, feeling relaxed, and I was buying what Dax was saying. I ordered another 1789.

It was going to be great.

CHAPTER 6

I AM NO STRANGER TO RUSSIANS, which is likely why I launched into this trip with so little trepidation.

In high school drama class, I was cast as Simeonov-Pishchik in Chekov's 'The Cherry Orchard." Likewise, my high school history class gave me the choice of reading a big fat book on Chinese history or Russian history. I chose the latter, the specifics of which I have retained little.

College was more or less wasted, as much on advanced alcohol consumption techniques as on a degree in creative writing.

Yet I was intent on learning from the masters of the writer's craft and so launched myself at reading and understanding the headiest authors I had ever heard of: Dostoyevsky and Tolstoy. There were courses in both, and I recall feeling that I was not smart enough to sit with the cum laude crowd and understand what I was reading. I took Dostoyevsky first because I had read "The Brother's Karamazov" and had found it to be fathomable

– it was more or less a murder mystery.

The class was taught by a Russian scholar named Ignaty Kalikov, who made a rather impressive entrance each week. He had some sort of problem with one leg, and he dragged the leg along as he went. The shoe's sole on that side had been reinforced with a steel plate so that we would hear *Screet! Screet! Screet!* as he approached. Further complicating this poor man's life was the fact that his eyes looked in radically different directions and I never did settle on which one to look at when speaking to him. Otherwise, he was bald with a white fringe and modest features – had he not been disfigured he was very ordinary to look at, a dignified man in a vested tweed suit.

The class began with only eight students, all the others wearing glasses and dressed mostly in black. *I'm screwed — these guys are all brainiacs!*

By the fourth week, there was only me – the rest had dropped out, possibly because Mr. Kalikov and I spent most of each class engaged directly in a protracted back and forth on symbolism and existentialism. For whatever reason, Boone the B student was adept at interpreting and embracing Russian literature and was suddenly an 'A' student. I read everything Dostoyevsky published.

The Tolstoy class transpired in precisely the same way as the other – a one on one discussion each week with Mr. Kalikov. Both classes required what amounted to a dissertation, and on both I got A+.

Again, this was not typical of me. This was a latent aptitude I did not know I possessed. Still, this was foundational knowledge, and other than Mr. Kalikov, I had not been acquainted with any Russians.

My experience in dinner theater is a matter of record. In high school, I made money on weekends as a pretend swordsman at a venue called Medieval Knights in lovely Ho-Ho-Kus, New Jersey.

In college, I worked the campus grill for money, which was greasy, lousy work. I was yawning one morning in one of my last classes with Mr. Kalikov, and apologized. I explained that I had worked a late shift at the campus grill. I mentioned that I wished that I could attain a job at a medieval dinner theater close to school because the hours and pay were better and that I had experience with sword play. One of his eyes considered me for a moment, and then he produced a note pad. He scribbled out a note and handed it to me, saying: "My cousin has what is like a dinner theater. It is Russian. I have recommended you. Go and see if the work is better and if he needs the help."

The restaurant was called 'Winter Palace' – the namesake is the storied residence of the Romanov monarchy in St. Petersburg. It was in a part of Brooklyn where there are Russians enclaves. It wasn't too far from a subway station – for the right money, weekend work might be worth it.

I arranged to meet Kalikov's cousin, a man named Peter Petrovich. Arriving early on a Saturday morning, I had little trouble finding the Winter Palace because the outward appearance was palatial and ornate. Three white arches formed the entrance. Tall white colonnades topped with gold pilasters flanked these arches. Between the colonnades were panels painted sea-green. It was the kind of place that if you were driving by, it would compel you to look twice.

I rapped my knuckles on the glass doors where the 'CLOSED' sign was and the cleaning staff unlocked the doors and led me upstairs to Peter's office. It was a small room, the walls crammed with costumes hanging from nails in the walls. There were also various Russian and Cossack hats. Peter was planted behind a desk flanked on one side by a crate filled with swords of various sizes. He was a burly, completely bald man who looked angry but had a very light handshake. I sat opposite him, and he leaned back in his office chair, which squeaked loudly. Mr. Kalikov's note was in his hand, his small eyes giving me the once-over.

"You are not Russian?" As you would expect, he had a heavy Russian accent.

"No."

"Linsenbigler is German, yes?"

"Yes, sir."

He leaned his large hairy arms on the desk and squinted at me: "Why are you here?"

"I have worked in dinner theater, at Medieval Knights, in Ho-Ho-Kus. Mr. Kalikov thought you might need someone. And I need a weekend job. I'm in college, and need living expenses."

He grunted, looked at the note again, and then cocked his head at me.

"What did you do at this dinner theater that I might need you here?"

"I did it all. I bussed, and then worked my way up to stage work. I eventually was a knight."

"A what?"

"I played the bad knight, and then the good knight. We did staged sword fights."

His eyebrows shot up. "We have Cossacks who do swords. You are not Cossack."

I took a breath. "Mr. Petrovich, if you think you could use a stage assistant of some kind, of any kind, I will have no problem handling that. If not, if you need all your talent to be Russians, I totally understand. Mr. Kalikov just thought you might need someone, that's why I'm here."

He leaned back, the chair screaming, and gave his pug nose a rub.

Peter plucked a short sabre from the crate next to him, admired it for a second, and then lobbed it across the desk at my head.

I snatched it by the hilt in front of my nose, midair. That may seem remarkable were it not for the fact that if you've done a lot of play acting with swords, it becomes second nature to be able to toss swords around.

His eyebrows shot up.

"The Cossacks rehearse in an hour." He grunted. "You work tonight, and if OK, I pay you, you work for me. If you no good, I not pay you, you not work for me. That's that."

I stood and shook his hand: "Fair enough."

As you may have guessed, I got the job working with his Cossacks and folk dancers.

In Russia and the Ukraine, Cossacks seem like Vikings – an independent-minded ethnic group that has mercenary tendencies. They are admired as much for their fighting spirit as they are mistrusted for their shifting loyalties. The hard-core Cossacks typically shave their heads on one side and have a long braid on the other. Elaborate whiskers are common, and they have their own style of dress, complete with tunics designed to carry many knives and swords. Their cylindrical wool hats make for easy identification, though the shaggy one worn by Dax was that of a particular subgroup of Cossacks – which one I'm unsure. I'm not by any means an expert in all this. Suffice to say, like Russia itself, Cossack history is complicated and murky and filled with as much passion as it is with romanticism.

At the Winter Palace, Cossacks performed acrobatic dances, often with swords in hand. I was told the squat-kick dance that Russians are famous for is actually a Cossack dance. The act also included a fair amount of sword twirling, swashbuckling, and juggling.

I didn't actually do anything more than toss swords of different sizes to the Cossacks for their various stunts and dances. When they were through with a particular blade they would toss it back. Note that these swords were real. Not particularly sharp, but real.

Assisting costume changes for the folk dancers was part of my duties. I had to deliver their change of costumes and take away the one they stripped off for re-hanging – they were usually in quite a hurry. Backstage areas were cramped and so you couldn't be overly modest about changing clothes in mixed company. That didn't mean I didn't take in an eyeful of some winsome lady dancers in their skivvies, but only surreptitiously. I had a feeling all these actors were relatives and Lord forbid I were to wink at a Cossack's sister.

While there were non-Russians who went to Winter Palace out of curiosity and for a change of pace, most patrons were Russians out on the town, and the quantity of vodka consumed was prodigious, as you might imagine.

I was treated politely but with little interest by my Russian coworkers, few of whom had much command of English. To make some inroads, I began growing my first mustache so that I would fit in better with the Cossacks, and grudging approval came when they began to shape my mustache before shows. Slowly, they began to say goodnight to me: *spokonoy*. Then after closing one evening, as I was leaving, the Cossacks were gathered around the bar. One of them nodded at me and growled: "Linsenbigler – come drink."

I unshouldered my backpack and approached the one who called me over. In his outstretched hand was a glistening, frosty tumbler of vodka. The others snickered, expecting me to drink and then vomit, I suppose. As I suggested, my college years were not wasted when it came to drinking.

The double shot vanished down my gullet with nary a blink – but it was strong, likely a hundred proof, and burned. But I set my jaw, and thanked them – *"Spasibo."*

I picked up my bag and left.

This rite of passage meant they were more open and friendly in the weeks that followed, even the dancers. They began inviting me to the bar after closing every Saturday. Interestingly, they didn't do it to try to get me drunk. They wanted to show me what it was to be a Cossack and to be Russian, and part of that was how to drink correctly. They don't stand around holding a cocktail. They only do shots (double shots, two ounces at least), and when the cap comes off a bottle, it does not go back on. The knack they have for hard drinking is that they keep eating certain foods when they drink, and they disparaged Americans for their sloppy habits of nibbling nuts and chips while consuming booze. Many of them favored hard-boiled eggs, others oily salted fish or dumplings. Some favored following each shot of vodka with a tumbler of milk. Following suit, I sometimes didn't arrive home until sun-up, yet for all that vodka, I was happy but not a stumbling drunk. They showed me that eating certain foods in direct conjunction with large quantities of liquor will keep you from getting overly sozzled.

Of course, I also began to pick up some Russian words, and they delighted in teaching me convoluted curse words, which when I repeated them aloud they exploded in laughter.

Every once in a while, they had a special act show up from out of town, and the crowds would swell: Boris and Bo Bo. Believe it or not, the special act was a dancing bear. You cannot imagine how much these people like dancing bears. By 'dancing' I mean to include riding a motor scooter, skipping rope, playing a horn and hula hooping. The Russians went bananas. I was of course unhappy when Boris and his bear Bo Bo showed up because it was decided that I was chosen to clean up after the ursine wonder, which pleased the Cossacks no end. They called me *medved' tualet*, or 'bear toilet.' That said, I also spent some time close to Bo Bo in the cramped quarters back stage, and Boris the trainer showed me something interesting about bears. Once they are on their hind legs, their center of gravity is low, and they need their forelegs held astern to keep their balance. So they can't do much with their front paws, or hack you to bits with their claws while standing. He said in the wild, when a bear confronts you by standing up, that's the time to head butt the bruin and knock him back. To prove it, he had Bo Bo stand in front of me, I head butted him halfheartedly and he stumbled and fell to the side. Rather astounding.

I avoided the girl folk dancers, but one of them did not stay away from me, a tiny blonde about my age named Anna. She didn't accost me, merely managed to be near me when I least expected it, and when I looked at her she smiled with her whole body. The large eyes looked up into mine: inviting, limpid blue pools. The Cossacks kidded me about this, and joked that I would soon be eating dinner at her parents' house.

By Zeus, I was! There's only so long a young man can resist the charms of a little blonde girl like that, and so we fell into some rather heavy necking and petting after closing one night in the wardrobe room.

When I saw her the next week, she pranced over to me and grabbed me by the shirtfront, those limpid pools imploring mine: "Boonie, you come to dinner tomorrow, yes?"

How could such a beautiful girl come from such grim surroundings and repugnant relatives? I found myself the next afternoon in a drab, brown Coney Island apartment with faded icons on the wall. A shaft of amber sunlight sliced across the room and landed on an ornate gold orthodox crucifix standing on an end table. About a dozen of her Russian relatives sat around a long table eyeing me suspiciously. It was a motley crew. One tall and skinny, the other squat and fat, the other bent and wizened, and yet another brooding and sexy. The meal began with cabbage soup and was followed by small courses, many of which I already knew I did not like from working at Winter Palace but was too polite not to eat. Vodka was heaven sent to help wash down the cod liver salad – to this day I can still taste that foul dish when I think upon it. Her ogre-like father gave me quite the interview. When I explained I was studying to be a writer his stomach gurgled loudly, and after he'd tossed back about six shots of vodka he muttered in Russian words that I was able to translate from some of the profanities I'd been taught.

He was smiling sadly at me when he said something in Russian akin to: *If you fuck my daughter in front of my God…*

He followed this open statement by tracing his thumb across his ill-shaven throat.

I learned a great deal about Russians during those years, and much of it I admired and liked.

Some of it was chilling.

CHAPTER 7

I DIDN'T REGALE Dax with any of my past experience with Russians simply because it seemed so long ago that it was irrelevant or trivial, and I was not conversant in the language but at one time could understand some of it.

The Aeroflot Airbus to Moscow was nothing special or much out of the ordinary. I was not able to secure anything above economy. True, the flight attendants in tight red dress suits and matching scarves and garrison caps were a little bit of a throwback. The in-flight meal seemed vaguely familiar dreck: beef stew, crinkle-sliced carrots and a cellophaned roll, with a side of ham slices and lettuce. The foreign fruit bar I tucked into my bag. Never know when you are fishing and will need a little pick-me-up.

We changed planes in relatively short order at Sheremetyevo International Airport for an overnight flight to Khabivostok. So, let's review: That day, I had gone from an ocean liner, to a limo, to a train, to a limo, to a plane and now to another plane. Mixed in there I had had a couple of drinks but as I set in for the longest flight – eight hours and change – it seemed the ideal time to tuck into some of whatever they had on the drink cart to help send me off to dreamland.

Dax and I were not sitting together. As I dropped into my seat and he passed by me towards his own, he whispered: "By the way, there are no cocktails on this flight, and you can't even drink your own."

This could not be.

I fumbled through the flight information pamphlets until I came to the dreaded sentences explaining that they have no bar service on that flight.

What unspeakable barbarity was this? As I said, the Russians seem like sensible people some of the time, yet this chilling development was entirely typical of their ironic nature. Here you have a people and nation utterly sodden in vodka and yet on their flights…

Once in the air, I gobbled down a couple of pills and propped myself in the corner with ample pillows and blankets to secure me in place. In my limited experience with long flights, and fishing directly after, it is highly advantageous to secure some serious shuteye. For me there is no other way than cocktails or pharmaceuticals.

I reflected on the dancing bear hula hooping before drifting off.

I awoke to sunrise shining in the window and a flight attendant leaning in with breakfast: strawberry blintzes, ham slices and lettuce, a roll, butter and some variety of cookie biscuit. In a pharma stupor, I ate it all, even the lettuce. I stared out the window at the snowy landscape sliding below me. *Good Lord, Boonie, what kind of maniac goes fishing in Russia in winter!*

I guzzled what I presumed was coffee and began to shake off the drug fog.

If I thought the previous day was full of interesting modes of travel, what lay ahead was to amply provide further novelty.

Khabivostok in winter was pretty much like what you would imagine – part *Doctor Zhivago*, part Soviet gloom. It began to snow while we were landing, so there were sleighs jangling along the snow-packed roads next to cars and scooters. Streetlights overhead were hung from catenary wires between buildings, and they swung in the white-flecked wind. Our minibus puttered along next to an ice-choked river on our left, golden onion dome churches and gaunt Soviet apartment blocks passing on our right.

The train station was anything but the grand St. Pancras in London, and a step down from even a Long Island Railroad platform. The concrete platforms had no canopies. Workers were shoveling snow from them, yet we had to slog through considerable snowdrift to reach our train – diesel Trans-Siberian railway cars decked out in blue. Once again, Dax and I were separated. He took his place in coach while I soldiered toward the head of the train and a first class compartment, which was not fancy but looked clean and smelled of solvent. It was wood paneled, bunks on both sides, table under the window. The best part was that I was alone as opposed to being crammed into an airline seat with hundreds of others, so I was happy for the elbowroom as well. I had taken the precaution of having our minibus driver secure me a bottle of brandy from a shop in the train station and I had snapped off some icicles from a downspout on the station. With lemon slices I had stashed from the Aeroflot ham and lettuce side courses, I was able to approximate a sidecar in one of my collapsible cups.

A whistle blew, and the train clunked forward.

I watched the snow swirl past the window and curtains as the station began to slip away. I sipped my drink, snug in the corner of my bunk, and kicked off my shoes, reflecting once again: *Good Lord, Boonie, what kind of maniac goes fishing in Russia in winter!* This was insanely far away from Brooklyn – I might as well have been on another planet. Everything smelled, felt and looked different. I admit to feeling a little afraid being that far away from New York, and with only Dax at my side. I dare say there was a part of me that would have welcomed a knock at the door and the appearance of my weevil publicist Terry.

Speaking of whom, my phone had been mercifully silent once on terra firma inasmuch as I did not have cell service in Europe.

Our destination was six hours away, and after a few impromptu sidecars, my fear abated. I left my cabin for the dining car – I had agreed to meet Dax there. As I was in first class, the dining car adjoined mine. It was what you would expect – tables on both sides by the windows with curtains, clean but nothing fancy. I could smell cabbage cooking, and was for a microsecond transported back to the Winter Palace.

Dax was not there, and nobody else either, so I proceeded through the car to the next one: the bar car, which was almost identical to the dining car except there was a small bar at the far end and barmaids moving about briskly.

You would not have known it was only noon, least of all because it was dark and snowing heavily outside. The bar car was half-full of Russians swilling beer and shooting their tumblers of vodka. At the booth next to the bar there was a knot of men who looked to me to be actual, non-theatrical Cossacks, one of whom was plucking a balalaika – one of those triangular guitars. The mood in the bar car was akin to a party early in the evening where you feel the festive mood is growing and likely to boil over.

I scanned the room for Dax and finally realized he was sitting with the Cossacks, so I approached and caught him mid-sentence. He was gesticulating wildly as he spouted Russian. "Linsenbigler! Join us!"

The Cossacks around him wore tall boots and large mustaches. They were not wearing tunics but shearling coats and vests over wool sweaters. I nodded at them, but was distracted by a barmaid at my elbow with a tumbler of icy vodka. She distributed glasses to the Cossacks and Dax as well. Russians like to drink in rounds.

I said to the barmaid: "*Spaceba.*"

Then I eyed my audience: "*Za vstrechu.*" Translated: *To our first meeting.*

I have mentioned the importance Russians assign to eating while drinking. However, it is worth noting also that the Russians I had known also insisted on toasting every single round. *Za vstrechu* was a very mild and formal one, but also not a toast that most tenderfeet know.

Tossing back the vodka, I smoothed my mustache and handed her the empty tumbler.

They all raised their glasses and followed suit.

Dax said: "Ah, Boone, I see you know a few words in Russian."

Standing before them, I smiled at the Cossacks, who were eyeing me with some measure of approval for my mustache, vodka etiquette and toast.

"*Konesho*." *Of course*, I said, following that with a relatively tame oath in Russian, the gist of which was that I hoped Dax's mother had been deloused.

Cossack eyes popped out of their faces at me.

They exchanged glances and burst into deafening guffaws.

The barmaid placed a platter of boiled eggs and fish on the table, and I deftly snagged an ovum and swallowed it while the laughter continued.

Dax had a grin from ear to ear. "So you do speak Russian!"

I smirked and shook my head. "I know a few phrases, Dax, enough to be entertaining."

One of the Cossacks blurted at me – something to the effect that he himself had gotten lice from Dax's mother recently.

Explosions of laughter.

The balalaika player then broke into a tune, which appeared to be a popular one that encouraged a group sing. It took me a stanza or two before I realized the Cossacks were singing the Merle Haggard song that begins with "I was drunk the night my Mamma got out of prison…" As it went on, the Cossacks expanded the song into numerous verses about what happened next after Mom got out of prison, each exploit more outrageous than the next. I couldn't follow it all, but certain words jumped out that indicated mother was very naughty as well as unlucky. The entire train car was now laughing and cheering the performance.

Just as the applause died with the conclusion of the song, two teenage girls approached me and held up a tablet with my picture on it. It was one of my TV commercials, and they hit play. Others crowded around to watch. It was a swashbuckling commercial where I'm defending a bottle of bitters from a gang of pirates trying to take it from me by force. Damned corny, if you ask me, and in the end I hop into a boat with a buxom maiden and slash the mooring rope, leaving the angry pirates ashore. As the girl cuddles up to me while we drift out to sea, I hold up the bottle of Boone Linsenbigler's Plain & Fancy Bitters balanced on the end of my sword, smile and say: "This treasure is too good to keep buried!"

The train car went quiet for a moment before one of the girls, her cheeks in full blush, asked if that was me.

The snow swirled past the windows, the train car swaying and clattering down the rails.

"*Konesho*," I said bowing. "I am Boone Linsenbigler."

It's an odd thing, fame. People react in unpredictable ways when they suddenly realize they are in the presence of a celebrity (such as I am, a puffed up barfly.) I think people suddenly think they need to do something, or behave differently. Under such circumstances, I like to try to break the ice. I put a hand on Dax's shoulder: "Tell them I wish to buy them all a drink and toast their good health."

He stood and blurted out some Russian, none of it I recognized except my name.

A cheer erupted, and the barmaids hurried to fill glasses and deliver large trays of beer bottles. A particularly scruffy one of the Cossacks called out to me, and Dax translated: "He wants to know whether you really know how to handle a sword."

I eyed the Cossack, and said: "*Konesho.*"

From behind him, the Cossack drew a *shashka*, which is a single-edged, guardless sabre of the type I used to handle for the Cossacks back in Brooklyn. He nodded at me and said something else.

Dax translated: "He wants to know if you have ever handled one of these."

I nodded politely at Scruffy and held out my hand. The sabre was passed to me, and I held it upright, examining the worn and lightly rusted blade. My next tumbler of vodka arrived, and I held it up next to the sword and toasted the crowd, who toasted me back. I ate another egg, and Scruffy asked Dax if I was going to prove I knew how to handle the *shashka*.

I asked Scruffy if any one of them had a second sabre, and one of his companions produced another from under the table.

Placing my empty glass aside, I asked those near me to stand back.

While I did not perform with the Winter Palace Cossacks, they did teach me some of their moves, but it had been a long time, so I started slowly to make sure I didn't send a sword flying into the crowd. The maneuver is windmilling the two swords so that the blades mesh and then unmesh as you draw them together and then apart. In essence, it is baton twirling. The ceiling of the train car meant that I had to squat as I twirled the blades to keep from hitting the ceiling.

The crowd clapped in unison, and I could see phones trained my way recording my performance. No doubt, this would find its way onto social media in a trice. Just wait until Terry takes an eyeful of this! Yours truly on the Trans-Siberian Railway twirling swords and drinking with Cossacks! You can't get much more Linsenbigler than that!

My performance lasted only about fifteen seconds or so as I was intent on not injuring anybody, to include yours truly.

Applause erupted again.

Scruffy came forward and took the blades. He cleared some space at the far end of the car, and did his own sword performance while doing a squat dance to the accompaniment of the balalaika. I led the clapping on this one, and made clear that Scruffy was the champion when he relinquished the floor.

The party was under a full head of steam, to be sure, but I was cognizant that Dax and I had only a few hours before we reached our debarkation. As such, and while the crowd was distracted by another rousing song, I had Dax settle my account with the barmaid and we drifted back to the dining car, which was dotted with people eating lunch. We secured a table, and the cabbage soup came without so much as a menu.

Dax laughed: "Boone, you are a man with cards up his sleeve! You would have done well in the foreign service."

"Don't believe it. I'm a drunkard who knows some bar tricks."

"Both of which saved your skin in the Caribbean."

I shook my head. "That was mostly retreating at the right moments and unadulterated dumb luck."

"I don't think you realize that both of those require a certain rare talent." He slurped soup, and swallowed. "Luck is never dumb, I know from personal experience. Luck is anticipating and taking advantage of opportunities other people don't recognize."

"My ardent wish is that I never need whatever talent that is again."

He waved his spoon at me, and almost said something, but didn't.

CHAPTER 8

SLEIGHS PULLED BY SNOWMOBILES were our next mode of transport. Stout men that looked to me like Eskimos in parkas piloted them. One transported us, the other our gear. The sleighs wound up mountain roads through birch and pine forests that were a dead ringer for Vermont. This last leg of the journey went on for over two hours until low-slung log cabins came into view as we crested a ridge. Then the squat main lodge came into view – all the logs used in the construction of these abodes seemed oversized. Even the main roof beams were better than two feet in diameter, and much of the wood was stained brown verging on black. The main lodge was two stories, the upper story sporting a large deck with gnarled log railing and backed by expansive windows. The chimney was also made of crisscrossed logs and wood smoke rose steadily from it. I had never seen a chimney made of wood and wondered how it was that it did not catch fire. To both sides of the main lodge were the guest cabins, black against the snowy woods.

One small flanking cabin directly next to the main lodge had steam rising from the roof and was obviously the sweat lodge.

Our caravan drove under the lodge balcony and came to a stop. A small elderly couple stood waiting for us, both slitty-eyed and rosy-cheeked. She had a headscarf, and he a pointed cap. Dax addressed the gnome-like couple as we stepped down out of our sleigh, and they bowed and yammered back at him as they alternately barked orders at our drivers. I stepped forward and shook their little warm hands: she was Alina, he was Anton.

There was some intense discussion between Dax and Alina before he turned to me and said:

"They are the caretaker and cook, they live here, brother and sister. They want to know what we would like to do between now and dinner a couple hours from now. They have the sauna up and ready for us, but I said I'd rather make a run down to the river and take a look."

I dug my hands under my armpits – it was much colder up in the hills than down at the train station, well below freezing and after all the travel I didn't hanker to move more than a few feet in any direction for a while.

"Dax, you go ahead, I think I'd rather get settled and maybe inspect the sauna, take the chill off."

The sled drivers had carted our luggage off to the two cabins on the other side of the sauna, with mine being closer since I had expressed interest in heating up.

Entering my cabin, I found a fire roaring in a stone fireplace, the log walls that same black-brown color. The walls were dotted with some old black and white photos of men with fish and dead animals, and there was an ancient rifle mounted over the door. Above the mantle was a mounted bear head that had been badly dried by the heat of the fire below it. The hide's shrinkage made the bear's eyes bugged-out and the lips and teeth exaggerated. Were the backside of the bear on the other side of the wall you would have guessed some sort of ursine proctologic exam was in progress.

A gigantic bed made out of girthsome logs just like the cabin dominated the center of the room. To one side was a long table where the sled driver had piled my stuff and lit an oil lantern – there was no electricity. There were small windows in three of the four sides that were frosted over with ice and snow.

The room smelled of eucalyptus, wood smoke and whatever fuel the lamp was burning. Perhaps whale? I had been transported back several hundred years.

The drivers trudged past me to exit. The hulking door was mounted on massive hinges, and it closed behind them with a colossal *WHUMP*.

Overall, if a man could hibernate, this would be the place to do it, just curl up in the over-stuffed bed piled high with comforters and animals skins and sleep until the snows melted. Talk about a man cave!

I sorted my cold weather gear and rigged some rods so that I would be ready to fish first thing the next day. Slipping on some swim trunks, I donned a heavy, rug-like robe hanging on the back of the door along with some wooden sandals. A course bath sheet slung over my shoulder, I emerged from my lair.

Like a pack of small cold dogs, the icy wind nipped at

my bare ankles as I trotted next door to the sauna. There was a sheltered entryway with an outdoor shower stall, the fixtures encrusted in blue scale from the mineral-rich ground water. Past that was an enormous wooden door and I shouldered it open. Inside it was toasty, steamy and dark.

There was an oil lamp in the corner beaded with water, and the same ice-choked mini windows, so I spent a moment adjusting my eyes to see if anybody else were in the room, which smelled sulphurous. There was a hot spring directly ahead of me in a circular stone well. Steam rose out of it. Beyond that on the far wall was a heavy plank platform for sitting. I circled the well while watching out both for the low beams and my footing on the stone floor. I disrobed, positioning myself on my towel on the platform. The sauna wasn't monstrously hot, but a half hour would be the most you would want to endure. My room was a cave, but this was a cave with a fog bank parked inside.

I heard a back door shove open, and some daylight splashed from beyond some heavy plastic curtains. As was customary, a towel draped my head and I was hunched. A hand rested on my shoulder and an accented woman's voice said: "Remove your trunks and lie on a towel face down."

I did as I was told, only catching a peripheral shadow of the woman, and she neither looked to be hulking or old. I didn't want to break any taboos so I soon had my head on my folded arms, my backside toward the ceiling.

She began rubbing my back and shoulders, and not in what I would call a workman-like way. Maybe this was just the way they did things.

The hands moved lower and just when I was beginning to think something more was in the offing, she stopped.

I heard some rustling, and then felt my back swatted repeatedly and none-too gently with a birch branch. Just as I was about to protest, she said: "Roll over."

I did.

Steam swirled around her, the face in shadow, the lamp flickering light across her pale naked waist, and then across her naked chest.

I recognized the bright red nipples and tits right away. "Katya!"

The woman turned, smiling slyly, and by God it was her face, slick with sweat in the half-light of the sauna, her long hair a wet copper curtain down her side. She leaned in and began massaging my pectorals. "Yes, it is Katya, Boone."

I tried to sit up but she pushed me down. "How are you all the way here, Katya? This is impossible. How did you even get here before me?"

"You obviously do not understand that your hosts wanted to make sure your entire trip was pleasurable. Is that wrong?" Her one hand drifted down to my thigh and she dragged her nails lightly, teasingly. "Boone, you are full of vitality and should let me please you."

Dumfounded, I realized she was as Hailey suggested, not just a crazed fan but sent to 'compromise me.' However, as I am not married, I really can't imagine how general knowledge of my fraternizations would have the least negative implications. To the contrary inasmuch as

Conglomerated has made me out to be the ladies' man par excellence.

She began to thrash my chest lightly with the birch branch with one hand, while the other had discovered that SS Linsenbigler's centerboard was deployed. If there were a camera in that steam bath, the only thing it would have recorded was shadows on the other side of a fogged lens. I have to say that while the intrusion aboard the Queen Mary was eminently thwartable, the exotic surroundings and erotic touch and thrashing was getting the better of me.

Damn the torpedoes, as they say.

It wasn't a particularly long coupling – it couldn't be in that infernal sauna or you'd simply pass out from heat exhaustion. She climbed astride my saddle and worked my pommel from a canter to a gallop, not sparing the birch crop. At a critical juncture, I flipped her – she resisting at first – and returned the favor, her bucking with fervor. When we cleared the last jump, I was at the point of fainting from the heat and exertion. That's when she led me by the hand back through that curtain to a discreet fenced area at the rear of the sauna, out into the swirling snow, which seemed impossibly bright. She gave me a gentle push and I fell into a drift of snow – talk about a whipsaw! Imagine not only the transition from hot to freezing cold, but also going from a steeple chase to a to high dive. Katya wiggled in next to me, rubbing snow in my hair – the icy cold didn't seemed to faze her a bit. No wonder her nipples were so red.

When I began to shiver she led me back inside, and from a bucket handed me a bottle of cold beer. She positioned me up against the wall and stroked me with the branch again as I began to warm up. I was handed a shot of brandy, which I downed, and shuddered violently.

That's when she began working my loins again.

I would never have thought this whole episode was possible – it was as intense a sexual encounter as most people would likely ever want.

As an aside, I cannot say that I have ever sipped beer while being serviced. That's usually frowned upon. Yet as you can imagine, from that time forward, it has been nearly impossible for me not to reflect on this encounter any time I sip a beer.

She arose, and whispered in my ear: "You had better shower and go to the main lodge. Dinner is in an hour." She bit my ear gently, and exited the rear of the sauna.

Showered and dressed a half hour later, I stumbled my way to the main lodge, the snow having turned to flurries.

I entered at the first floor where a long heavy wooden table was set, and at a wood stove where Alina and Anton worked steaming pots and fry pans. They turned, smiled and nodded. I felt like I had just entered the base of a tree where the gnomes live. Anton gestured for me to ascend a steep hewn-log stair. As I went up the stair, I was aware of the pounding that my loins had sustained and did my share of grimacing as I went.

The second floor was arranged with lounging furniture in a semi-circle around a fire pit blazing in the center of the room, the large glass windows beyond with a commanding wintry view of the valley below. There were many lanterns lit, so it was not as dark an interior as that to which I had become accustomed.

"Boone!" Dax jumped from a seat by the fire and approached with a glass extended in his hand. "Brandy?" He was the only one in the room.

I took the glass and pulled a mighty swig from it. "Don't mind if I do."

"How was your sauna?"

I cleared my throat. "First rate."

"Come over here, to the windows."

The valley was in half-light, but I could make out the river below. I gestured with my glass: "That's the Goryachiy River down there?"

"Indeed it is." He gripped my shoulder. "Boone, I scouted out a few runs this afternoon. Some of them are just packed with char."

Having tangled with Katya, the heat, the snow, and then Katya again, I was having trouble focusing on the importance of fishing. "So, Dax, where are the other anglers?"

"Delayed. There was an avalanche on the tracks that has to be cleared."

"So is it just you and I for dinner?"

"I would guess so."

I lowered myself into a chair, my gonads complaining.

"Boone, are you in pain?"

"It's nothing, Dax. Oh, I have a question: did you tell anybody I was taking the Queen Mary?"

He shrugged. "No. Why?"

How the devil did Katya know to follow me onto the boat on such short notice? Unless someone was reading my emails as I typed them. Hailey claimed that might be the case.

"Oh, just a coincidence, I ran into someone I know on the ship. You mentioned that they have the heavy winter gear for us? I've got all the base layers and such."

"Yes, they supply the fur hat, coat and boots."

"Do they ever fly helicopters in here? I see that at the peninsula lodges."

"They plan to do special side trips to another river by air, and I'm told they have a clearing for that purpose. But for now they only use the train to get people here."

"Interesting. So what rods do you plan on fishing?"

Our conversation devolved from there into technical angler talk and continued through dinner. Though to be honest, char fishing tends not to be that technical – the quarry are known to be indiscriminate feeders. *Salvethymus romanov* are sea-run char that are related to Arctic char. They move up into the Goryachiy River in the winter, chasing a kind of herring that spawn that time of year in the warmer thermal waters. Likewise, the local Tetrov Lemmings (to the untrained eye, a mouse) make for ample prey. The lemmings do not hibernate, and remain quite active in the snow. Inasmuch as most of their summer feed plots are fallow beneath several feet of snow, they find it productive to work the edges of the warm streambeds looking for green shoots and watercress. As such, the Goryachiy is said to have a 'lemming hatch' very loosely comparable to an insect hatch. The char will jump on anything dragged across the water that looks like a cat toy mouse.

Trout back in the States require delicate presentations of just the right insect in just the right size and color at just the right time. Likewise, many Caribbean and other fish require delicate presentations or precise imitations of the bait. That kind of fishing has its rewards. However, so does fishing for hefty fish that hit anything you throw, which is ostensibly why I had traveled half way around the world to the snowy nether reaches of Russia.

The most technical part of the fishing would likely be just dealing with the cold, the snow, and the ice forming on the line and rod guides.

As just the two of us ate at the giant table, Dax prattled on about his adventures chasing an obscure, oversized perch in the Philippines, and I was only half listening.

If Katya was connected to my 'hosts' for this Russian jaunt, that meant my hosts had access to my email and web browser and were able to deploy her to be on the same voyage in an instant. Likewise, for her to reach the lodge before me, it meant that she had to be flown in by helicopter. While I'm sure the lodge owners are well versed in the finer hospitality arts and wish to please a famous guest, that level of service seemed a tad beyond the pale.

Something was up.

CHAPTER 9

BRACING BLUE SKIES greeted us the next morning, with a light breeze and hovering ten degrees below freezing. Our two Eskimos (Dax identified them as native Udege, which he pronounced *OO-de-gay*) drove us on their snowmobiles down to the river, which was narrow enough that you could wade across certain parts but not others. There were some long pools and steep riffles and deep blue undercut banks. The water was an aquamarine color and utterly pristine. Fresh snow hemmed the banks unblemished, a tree line of birch and fir nearby. On the other side of the stream was a series of piney hillocks backed by snow-flanked mountains – not the Himalayas but certainly the Rockies.

I wore my chest waders and several layers of thermal gear, plus a voluminous white fur coat and white fur hat, complete with earflaps. In the mirror, I looked like a giant marshmallow. My hands sported neoprene gloves. Under a fleece facemask, I wore my darkest polarized sunglasses to cut the snow glare and look deep into the water. I did not see or spook any fish as I waded the shallows upstream from the base of a pool. Dax was working a pool directly below mine.

All it took was a 'mouse fly' (I call them cat toys) thrown center stream and moved two feet before a char arced out of the water and crushed it. Char don't have a reputation for jumping, but these went aerial, and until beached you would have thought these were Atlantic salmon. Their sides had the customary silver with white spots but the belly was violet – Arctic char have vermilion bellies. That first lively fish was likely fifteen pounds and measured the length of my arm, shoulder to wrist.

Our Udege guides sat and watched from their snowmobiles, arms folded, Kalashnikovs propped in the snow by their sides. I daresay that seeing a tiger in those surroundings certainly seemed as remote as seeing a tiger at a Colorado ski resort.

When my second fish jumped, a dead lemming actually flew out of its mouth! I lost that fish, but the sight of an actual lemming inspired me to inspect the edges of the stream. Wouldn't you know it? When I looked closely, I could see lemmings all over the place scurrying along the river edges. I'd never seen anything like it. Astounding.

Eventually we took a break for a thermos of coffee and jerky. Dax and I were beside ourselves as we had each of us only worked the one pool all morning and each had twelve or so fish up to eighteen pounds. Our Udege put us back on the snowmobiles and took us downstream to another set of pools with the same result.

This is why I had come to Russia in the winter. We

were slaying them.

By early afternoon, we were exultant and ready to head back to the lodge. Dax in particular wanted to have a sauna, which had me wondering about where Katya was and whether she would make another appearance. I had not seen a wit of her since the sauna – no idea where she was staying and she did not come to meals.

Alas, the sauna was uneventful, and we sweltered, just the two of us. I left the snow diving to Dax and went instead for a shower and then my room, thinking I would take a snooze before dinner.

I was startled when the covers on my bed moved, and Katya sat up, one of the bed furs fetchingly held across her chest, the small dark eyes looking at me from under the copper hair. Beside the bed was a bottle of open champagne and two glasses.

In a breathy, Russian accent, she purred: "You kept me waiting."

Had she been holding any tree branches, I think I would have had a second thought. However, this apple was already bitten, and I could not think of a reason to refrain, this time perhaps with a bit more élan.

Yet she was still quite spirited, so in deference to my gonads I managed to moderate the pounding, which in the result I would have to guess was better for her.

When we paused, we drank champagne while she toyed with my loins trying to get me started again – a persistent lass if ever there were. Yet I was distracted. Who were the hosts? When would they show themselves and tell me what they wanted? I asked her.

She laughed lightly, and said: "Soon."

As if on cue, there was a thumping sound in the air. I asked: "Is that a helicopter?"

"*Koresho.* But we have time, why waste it?"

"Katya, you're saying they do want something?"

"Boonie, everybody wants something. I want something."

The helicopter got louder, echoing through the valley, and I would soon know why I had been brought to East Russia. I was fairly positive that I hadn't died and gone to heaven. Otherwise there would be a full bar.

Completely in the dark as to what would happen next, my calculus was simple. If what was coming was bad, what's the worst it could be? Well, I might be held captive, maybe have my life hang by a proverbial thread… wouldn't be the first time. If that were the case, and I had the ability to grant myself a last wish, what would that be?

So I gave Katya what she wanted.

CHAPTER 10

I ENTERED THE SECOND FLOOR of the lodge to find Dax flanked by six men in heavy sweaters and shearling vests – five were large. The sixth was the only one still wearing his fur hat, and his bored eyes only glanced in my direction. The other men kept their eyes on me.

Dax gestured to the empty chair between him the first large Russian. However, as I approached, I noticed a side table had been arranged as a bar. In addition to vodka and brandy, it was complete with bourbon, single malt and port.

I was understandably nervous, a circumstance under which I often act very flip indeed. It's a defense mechanism, I suppose. It remained to be seen whether it was an effective mechanism. Were these men my hosts or my fishing companions? Both?

I veered to the bar. "Can I make anybody a cocktail? Dax? I'll be right over for introductions. My apologies if I'm tardy for cocktail hour." The first ice cube I tossed in my glassed popped out and vanished under the bar. So did the second, so I shoved a fist full in the next time and splashed some PennyPacker bourbon on top of that. You don't see that brand often in the States as it is mainly for European consumption. But it was a welcome old friend at that juncture.

I approached Dax with a smile and bright demeanor. "Gentlemen! Pleased to meet you, I'm Boone."

I went down the line shaking hands and none of them uttered their names.

When I got to the last one, the smaller man with pointy nose and dull eyes, he stood and said: "Vlad."

"Vlad! Well, pleased you finally made it." I noticed nobody but Dax had a drink, and it looked like vodka. "We certainly had some great fishing today, didn't we Dax?"

"We did! Say, Boone, I know Vlad is a big fan of yours and is hoping you might honor him with one of your cocktails. He's generally a beer drinker."

"At your service!" There was bottled Pilsner in a wooden bucket filled with snow beside the bar, so I opened that and poured it over some rocks in a glass. Looking over the other bottles, I noticed some Barenjager (a honey liqueur) and recalled a Russian fondness for honey, so put a splash of that in along with a dribble of what appeared to be a very old bottle of Cuban Amaretto, and a drip of orange liqueur. There were no garnishes to be had, so I suppose that would have to be that. Pilsner can be a surprisingly good base for a mild, sweet cocktail.

When I sauntered back to the group the only open chair was next to Vlad, and Dax had moved to the side of that so I would be between them.

I sat in my spot and handed Vlad his cocktail. His dull eyes inspected it by the lamp light, and then the eyes inspected me askance. He drank while keeping his eyes on me, and then looked at the ceiling, his eyes showing some life. "*Osvezheniye.*"

Dax translated: "He said it's refreshing."

I clinked glasses with Vlad and looked at the other large men, who sat motionless, staring at me. Was I mistaken or were these Vlad's bodyguards?

Vlad cleared his throat, looked at Dax, then at me, and blurted some Russian.

Dax: "Vlad would like to fish with you tomorrow. He has heard you are very good at fly fishing. He does not fly fish but uses a spinning rod as he finds it more efficient."

"Capital!" I chirped.

Vlad sipped his drink, grunted with satisfaction, and then removed his fur hat to reveal thinning blond hair swept to the side. He hooked the hat on the back of my chair, leaned in and asked (through Dax, of course) about fishing for permit, which he had heard much about but knew little. The fish is not native to Russian waters.

This is a topic about which I am not expert but have my share of experience, so I explained the looks of the fish, how they cruise the shallows looking for crabs and shrimp with their dorsal fin and tail fin sticking out of the water. I also explained that another way to fish for them is to look for manta and other rays as permit often follow alongside the rays to scoop up crustaceans the rays miss, and that for my money, permit were much easier to catch in this situation.

Vlad responded: "Yes, of course it would be, there is turbulence, and the fish would be focused on the ray and not spook so easily, yes?"

"Exactly. And if you get a big one, at the end of the fight, they sometimes just lie on their sides on the bottom and it is very hard to move them."

Vlad slapped his knee. "Fascinating. All this is not too unlike life, is it not? Like in judo, maybe. The best way to take advantage of an opponent is to use a distraction or to assume a defensive position that makes your opponent wear himself out."

I then explained that the first permit I ever caught was the product of dumb luck. The guides and I had been casting to tailing permit – those eating off the bottom in such a way that their tails stick out of the shallows. The fish would look at and follow my fly but would not attack it – my guess was that they would not eat it because it did not smell like a crab. My contention is that tailing permit rely in large part on smell to identify prey. So I was standing on deck, holding the fly, ready to cast at another fish in the shallows, when in my peripheral vision I saw a permit coming toward the boat from deep water. Only twenty feet from the boat, the fish could not see us because the sun was in his eyes. I had been making eighty-foot casts all morning to no effect, and now I just flipped my fly over my shoulder and this permit dashed in and ate it. He ate my fly based on sight, not with his nose pressed to the sea floor.

Vlad laughed, though the laughter stayed in his chest, his grin exaggerating his cheekbones. He threw out a hand: "Again, how like life is this? The accepted approach to a problem is not always the one that gets you what you want. Sometimes it is best that you position yourself so that the fish comes to you."

As ever, fish talk had the capacity to engross me to the extent that all else faded from importance. Talking about fishing utterly consumes me.

In this instance, however, I suddenly realized who Vlad looked like. I turned to Dax: "Am I crazy, or does this guy look like Putin?"

Dax looked amused, his eyes darting from Vlad to me.

"Boone, this is Vladimir Putin."

I searched Dax's eyes a moment, and then laughed. "No! Come on!" Then I glanced at Vlad, who also looked bemused, a knowing grin beneath sleepy eyes.

Dax tented his fingers. "Boone, that's what this trip was all about. Putin wanted to fish with you. He felt that if he asked directly you would be told not to come. This is effectively his lodge, his *dacha*, and there are no other anglers coming."

I squinted at him. "But why on earth would he want to fish with me?"

"I'll ask and see what he says."

As Vlad was responding, I was in wonder at what an unassuming figure Putin was. I had no idea he was not particularly tall, or that his voice was relatively high, like a high schooler. This was not the commanding presence I would have imagined. Could this be an imposter to try to get me to do something?

Vlad said: "While I know Mr. Linsenbigler is an actor for his company, I also know that his exploits in the

Caribbean were very real, and that he is a man's man and intrepid angler and swordsman. These are things I admire, and in my own way, I feel we are kindred spirits. The talk of how permit operate we both find fascinating. I like to think of fishing as a brotherhood where there is mutual understanding. Once when I was in your country, I went fishing with George Bush, the elder Bush, while his son was President. You know, the simple act of catching fish together…it was as if we were not enemies and understood each other and did not have to play games. I don't like to think of us as enemies, but I feel your political system and election process demand polarization, that the U.S. makes Russia the bad guy because it makes a candidate the good guy." He flashed a grin, reached out and prodded his white fur hat. "You notice, Linsenbigler, my hat is white. I do not wear a black hat."

I nodded, studying Vlad. Then I turned to Dax: "So you're a diplomat. The State Department had you deliver me here?"

Dax bobbed his head apologetically. "I never said I *still* work for the State Department. I guess you would call me a freelance diplomat."

I paused. "You work for Russia, then?"

He shrugged. "At this moment, yes, they asked me to get you here."

"How on earth did you know I would accept, and on New Year's Eve of all times?"

Vlad cleared his throat, and said in broken English: "I understand question." Then he resumed answering in Russian: "I saw you on that stage, in Times Square.

Knowing what I know about you, I can see that this fame, this acting, this cartoon imprisons you as an adventurer, as an angler and man of the world. As with the permit, I saw that the sun was in your eyes, and I flipped you the crab. To my astonishment, you took it. So here we are. Is this not good? Is the fishing not good? I made sure to have better liquor for you as I know your tastes. I hope also that the female companionship is to your liking."

I leaned back, smoothing my mustache, trying to take this all in. Sipping my drink, I was amazed that I had not only somehow captured the imagination of the people all across the United States, but of Vladimir Putin! He thought of me as an 'adventurer' and 'man's man.' What does one say to someone like him under such circumstances?

Yet there I was, halfway around the world in the company of the president of Russia. I knew him, of course, by reputation as filtered through politicians and the media as a slippery and manipulative autocrat. I had been dimly aware that he was also an angler, and believe I had seen a picture of him holding a large pike. As I am not political, it serves me no purpose to judge people based on political philosophy. I don't make it my business to follow international events closely or to take stands on who is good or bad – many professionals make that their business. So while I knew Vlad was supposedly a 'bad guy,' there was no imaginable reason to refuse his hospitality, especially after I had traveled so far. There was no walking out the door to the nearest subway stop because of whatever was going on in Crimea or elsewhere.

I leaned in to Vlad, and Dax translated: "Well, I have to say I'm a little embarrassed that I did not recognize you right off. I would never have imagined that I rated the admiration and kinship of a man of your stature. You will have to excuse me – I am completely stunned by my circumstance. As you say, anglers are a fellowship, and it is clear that we share a worldview of fishing. Your bringing me to this exquisite lodge honors me all out of proportion to what I deserve."

Vlad looked very pleased by this, then cocked his head with curiosity: "Why do you say you do not deserve this honor?"

"Because – as you say – I am merely an actor, and while I have managed to escape with my life from that terrible situation in the Caribbean, at heart I am only a drinker and angler."

"Ah!" He held up a finger. "Then how is it you are also a Cossack? I saw on the internet the videos from the train. You are not a stranger to Russia."

Anton appeared at the top of the stair down to the kitchen. Brandishing a carved sheep horn, he blew into the small end: *BLAAAAT.*

The horn indicated dinner was served, and we were soon downstairs with me sitting to Vlad's right at the head of the table. Dax sat opposite me, and the henchmen filled in the rest of the table, utterly silent.

The Udege had harvested one of our char for dinner, and it was cooked on a long platter with turnips and herbs and artisan bread. Through dinner, Vlad and I discussed fishing, and because Dax had to translate, he had difficulty eating. Putin regaled me with his adventures with pike, and it was clear by his flashing eyes that this was his favorite fish, though surprisingly he was also quite fond of yellow perch in the Volga. He described his favorite lures, many of them spinners and spoons, about the rods and qualities of fishing lines. We discussed the merits of braided fishing lines and knot strengths. He asked about fly fishing, and said that he had tried it but could not get the knack of it – yet it looked simple. I went on to describe in detail the mechanics versus spin fishing, adding that I was not a snob about fly fishing and would use a spinning rod if it meant the difference between catching and not catching. He explained that he had so little time to take off to go fishing he needed to make the most of it and did not have any time to learn to fly fish.

Our conversation eventually turned to Cossacks and my history with Chekov, Dostoevsky, Tolstoy and the Winter Palace in Brooklyn. By this point pistachio ice cream was being served, which he said was one of his favorites, that he did not like sweets except ice cream. He was fascinated with my experience with Russian studies and Cossacks, and that it was to my credit that as an American I took a genuine interest in Russia.

His ice cream dispensed, Vlad stood: "Linsenbigler, it has been a long day, and I look forward to a productive day fishing with you tomorrow. I admit that one of my failings, as an angler, is that I sleep late, so for me to arise earlier than I am accustomed, I must retire earlier. It has been a pleasure having you as my guest, more so than I even anticipated. *Spokoynoi nochi.*"

With that, he and his five bodyguards donned their fur coats and hats and left the main lodge.

"Dax, can we go upstairs for a nightcap?"

Still chewing the last of his food, he agreed by waving me on.

Once we were situated before the fireplace, the dark, snowy windows whistling with the wind, I swirled my freshened glass of PennyPacker and got to cases with Dax.

"Dax, if you were me, would you be just a tad miffed at being lured half way around the globe on false pretenses?"

"I said the fishing would be awesome, and the fishing is awesome. I said there would be other anglers, Russians. OK, so there's only one, but he's the undisputed ruler of the largest piece of real estate on the face of the planet."

"I must say Vlad seems as natural and friendly as can be, Dax, but I'm concerned that there's something more involved."

He sipped his vodka and said flatly: "Like what?"

I thought about telling him of my conversations with Hailey, but then thought better of doing so. If indeed she were my guardian angel, it would be best if my hosts were not the wiser. My retort: "I suppose that I'm concerned with being used as some sort of prop to color Putin's reputation. We've seen him cozy up with some American expatriate celebrities and I don't really want to become part of that club. I don't want to be involved in any geopolitical gamesmanship where I'm made to look sympathetic to a foreign country."

He shrugged. "He will certainly want to show you to

the press, that you fished together. Look, he's a nice guy, and although he likely does have an agenda, that doesn't mean the agenda needs to be yours. It will be up to you when you return home to say what your position is. And it isn't as if you have a lot of choice right now."

"Precisely." I knit my brow. "I don't cotton to being put in this position."

"Oh, really?" He laughed. "You get to fish and fuck a sexy red head and fraternize with Vladimir Putin. Don't you think pictures of you and him fishing together will make the news, help promote your brand?"

"My brand?" I rolled my eyes. "I hardly need any more promotion. Look, there are certain quarters that have been attempting to get me into politics, and I fear this trip is somehow engineered as a result of that."

"Look, Boone. Tell Vlad what you told me. I think he will respect that you don't have any political ambitions, and if he has some sort of designs on you in that regard, it will have been well worth it to get you out here to find that out – as a process of elimination. I honestly think the reason he brought you here is mostly for the reasons he stated. He wanted to meet and fish with you."

I stood and recharged my drink, then paced a moment before the fire.

"You know, Dax, as much as I'm a bar fly and addled angler, I'm not stupid."

"What is it you're afraid of, exactly? He can say what he wants, but when you return to the U.S. you can say whatever you like about your relationship with him and Russia."

I sighed. Perhaps he was right.

With the remainder of my drink in hand, I returned to my cave and was grateful that Katya was not there.

Burrowing under the blankets and pelts, I downed the last of my bourbon and blew out the lamp.

Firelight danced on the cave ceiling and across the old pictures of men long since as dead as their fish. The wind whistled across the giant black logs of my cabin and rattled the icy windows. As I drifted to sleep, and through a pleasant bourbon fog, a small catch in Dax's logic occurred to me.

What if they didn't let me go home?

CHAPTER 11

THERE WAS A FLEET of five snowmobiles to transport the three anglers, five bodyguards and two Udege down to the river. This time we went farther downstream than the day before. Overcast skies littered us with a light snow as we lunged and jolted along the river, the roar and whine of the engines shattering the icy silence. Dax and his Udege stopped at a slick bend, but the rest of us charged onward downstream to a complex series of stepped blue pools connected by silver riffles like a giant sapphire necklace.

Vlad dismounted, accepted his spinning rod from a bodyguard, and swaggered toward the stream edge. 'Swaggered' is perhaps an exaggeration – he rocks side to side as he walks in a very purposeful gait, but there is no bravado to it. As I said, he is not a tall man, but with the fur hat and coat and snow boots he looked much larger.

As I rigged my rod, I kept an eye on him. He had a small plastic case of lures in his hand, and he looked carefully for just the right one before tying it directly to his monofilament line. I could see that the lure of choice was a steel spinner with white bucktail tied to the trailing treble hook. I had little doubt that just about any lure would work.

When my fly rod was rigged, I trudged through the snow and up near him, watching the flash and flicker of his silver lure as Vlad reeled it toward him through the water. He muttered to himself in Russian, and I noticed that the char were following his lure but ducking away from it. If I had to guess, the vibration of the spinning blade wasn't to their liking. Continuing downstream below him, I situated myself at the second blue gem in the necklace, perhaps a thousand feet away.

Once again, lobbing my cat toy into the center of the pool resulted in an explosion of char. I hooked one, and shot an eye upstream to where Vlad was changing lures.

Out-fishing a man like Vladimir Putin was something I did not relish. To be frank, I don't like out fishing anybody. Fishing is not nearly as much fun unless everybody is catching. After I had landed three (and one that tipped twenty pounds,) I could see Vlad still struggling. So I reeled up and began to approach him to see if I could help. He was in the midst of changing lures for what must have been the tenth time, his bodyguards sitting on the snowmobiles behind him, arms folded.

He saw me coming and held up a hand.

I put my arms out to say: *Are you sure I can't help?*

He waved his arm to signal he was OK, and then waved me off.

The least I could do under the circumstances was to catch my fish out of sight, because I had seen men in his predicament before and they rarely find the lure that works. The mechanics of 'why' stems from a rather disheartening loss of mojo. Much of angling success is positive attitude and a belief that a fish on the line is inevitable, a box of lures notwithstanding. I have seen men casting bare hooks outperform men with the most advanced and time-tested lures and flies. So there are days when an angler succumbs to frustration, self doubt and indecision, wherein technique withers. Making matters worse is when – like Vlad – you see the fish chase and break away, making the exercise that much more maddening. The way to regain your mojo is to swallow your pride and ask for help to catch that first fish, or first couple of fish. Once accomplished, the self-doubt usually subsides and the bungling ends. True, there is residual humiliation in needing help, but that is an easier emotional ice cube to dissolve in your evening cocktail than the cold pebble of failure. You would not have thought that this would happen to a man like Vlad. Alas, it happens to all anglers now and again. Any angler who says otherwise – no matter how seasoned – is a liar.

I fired up a cheroot and slogged along the snowy riverbank, puffs of cigar smoke in my wake. I pushed on around a bend, a steep hillside across from me overhung with birch, the mountain peaks around me invisible in the clouds of lightly falling snow. I was completely alone, and took a moment to hear my own breath contrasted against the snowy hush and the burble of the icy blue water. *If only this were Vermont!*

Please dear God let Vlad start catching fish. It is bad enough when you are on a trip with men of lesser stature that are skunked. Then come evening, they must listen to the triumphs of their fellow anglers. Perhaps Vlad was self-effacing and magnanimous enough an angler to be able to brush it off. While I'm not student of such things, those characteristics did not seem entirely simpatico with a Russian tsar.

My cat toy continued to work marvels, the silver and violet char bursting upon the fly and once hooked jumping repeatedly, one of them pirouetting up through the branches of a leaning birch tree and breaking me off. That was fine, I had more cat toys, and as I was tying a new one on, I heard snowmobiles approaching, and soon saw four of them loaded with men in fur approach.

I paused and awaited their arrival.

Vlad dismounted, smiling and half-lidded and I assumed he somehow got his mojo back and caught some char. He tromped toward me and asked in English:

"How is fish?"

I flashed a thumbs up, and he clapped his mittens with applause.

"And you?" I asked.

He rolled his eyes, and attempted his English again: "Old Russian saying: A wise person not climb mountain; wise person go around mountain."

Vlad opened his mitten and held out a dark egg-shaped object in his hand.

While I have never been in the military, it was immediately obvious by the split ring, handle and "pineapple" steel case that what was in his mitten was a hand grenade.

Smiling he began to toss it in one hand. "We name

these *limonka.* Small lemon."

Without much ceremony, he held it up, pulled the pin, cocked back an arm, and threw it through the swirling snow toward the pool I'd been fishing. When the spring-loaded metal handle separated from the grenade, there was a loud snap like a .22 rifle firing. I supposed that the snap was something setting the fuse alight.

I was unaware of exactly what the impending explosion would be like but did not hesitate to drop to the ground.

BOOM.

I had my head tucked down so could only hear the enormous plume of water erupt from the pool.

Vlad laughed and said something to his bodyguards, and then to me. "Not frightened, Linsenbigler."

I slowly rose to a crouch and saw the surface of the pool covered in white foam and the forms of slowly rising dead char, most of them tattered.

Vlad helped me to my feet and placed another grenade in my glove. It was both smaller and heavier than I imagined it would be. He pointed at the pool, his eyes inspecting mine curiously. I looked back at the bodyguards and two of them had their phones out. They were recording.

Imagine Terry's dismay once a video of me grenade fishing hit the internet?

Imagine the uproar in the fishing community? I would be vilified to no end.

Was this something that was supposedly going to be used to blackmail me into being a Russian sympathizer and shill?

Vlad leaned in, and whispered: "I insist."

I was petrified that I would drop it into the snow or bobble the bomb somehow, so I gripped it tightly and pulled the pin, which was much harder to remove than I anticipated. I recall seeing pictures of GI's pulling the pin with their teeth – to do so with the grenade I had would certainly be at the peril of any man's teeth.

Pausing, I glanced at Putin, who was grinning, and he said: "When there are wolves, to survive, you must run with them, not away."

My arm cocked, I sent the grenade sailing – *SNAP*. It tumbled end over end against the gray snow-flecked sky, a thin seam of smoke corkscrewing from the explosive. Too much arm – the grenade headed for the far shore, but it became entangled in the birch branches and plopped into the river.

BOOM.

The plume of water was at least five feet high.

Vlad waved to the Udege, who scrambled down and pulled a damaged char from the water.

They took photos of me holding the shrapnel-torn fish.

One might ask why I complied with the charade.

One might also recall that I was keen to make it back home. There's no purpose blackmailing a dead man. Let them think they can manipulate me and they will send me back home. If I were to remain proud and resolute, what good was I to them alive? I would in fact be a liability as I would return home and tell the tale of how Putin had some hard-luck fishing and so resorted to grenade fishing.

As I have asserted many times regarding my previous trials and tribulations, my so-called heroics are little more than the mechanics of saving my own skin.

There was a small part of me deep inside that would not have been sorry to be stripped of my fame and sent packing. I hadn't squandered my money, and there could be enough to retire on, modestly. I could buy an obscure bungalow on an obscure Florida key. I could fish all day and haunt the local tiki bars all night for the rest of my days. One might imagine that such thoughts were utter folly – yet look where my fame had landed me? My fame had put me in the middle of Siberia in winter at the mercy of Vladimir Putin! It had put me in the cross hairs of political ambition!

Vlad and his bodyguards laughed as I finally dropped the destroyed fish into the river, their chuckles quickly drowned out by the thump of an approaching yet unseen helicopter. The lot of them scanned the skies as they mounted their snowmobiles, revved them up, and charged back in the direction of the lodge – without a second glance at me and my Udege.

I climbed the river embankment, glancing back at the exploded fish littering the stream's edge, my breath loud in my ears. The Udege began to walk back to our snowmobile, and I bent down to pick up my rod.

On the snow next to it, half buried, was another grenade.

It must have fallen from Vlad's pocket.

Glancing at the retreating Udege, I tucked the grenade into my tackle kit and slung it over my shoulder.

My Udege and I took a leisurely trip back to the

lodge, and upon arrival I learned that Putin and his guards had flown out on the helicopter.

That came as some relief, as I imagined that meant they felt they had what they wanted from me.

My cabin was devoid of Katya, and again I was relieved, and not altogether surprised. Her purpose had been to keep me off balance, and that task was done. It meant they had what they wanted and didn't need to invest any more in feigning to entertain me anymore. I had little doubt that had Vlad caught fish he still would have pulled that grenade stunt; I had been brought there to seem like a Russian sympathizer.

I went up for cocktails a little early and found Dax upstairs at the lodge by the fire.

"Well, Boone, it sounded as if you were introduced to the fine art of grenade fishing."

I took a breath. "So you knew that would happen?"

"Nothing is certain with Vlad." He shrugged. "But he's gone and we have the lodge to ourselves for the duration."

Part of me wanted to plant a fist in his face – the stupid part. Fortunately, the smart, self-preserving part of Boonie prevailed. I was still in the middle of nowhere, and even if I were not at the mercy of Vlad, I was at the mercy of Dax. I had to assume that as a 'freelance diplomat' he was more devil than angel. I had to play through this episode and find my way back to Brooklyn, even if it meant playing nice with the miscreant that got me into this jam. Perhaps somewhere down the road I could find a way to fix Dax's wagon, but that would have to wait.

Turning toward the bar, I poured myself a stiff PennyPacker, sipped, and resurrected my Linsenbigler composure. "Damned shame to blow up those char, though I would imagine there are more where they came from."

He patted me on the shoulder as I sat back down, clearly pleased that I was the fishing, drinking fool he wanted me to be. "That's the spirit! I know you have some experience with Russians, and when in Rome... Do you know how many Americans died in World War II?"

"Not off hand."

"About a half million. How many Russians do you think were killed, by comparison?"

I shrugged, and he continued, his eyes on the fire.

"Twenty-seven million. They lost fifty times as many people as we did. But that was just the beginning of the carnage. Any idea how many died under Communist rule, to include those slaughtered by Stalin after the war? Another twenty million, at least. So in round numbers, let's just say fifty million were killed from the revolution onward. That's a hundred times the number of U.S. casualties in World War II."

Dax stood and moved past me to the bar, filling his glass, vodka, no ice. "And then there were the atrocities. Prior to the war, one million were imprisoned or exiled; another eleven million peasants forced off their lands. Three million were arrested or exiled in collectivization programs. Seven million were killed by an artificial famine; one million exiled from Moscow and Leningrad. Six million were sent to labor camps. Twelve million were forcibly relocated during World War II; and at least one million were arrested for various "political crimes" in the years just after the war. Millions upon millions unjustifiably enslaved, disenfranchised and murdered."

My sip of whiskey went down hard. "Tragic all around. But why are you telling me this, Dax?"

He slid past me and dropped back into his seat by the fire, his eyes on the flames. "I'm telling you this because I believe it is critical to understanding Russians. Those who survived have endured atrocities like no other, and not by being the nice guy. It's my theory that Russians today are effectively genetically engineered through natural selection processes to have the capacity to act like your best friend one moment and in the next be your worst nightmare. What's more, I think they are proud of this trait. That's why they like Putin."

My jaw tightened. "It doesn't make blackmailing me or anybody else justifiable."

"A man climbs into the tiger enclosure at the zoo, and the tiger tears him to shreds. Is it the tiger's fault the man is dead? Global politics is a tiger cage. Come ready to fight, or die."

"Metaphors make for pretty speeches, Dax, but I'm not in a tiger cage, and Vlad is not a tiger. He has the ability to choose how he acts."

Dax looked at me with a sad smile. "That's what I'm trying to say, Boone. He's Russian, so he's been bred *not* to choose. He could no more *not* use or manipulate you than the tiger *not* devour an intruder in his cage."

"This isn't worth debating, not to me, this isn't my world. So now that Vlad has had his way with me, can we dispense with this charade of being on a fishing trip and send me home?"

"What? You come all this way, and you have Vlad behind you and now you want to go home? Shake it off, Linsenbigler. Tomorrow we get to take a little helicopter ride all our own. There's a stream with sea run browns calling us."

Brown trout have chocolate backs and golden sides dotted with black and red dots. The anadromous variety that run to the sea are more silver. They are a bucket list fish and much sought after by anglers.

"Stupendous!" I smiled, on the outside.

I wasn't sure how I was going to endure the rest of the week, or even make light conversation through that evening's dinner, though I hoped that if things remained uneventful and jam-packed with spot-on angling, I could recover from my encounter with Vlad.

Sleep came little to none that night, the dead men on the walls foreboding wraiths.

CHAPTER 12

THERE ARE HELICOPTERS, and then there are Russian helicopters, specifically the hulking Mi-8. It is the shape of a gigantic baking potato on three wheels. On top of the potato lengthwise are twin turbine cylinders, and on top of that a floppy five-blade rotor. Along the sides are portholes for passenger windows. Known as a veritable workhorse throughout Russia and the world, it functions at Russian fishing lodges as floatplanes do for Alaskan lodges: sturdy air transportation.

Unlike the previous day, the skies had cleared, and the wind was up, creating drifts of snow in every doorway. Dax and I said little as we gobbled down our breakfast of what amounted to porridge and coffee. We donned our winter gear and hoisted our tackle, the Udege loading us onto their snowmobiles for a trip to the helicopter pad.

As we broke through a line of trees at a hilltop saddle, the Mi-8 hove into view in a clearing before us. Its enormous exhaust-streaked sides sported faded red racing stripes. The blades began to turn ever so slowly, and by the time our snowmobiles came to a stop next to the leviathan, they still were not turning very quickly, and yet the machine emanated a deafening whirr and "TWEEP TWEEP TWEEP" with each turn of the blades. We were urged up a folding stair onto the craft, whereupon the Udege hoisted the steps up into the hands of the co-pilot, who wore a white helmet and orange flight suit. He stowed the stair and struggled to shove the sliding door shut. Dax and I took a seat opposite each other on the bench seating that were aligned on the walls. My guess was that it could seat sixteen easily. In the back were some boxes by cargo doors that opened at the rear. The co-pilot flashed a thumbs up and we returned the same.

Yet the blades still seemed to be struggling to turn and I wondered if they ever would gain sufficient gusto for a lift off. It seemed like it took five minutes before they began to make chopping sounds and we felt the hulking rattletrap begin to lift.

I looked out the portal as we topped the trees and could see the lodge and our cabins. For the first time in days I saw Katya. She was some distance from the cabins at a location I had not observed in my stay there: a shooting range. Katya was firing a pistol at various man silhouettes against a wooden wall, but as the copter turned she swung out of view. Well, she was a fine one! Say what you may about the rest of the trip thus far, but there had been no downsides to Katya.

The snowy forest of fir and birch raced by as we turned west, climbing to ascend over a series of hills. Vibration of the aircraft's fuselage and roar of the turbines made any conversation with Dax impossible, which was unfortunate because I wanted to discuss the particulars of where we were headed. While I was still perturbed by the previous day's exploits, I felt that I had the capacity to shake it off and enjoy some fishing and let the chips fall where they may. Bothering me most was Dax's subterfuge, and he seemed to think nothing of the fact that he lured me to the wilds of Siberia to be blackmailed by Vladimir Putin. All he really seemed to care about was the fishing, which was what I usually really care about, so it was somewhat easy to forgive him.

My stomach rose to my throat as we topped the hills and began down the other side. Through the window, I could see what looked like streams in the distance, now flowing west instead of east, and the hills had given way to rolling wooded hillocks and spaces of grasslands. There were no buildings, no railroads, no civilization in sight. The forest now was less piney and more like the canopy you would see in Pennsylvania. It came as some surprise when the Mi-8 hovered and then sank with a jolt to the ground at a clearing.

I had not seen any streams nearby.

The co-pilot reappeared and struggled once again with the door until it cooperated. He kicked the stair down and gestured for us to exit, the blades of the craft still swirling mightily. I grabbed my rod cases and tackle bag, heading for the exit, Dax in my wake.

I trotted through the a thin blanket of snow away from the craft until I was away from the influence of the enormous blades.

When I turned, Dax had also stopped, and I noticed he did not have his tackle.

In his hand was an automatic pistol.

Behind him, still in the door of the helicopter, the co-pilot was casually cradling a Kalashnikov.

I scanned my desolate surroundings. You might think a shiver raced up my back, but instead I felt suddenly quite hot with the realization I was going to die.

What does one ask when it is obvious what the answer is. *So, I guess we're not going fishing, then, old chap?*

Dax saved me the trouble: "Sorry, Boone, but I'll have to ask you for that coat."

My exasperation found a voice.

"Good Lord, Dax, you can't mean this! What was the point of blackmailing me if you're going to kill me? This is insane!"

"I don't call the shots, Boone, you know that." The bastard's tone was utterly conversational as it had been before the fire with a drink in his hand. "He could either blackmail you or humiliate you and America. He chose the latter because he didn't think you were going anywhere politically. Our story? After the grenade fishing, you got drunk and wandered away from camp and froze to death. Give me your coat."

He fired a shot at the ground near my feet and I must have jumped five feet in the air.

So much for the Brotherhood of Anglers. Remind me to shred my membership card.

I took off my tackle bag, put down my rods, doffed my gloves and removed the heavy fur coat. I only had on thermals and a fleece jacket under that.

At most, it was twenty on that windswept plain. Without the coat, I was a dead man.

"Can I keep my tackle?" I shouted, my voice cracking with desperation.

He shrugged his answer, turned with my coat under his arm and without so much as an apology headed back to the helicopter. I picked up my rod cases and strapped the tackle bag across my chest, following him slowly. "You know, Dax, I'm a rich man, and I'd pay to save my life right now."

He didn't turn, but I followed until he reached the steps and climbed past the co-pilot and onto the Mi-8. I stopped about ten feet back, and the co-pilot began to struggle with the door. The blades of the craft chopped furiously at the air and the Mi8 began to lift off the ground.

I put my hand into my tackle bag and grasped the *limonka* Vlad had dropped in the snow the day before.

SNAP.

The co-pilot managed to coerce the door to close just as I tossed my little lemon underhand toward him, smoke corkscrewing in its wake. He had turned by the time I tossed it, and if he did see the grenade as it rolled past him, he clearly was unable to react quickly enough to halt the door closing, much less reopen it.

The door slammed shut.

A whirlwind of snow and dirt blinded me to the Mi-8, and I covered my stinging eyes. All the same, I knew enough to turn and run.

The roar of the craft lifting off overwhelmed the noise of the explosion because I didn't hear it.

What I heard was the whine of the turbine stutter, and the blades slow.

Turning as I ran, I saw that the craft was still only ten feet off the ground and racing away from me in a fog of snow, black smoke trailing out a broken porthole.

Abruptly, sparks exploded from the tail rotor and the craft spun around to face me. The windshield was cracked, and there was blood spattered on the pilot's side. I could make out the co-pilot struggling with the controls, or to get out of his seat, I could not tell which.

Then the Mi-8 tilted toward me, an angry wounded dragon, snow on the grass bursting from its side in an enormous white V.

I began to run from the path of the raging beast as it sped toward me, the chopping blades tilting ever closer to the ground. A few hundred feet out, the blades made purchase with the earth. They burst into a thousand black shards that shot into the air like a flock of bats.

Spinning away from me, the helicopter's long tail section jammed into the ground and snapped off with the starboard rotor buried in the ground.

The brute heaved and somersaulted end over end in an eruption of dirt, the turbines howling as the dragon flopped end over end until it landed on its roof with a stupendous and resolute *THUD.*

Shattered blade shards and debris rained down on the belly of the monster, wheels in the air like the serpent's lifeless claws.

The only sound that remained was the wind and the ticking of overheated metal.

My breath came fast, and likely as not I uttered a lengthy string of oaths that would have made any seadog blush.

I surveyed my surroundings again.

To my east: snow laden mountains

To my west: snowy, brushy plain and hillocks

In the middle: me with no coat.

I needed a coat.

Running past where the tail section was jammed into the turf, I approached the helicopter, wary of survivors with weapons. It was hard to imagine anybody could have survived those smash-up acrobatics.

Redolent with aviation fuel, the crushed Mi-8 carcass was not on fire that I could see.

The pilot was in a bloody jumble on the ceiling of the cockpit. The co-pilot's windshield had been blown out, and as I circled to one side I could see his body in the orange jump suit had been flung a hundred feet to the other side. No surviving that.

Circling back to the front, I peered into the broken windshield. Dax was nowhere in sight.

Yet the back passenger compartment of the Mi-8 was in shadow.

What I could see was the Kalashnikov jammed in next to the co-pilot's seat, and I reached in through the missing windshield and wrestled the rifle free. I had never fired one, but I was sufficiently familiar with guns to know that there was likely a way to cock it and load a chamber. A handle on the side, when pulled rearward, did exactly that. A test fire into the middle distance confirmed that I succeeded in figuring out how to fire it in single-shot mode – that was all I needed as I hunted for a coat.

The Mi-8 door frame was mangled and I did not even

attempt to open it. If it was hard to open before it would have been rendered impossible from the damage.

Circling carefully to a broken porthole, I came close to one side and just listened. Mostly what I heard were my teeth beginning to chatter.

Was my caution idiotic, I wondered? I needed that coat. Certainly, Dax was dead or utterly incapacitated.

Certainly.

No sound of life, and the sweat on my torso was cold enough to make me shiver violently.

CRASH.

A back part of the helicopter gave way and I jumped right out of my skin. When my vision returned and my heart started beating again, I took a deep breath and circled toward the rear of the craft – ever so carefully.

The back cargo doors had fallen open.

I listened, shivering.

Something shifted inside.

Then again.

I drew closer to where the copter's tail used to be, my back against the fuselage.

Something shifted again.

Rifle at the ready, I brought an eye to where the metal doors had fallen away, and pivoted to try to see an ever larger area of the interior.

Dax charged out of the craft, tripped and stumbled. His white fur coat was splattered in blood, and his hair matted with red gashes. Not thirty feet from me, he had fallen on his back, fitfully trying to right himself, pistol in one hand. His head jerked side to side as he tried feverishly to take in his surroundings – perhaps he had blood or dust in his eyes but it was clear he had not seen me – yet.

Don't let anybody kid you: this is ugly stuff, and it is not in the least fun or exciting or cool.

It is just devastatingly grim.

The worst part of it is not the gore or any guilt or anything of the sort. Killing another person reduces you to a vicious animal. In that moment, I was not angry with Dax for trying to kill me or for deceiving me. All I knew in that instant was that he stood between me and the coat. He stood between me and survival.

With less consideration than the situation may have been due, I shouldered my weapon and fired twice, both rounds finding their mark with a decisive *THAK-THAK*.

One round hit him in the neck even though I was aiming at his chest.

Dax died quite quickly, and ceased breathing within moments after a loud gurgle, bubbles of blood emerging from his mouth. Just to be sure that he was no longer a threat, I trotted over to him. Averting my eyes from the grisly startled expression and pathetic mustache, I plucked his pistol from where it lay next to him.

I would need it.

A cursory inspection of his coat pockets did not result in any spare ammunition. I checked the magazine and it looked as if it still had in excess of twelve rounds.

In moments like that, the small child in you wants to break down and blubber about how unfair it all is and that you wish this had not happened or that you had not come to Russia in the winter to fish with your angling brothers like a complete idiot.

Oddly, I find an odd sense of clarity of purpose in such circumstance. There is much to do, and little time to do it.

They would come looking for the helicopter before too long, so I needed to be as far away as possible, and equipped with whatever I could salvage from the craft that could help me survive.

No matter where I was in Russia, it was a safe bet that the military and police would have an eye out for Ol' Boonie. I had to get out of Russia, pronto. At the same time, I also had to be clever.

While aboard the Queen Mary, I had studied my destination's local geography. The lodge was located on a finger of land between China to the west, North Korea to the south, and the sea to the east. To the north, Russia extended all the way to the Arctic. The Mi-8 had transported me from the mountains next to the sea to a series of hills and valleys stretching west. There would be towns north and south on that side of the mountains, places that were likely only a day or two away on foot but loaded with police. If I were them, I would concentrate my search for Linsenbigler there. Due west was less populated, and likely three or four days to the border with China, which was defined by a navigable river and railroad. They would be expecting me to seek the fastest route out of the country. My tactic would be to engage the unexpected route of escape and hope that by the time they started looking westward I would somehow be gaining entry to China.

In the helicopter, I found my coat, which had some shrapnel holes through it but was otherwise a welcome find. The co-pilot had a knapsack affixed behind his seat. It contained an extra ammunition magazine for the AK-47, a mostly full bottle of brandy, cigarettes and a lighter, a coconut bar and a wallet with identification and cash, some magazines and a cell phone. I liberated the lot, along with the pilot's compass watch from his bloody wrist. I added the first aid kit to the knapsack, as well as a combination fire hatchet and pry bar from next to the fire extinguisher. There was no food, other than the candy bar, which as we used to say in New Jersey, *sucked*.

My tackle bag revealed some useful items other than some boxes of fishing flies and associated gadgets. Whenever abroad, I am never without my passport, wallet, and phone, which I kept in a waterproof bag. There was a brace of cigars and a powerful lighter; a cap light; a multi-tool with plyers and knife and whatnot; chewing gum; the fruit bar from the Aeroflot flight and a half-eaten pack of sunflower seeds. Also along for the ride were my birding binoculars. I'm rather keen on taking a break from angling now and then to inspect local birdies.

With my phone, I took pictures of the crash site, some selfies. For whatever reason, I felt I might have to prove what happened, assuming I miraculously made it out of that mess alive.

Pushing and shoving, I rolled Dax's body back into the helicopter. This was made forbidding by the fact that as I did so, his body farted with each tumble. Quite revolting.

Then I lit parts of a magazine and tossed it in after him.

The gas fumes had been getting stronger as the fuel tanks leaked, and the interior burst into flame just as I was beginning to consider trying something else.

Smoke would draw them to the crash site sooner than later. That said, out in the open, the crash would be obvious in any case. What I hoped to accomplish was to cover my tracks even just a little. That is, would my pursuers be able to determine immediately that I had survived the crash and escaped? If they found Dax outside the craft with bullet wounds that would make that determination an easy one. The wind was blowing steadily and I could see that my tracks in the snow from when we first landed were already disappearing. Given an hour, they would not see that anybody had walked around the crash site.

I slung the AK-47, knapsack, tackle bag and rod cases across my back. The rod tubes, parenthetically, are a little less than three feet long, two of them strapped side by side with a shoulder strap, so not hard to tote. Carrying my fishing equipment may seem absurd under the circumstances but doing so had a way of attesting to myself that I would indeed find a way out of this. An angler loves his rods like his children. And who could say? I might need to eat a fish or two along the way to go along with my candy bars and sunflower seeds.

With the birding binoculars from my tackle kit, I inspected my western horizon, the sun over my shoulder and the mountains behind me. In the distance were hills, not mountains, and they appeared forested. I was guessing that Brooklyn was only seven thousand miles away. If I walked twenty miles a day that would take me…what, about a year? You know, assuming I could walk across the Atlantic. I'd have to cross China or Mongolia. Many unfriendly countries to the southwest, and India was blocked by the Himalayas – I did not fancy crossing those. As far as I could recall, some sort of Whutzitstan was on the far side of Mongolia, yet the latter's capital city Ulaanbaatar might have a Holiday Inn and was possibly only a thousand miles distant. This was all assuming China would let me in with a passport and no visa. Who could refuse Boone Linsenbigler?

Of course, this flippant inner dialogue was to put it all in perspective: I hoped to find some reliable and fast transport to a city where I could charter or book a flight.

When we were kids, my parents would load us into the station wagon for a camping vacation. With me and my sister Crocket piled in the back seat, my Dad would start the car, a pipe clenched in his teeth. He would then invariably say to no one in particular:

"A journey of a thousand miles begins with a well stoked pipe."

With a sense of adventure and delusional optimism suppressing the realities of my predicament, I lit up a cheroot and began my march for freedom, the Mi-8 an inferno at my back.

CHAPTER 13

IT WAS A GOOD THING that I still had my waders on because after several hours hiking I found myself in the woods and rolling terrain, and then at the edge of a rushing stream. The tree canopy was welcome camouflage so that I could not be spotted from the air – they likely would be coming at me with a helicopter. I only hoped what footprints I'd laid prior to entering the forest were no longer visible.

As I observed from the airborne Mi-8, the woodlands on this side of the mountain differed from that at the lodge in that it was predominantly birch and firs, yet it was thicker with the occasional maple and poplars. This made hiking cross-country slower going as the trees were closer together. Yet I had the pilot's compass watch, and there was no underbrush, just leafy moss. I was determined to head due west and hoped to intersect some sort of road or path. There was an angular hill in the southwest that I used to stay on course. I caught glimpses of it whenever I could. Where I hoped to end up was an open question, and it depended on how intense the search for me would be – would they assume I had died in the crash and fire? Presumably, if I were to stumble upon a small town where there was a phone I could call Terry for help – though if the local constabulary was on the lookout for Ol' Boonie I might not get to make that call. Under optimal conditions, I might then be able to find my way to a train or chartered plane and fly as far away as possible. It was in that frame of mind that I tromped through the trees and moss and a thin crust of snow hither and yon, crossing streams at will in my waders, expecting at any moment to stumble upon a road or path.

Two days later, I was still in the woods, and I don't mind telling you that my optimism was wavering. I had become keenly aware of the presence of bears by scat I was finding along riverbanks. I would have thought that they would be hibernating, but it was a relatively warm, sunny day, and I knew they sometimes got so hungry in the den that they ventured forth.

I had sheltered two nights, making a simple lean-to by affixing a branch between two trees with very expensive fly line I had been compelled to sacrifice to the mission. I then leaned branches on that, and piled leaves up into a sort of nest into which I curled. Fire was made eminently more possible by the magazines that were in the co-pilot's bag and the paper proved a very helpful fire starter. Dry grass or other starter would not have been available. For firewood, I used larger sticks and small logs that I was able to fashion using the fire axe from the deceased Mi-8. Conscious that fire made light and smoke that might direct people to my location, I did my best to shield the light by piling branches around the fire. There was no choice but to have a fire, really, I needed the warmth, and my guess was that at night it was in the single digits. Sleep came and went with my ears interpreting woodland snaps and pops as the approach of a bear or tiger. The only critter I had encountered in my travels were deer and a sable ducking into a hollow stump.

On the second night, I resigned myself to calling off the hike early when I came upon a stream midafternoon. I determined it was more critical to attain sustenance than mileage, and the creek looked like an ideal spot to catch some trout. My snack food was utterly depleted after two days hiking. Also, my charted course due west put me at the base of a hill that needed climbing, and I wanted to tackle that in the morning and be on the other side by the next evening.

The location in question was particularly inviting as there was a bend in the stream and a tight bunch of pines opposite that would make a nicely secluded campsite. In a couple of hours, I had my shelter constructed and fire pit set.

I rigged up a fly rod and approached the stream. It was no wider than a city bus is long. The deep green undercut bank opposite me looked to be the perfect lay for a fat trout, and was free of slush and ice. Now, I had never had to fish for food before. As such, I was somewhat apprehensive of having an episode like Vlad's wherein I couldn't manage to catch a damn thing. I did not imagine char on this side of the mountain as I knew this stream and drainage was many miles from the sea.

Complicating matters was that most native trout in winter are only half-awake and fussy eaters. My fly choice was critical.

First, I swung a drab, shaggy wooly bugger through the deep spot a few times. Then I attached to the bend of that hook some more line and a small nymph – tandem flies. The idea behind the rig is that the first fly draws a fish's attention and then the second one – a teeny-tiny, delectable morsel – presents itself immediately afterward. Who could resist?

They could. So I tried what's called Czech nymphing in which you delicately drift two or three nymphs through the feeding lane. *The subtle approach must be the ticket.*

Subtlety was to no avail, so I tied on a succession of streamer patterns meant to look like minnows: Grey Ghost, Mickey Finn, Muddler Minnow. No go. Next at bat was a caddis pupae peeking out of its shell, then a pinkish freshwater shrimp pattern known as a scud, and then a black ant, and then the smallest of the small: a size 24 zebra midge no bigger than a crumb. What self-respecting trout could pass up a salty little peanut like that?

They did.

As I went through this process, the scene at the helicopter crash kept trying to intrude. A forbidding business indeed. Believe it or not, my frustration with the fish found me mumbling epithets with regards to Dax: *Stick me out here in the wilderness with picky trout will you? Take that you so and so! I should have shot you many more times for all this misfortune. Well, I'm not Vlad, I'm not skunked, I can figure these trout out if it kills me. But it won't!*

While searching my tackle kit for the miracle fly, I discovered a fly that should not have been there. It was a tropical fly called a Ginger Tonged Pizzer and a pattern of my own invention. It resembled a thin, flattened mouse with its tongue sticking out, and I had created it on a drunken wager that I could tie the most implausible fly imaginable and still catch fish on it. That harebrained wager was predicated on catching saltwater fish in the flats and mangroves – surroundings markedly different from those I found myself at that moment.

I lost the wager.

As my father would say: *When donuts block the view, look through the holes.* So I gave it a try.

Fish on!

By Jupiter, a Ginger Tonged Pizzer seemed to be precisely what the brook trout had been waiting for, and I caught four foot-long fish!

Trout can be cooked and eaten without scaling, so preparing them was a rather simple affair of gutting them. With my multi-tool, I cut some green branches to make skewers for my catch and then laid the ends of the skewers in a 'Y' shaped stick plugged into the ground on either side of the fire.

My anxious mood had been greatly improved by my accomplishment, and I took the opportunity to smooth my bedraggled whiskers and snap a few selfies for posterity. I took the precaution of circling my small camp with fly line dangled with knee-high sticks. I hoped the sound of the sticks moving against the ground would alert me to the approach of any hungry beast. I was hoping to get a better night's sleep than the previous evening, pistol at my side.

Fire going and fish grilling, I daresay I fancied a cocktail. As such, I emptied a cellophane envelope containing leader material and packed it with snow and a stick of chewing gum. I topped my snow cone with brandy. Voila, a Siberian Julep!

I cannot adequately express how satisfying both the cocktails and fish were that evening. I have no doubt that under any normal circumstances neither delicacies – charred brook trout and Wrigley's flavored brandy – would meet muster. Yet alone and adrift in the Russian Far East, the combination was utter ambrosia. Perhaps I was a man in denial of his plight. If so, one might also imagine that it is easy to delude oneself when outward signs of danger are so lacking, and my surroundings so serene.

When I was done with my fish, I built up the fire and burned all the remnants of food and the sticks they were cooked on so as not to attract any critters.

I enjoyed half a cigar and some more brandy by the fire, and reflected on the tropics rather than recent events. I thought of Tanya and our Christmas on her little sailboat in balmy Nassau. She had a small Christmas tree mounted on the bow, and one evening while I was giving her lessons in swordplay, she reflexively reacted to one of my lunges by kicking my legs out from under me. I pitched head over kiester into the drink! She laughed and hopped in after me with a bottle of champagne, and as we swam, drank bubbly and watched the sun set. Her little tree slowly lost its center of gravity and pitched into the water along with us, the lights flickering out. Damn, that was funny. And warm. Warm in all the right ways.

If she could only see me now in this snowy Russian boondocks! Good grief! Though knowing her rough-and-ready inclinations, I have no doubt she would be proud of how I'd made out so far, especially with the grenade.

My belly full, and the brandy half gone, wind whispering between the branches high above, I curled into my nest, collar up, fur hat pulled down, whiskers at half-mast.

To this day, I can't say I ever slept better.

CHAPTER 14

THE THIRD DAY was yet another sparkler, bright sun and blue skies, and slightly warmer, so much so that I had my coat open as I ascended the hill that lay in my path westward. I cannot say how tall the hill was, just that by the time I began to reach the top of it, I began to catch glimpses of a commanding view of my path from the east.

Rock outcroppings at the top of the hill provided an open view. While I rested and quenched my thirst with snow, I took the opportunity to inspect whence I'd traversed the last days, my birding glasses at the ready.

As I did so, my attention was directed to some commotion in a stream that I had crossed the previous day – but not where I had just camped.

My breath caught. I adjusted the binoculars.

Horses, about a dozen, all but one affixed with armed Cossacks. They wore dark tunics and furry pillbox hats, each with a full beard, sword scabbards flanking their saddles and rifles slung across their backs. At that distance, they all seemed to be moving in slowed motion.

The twelfth horse led the pack, and was ridden by none other than Katya in a camo snowsuit and sable hat, a Kalashnikov in a scabbard at her side.

My jolly little camping trip through the wintery Slavic woodlands faced the stark reality that I was being hunted. Making it worse, I was being hunted by Katya. Clearly the entire situation had been engineered. Even while we were sharing a sauna and a roll in the proverbial hay, Katya was preparing for this. Could anything be more sinister?

You don't suppose that Vlad – out of sheer perversity – left the grenade for me to find? That he did so just to see what would happen, to see what I would do when Katya came to hunt me down? Whether I would prevail? Or would it have been to further demean me, making him more of a man's man? Then Hailey's words came back to me, about her crew wanting me to go fishing in Russia in the winter 'to see what happens.'

Dax's little speech about the feral nature of Russians echoed in my mind. When he was blathering on about it, I did not take him seriously. Or rather, I think I was too distracted by the events of that day to comprehend the logic of it all. It still didn't gel, but it added to a growing anxiety that there was still much about this fiasco that I did not understand and might not ever understand once charging Cossacks summarily ran me through and left me for raven chow on the moss.

I watched as the line of horses vanished into the woods, headed my way.

Given my circumstance, I made a mental note that – should I survive – I would recommend to the boy scouts that they include some instruction on eluding pursuers.

Nothing they taught me about lean-tos and fires were of the least assistance in that regard. Countless accounts of escaped convicts provide some assistance when evading hounds, but all my pursuers had to do was follow my footsteps in the snow, which were protected by the woods from the wind's erasing effects. Likewise, I had no way to judge how much time I had before they caught up to me, though the calculus of utmost haste on my part was an easy equation to cipher.

The only hope was that there was something, anything at all other than open country, on the other side of the hill. Scrambling over the rocky outcrop, I made my way to the far side of the hill and began down a steep and rather treacherous slope that I hoped would significantly slow the death squad in tow.

A clearing in the trees afforded me a view of the next valley, and I had to wipe the sweat from my eyes to get a clear view through the binoculars of what was ahead.

Smoke. I could see smoke. Then a cabin. No, several cabins. Cows. By Jove, if there was a way out of this, I had to find some mode of travel that would outpace the cavalry. There might be a car. Or a canoe. Or gyrocopter or rocket ship that could whisk me out of that bad neighborhood.

Down I went, steady as she goes, conscious that it would not pay to descend into panic mode and trip and sprain an ankle.

Hazzah! A path lay ahead that angled down the slope toward the cabins, and my progress was of course greatly improved.

Improved until I heard a shout.

Stopping, I surveyed my surroundings.

I heard the shout again, a high voice, seemingly a child's, coming from down slope off the path and toward a rock outcropping.

Continuing on my way, I heard it again, and even though there were no words that I understood, I knew it for what it was.

It was a child's cry for help.

Cursing, I wrestled with my conscience. *Not now! Blast!*

Veering from the path, I headed toward where the sound came, telling myself that this would probably take only a little time, and might even buy me some good will with the parents of the little darling.

A rock outcrop emerged from the hillside to my left, and the cry came again, but around the corner of the outcropping. I broke into a trot and turned the corner where the rock face ended.

Better sense would have dictated that I round the corner with more caution.

Not five feet before me was a brown bear standing on his hind legs. His forepaws were clinging to the face of the outcrop. On his hind paws, he stood maybe seven feet tall.

His yellow eyes: fierce.

His bared teeth: gnashing.

My flight instinct was little match for the quick reaction of the bear, who reared back from the face of the rock, towering above me, claws and paws out to the side. All he had to do was tip forward off his two hind legs to be on top of me.

The fundamentals of bear encounters dictate that you do not try to run from them. They have four legs, you have two. They are faster than you are and will catch you. Such rules are not at the fore in the moment of panic. Yet, he was so close to me that I knew there was no time for guns or running. Or even a prayer.

There was time for only one thing.

Reflecting upon the demonstration by Boris the dancing bear instructor at the Winter Palace, I ducked my head down and shot into the creature's chest with all of my weight. My face was buried in the course fur, which smelled slightly musty, and of clay. From the bear's chest came a mighty *WHOOF!*

I recoiled from the force of the impact and did not fall forward, rather I bounced back and kept my footing.

The bruin, still on his two small hind legs, reeled backward, his paws waving in the air as he tried to regain his balance or at least fall forward. Yellow eyes wide, he grunted with effort, the hillside behind him getting the better of his center of gravity. When I think on that part, it was really quite hilarious to witness this mighty beast stumbling about on those little legs, he looked exactly like Boris's Bo Bo except without the tutu.

His bruin ballet came to an end when he tripped on a log and collapsed backward into the leaf litter, rolling end over end.

Atta boy, Boonie! One minute you're catching trout and living on the land, the next you're subduing bears with nothing but true grit! Wouldn't your namesake Ol' Danny Boone be impressed?

Mr. Boone may have been more so had I taken

advantage of the pause in the action to pull Dax's automatic and prepare myself for what was to come next.

The bear rolled back onto all fours, shook his head, and fixed his irritable eyes on me. With a massive huff, he lunged back up the slope.

Fumbling for the gun in my coat pocket, I heard a shot.

Half By Hades! I've shot myself!

Not ten feet in front of me the bruin's lunge resulted in his collapse, a bullet hole and blood on the side of his brown furry noggin.

I didn't move. Had I shot the bear through my pocket? I removed the weapon and could see it had not discharged.

A whimper sounded overhead, up on the rock face.

Turning my gaze upward, I saw an Udege boy clinging to the rocks, tears staining his face. He wore leather pants and – oddly – a Falcons Super Bowl Champs hoodie sweatshirt.

Footsteps tromped from behind me, and I reacted by swinging my pistol toward the sound.

An Udege man with shaggy black hair jutting out from under a mottled fur turban ran toward me, a rifle out to one side. He wore a fur coat, dirty sweat pants, and muddy Wellingtons. A significant diagonal scar hashed the bridge of his nose. I noted once again the remarkable resemblance between the Udege and Inuit or Eskimos. Well, I'd never actually seen any in person, and am no anthropologist, but to my untrained peepers they were mighty similar.

He gestured toward the boy, who was now in tears,

and I lowered my weapon.

Scar Nose rushed past me, stepped over the bear, and began jabbering at the boy, who clambered down the rock face and latched himself onto his father's back for dear life. The Udege stooped over the bear to give the deceased a quick once over.

When he stood again, he gestured at the bear, and then me, and blurted out more gibberish, his eyes beholding me with wonder. A question was asked that I of course did not understand, and I countered with: "I'm American."

He squinted at me incredulously, then with resolve, Scar Nose stepped up and clapped me on the shoulder. He gestured for me to follow him back down the hill.

As I walked behind him, the little boy on his back unlatched a hand to wipe away tears, the soft amber eyes inspecting me. "Am Arican?" He said.

I nodded. "You speak English?"

He shook his head, but pointed down the hill. Perhaps that meant there was someone at camp who did.

In fact, it was more than a camp, it was a regular hamlet of log cabins with white chinking, wood plank walkways connecting them, and enormous stacks of firewood at every turn. Curly-tailed mutts sniffed me doubtfully and darted away. I was glad to see junked pick-ups and SUV's, and hoped to spot one that seemed to function. As we came down the main thoroughfare, villagers began to appear in doorways, most of them old women with brightly-beaded pillbox hats and bony fingers pointed my way. They flashed gold teeth as they smiled and shouted to one another – I was big news.

Mounting a plankway, we tromped past a rack of sable pelts arrayed on pegs.

Cabins ahead were on stilts, pens of cows and fowl on the sides, with yet more firewood, and one cabin at the end was on higher stilts and directly next to a river. Not a stream as I had been used to seeing, but a watercourse a hundred feet wide – nothing that I could have crossed in my waders. While this did not look large enough to be the border river with China, it had to be connected to it.

Wood smoke drifted everywhere in thin, suspended layers.

My heart skipped a beat – I spied long, squared wooden boats docked at this end cabin. Boats thirty feet long and four feet wide with outboards.

We mounted the steps to this last cabin, which had a sign in Cyrillic above the rough-hewn door. On the porch, sitting on upturned logs in the sunshine, was a line of six wizened male Udeges smoking pipes and cigarettes. Wardrobes for them were like others I had seen in passing – warm, rustic clothing and mud boots. The only traditional tribal gear I had seen were the hats on the old women in the doorways and on the wizened coot at the end of the porch. He wore a colorful beaded peaked cap with a squirrel tail sticking out of the top. These were clearly the local gentry at the country store solving their world's problems over a cracker barrel. Yet no black and red checkerboards were evident. Just mahjong tiles on a crate to the side.

We stopped in front of the central gent closest to the cabin door. He had close-cropped white hair, a dirty plaid down vest, no hat and one cataract eye that looked like a milky marble. Scar Nose swung the boy off his back to the deck and launched into an animated telling of the episode with the bear.

The old man's good eye dipped slowly around Scar Nose's side to focus on me. Nested in a basket of wrinkles, the watery eye was calm and utterly dispassionate. Without interrupting the vibrant tale, the chieftain said something to the gent next to him, who passed it to the one next to him, until it reached the railing and a fat middle-aged Udege in a torn fedora – who promptly waddled away toward main street shouting.

Finally, Scar Nose stepped back and waved at me.

The Chief was intent on rolling a cigarette with a small square of newspaper, so I fetched the pack of store-bought co-pilot cigarettes from my satchel and held them out to him. He was startled by my offer, but reached out and took the pack without really looking at me and handed them to the geezer next to him, who proceeded to pass them out to the whole gang. Shortly, they had all lit up, and as they inhaled, they smiled and nodded with approval.

Footsteps approached from behind on the plankway. I turned to see the fat man in the torn fedora approaching with a lanky mop-top teenager in a "Falcons Super Bowl Champions" hoodie much like the littler kid. Fedora broke away as the kid hopped up the steps, his pants and Wellingtons muddy. Our eyes met, his hooded but curious. He turned to the chief and Scar Nose and blurted something – the latter launching into his story again, but more quickly. The kid looked back at me, cleared his throat, and said gently:

"I speak little English. How you here?"

"Long story. I would tell it except that there are Cossacks on horses chasing me. They are trying to kill me."

His response was a sway of the head that said *dude?*

I added: "I need to keep moving. Can your people take me down river as quickly as possible? I can pay you."

The kid scratched his head, thought a moment, and said: "Cool Hand Luke?"

It took me a moment to think of the reference. He was referring to a famous old movie in which Paul Newman was a frequent escaped convict. I snapped my fingers: "Yes, like Cool Hand Luke."

The gentry puffing away on their cigarettes seemed to know these words, and the kid turned to them and began to explain. When he finished, the Chief mumbled to him and looked at me.

The boy translated: "Why Cossacks kill you?"

I shrugged at the Chief: "I am a famous American, and Putin seeks to discredit me, but I bolted from his fishing camp far to the east. I had to destroy a helicopter and kill three men to escape." Even to me, who had lived through that terror, the words sounded like a lie. *I blew up a helicopter? By Jupiter, I suppose I did.*

It might not have been the smartest choice on my part to mention Putin as it could have had the capacity to intimidate these tribespeople from helping me. But in the moment, I could think of no faster way to justify what I had done.

The kid actually laughed and said: "No!"

I looked at him levelly: "Yes."

He shook his head and explained to the gentry, who all went wide eyed and began to mumble: *MacGyver*.

Before they could say any more, I had to ask the kid: "Can you tell me your name?"

"Yavit."

"Yavit, how is it you know the movie *Cool Hand Luke* and the television show *MacGyver*?"

He gestured to the roof the next door building the building and I noticed the first sign of modernization: a satellite dish. "We have a television. I translate. Richard Dean Anderson MacGyver very much good."

"And your shirt?"

He looked down at it, then me. "Little money."

It was then that I recalled that the merchandising for the Super Bowl required the production of team wear proclaiming either side's win. As such, the gear for the losing team is sold overseas. Ostensibly, nobody overseas will know what it means and no NFL fans will see it. As of that juncture, at least, the Falcons had not prevailed.

The chief stood on bowed legs, spewing a long diatribe, one that included a lot of gestures and finger pointing. The kid finally turned to me and said: "Village not like Putin. Take trees from forest where no trees to take. How far Cossacks?"

"Two hours ago they were approaching the other side of the mountain." I annotated my explanations with hand gestures to help Yavit understand.

He relayed that tidbit, and the Chief gestured at Scar Nose and Yavit, yammering at them and then at me.

Yavit: "He says Glegov [he gestured at Scar Nose] is

obligated to take you down river because you confronted the bear to save his son. You have spirit of bear inside you, very powerful and not killed by the Cossacks, bad for the village, the bear spirit is with us. You are famous? What is your name?"

I told him, and the gentry leaned in to hear it repeated several times. They tried mumbling 'Linsenbigler' but could not get their mouths around it. Then I said my first name, and they all liked that, and a chorus of 'Boone' arose.

Yavit: "They say you are Boone the Bear. If you are famous, we have not heard of you, and apologize. Glegov and I will take you down river where there is a town with telephones and maybe help for you." He gestured at his little village: "We simple people and help simple, you have go your way where we take you."

I laughed, mostly to myself. Of course they would not have heard of me or my products as I could not imagine their commercial breaks containing a pitch for cocktail amenities. Imagine even finding a martini glass within a hundred miles? "That's OK, Yavit, I am famous only in commercials. Please thank everybody for the help. I am humbled that they have been so generous to a stranger."

While he relayed this, a stout woman in what looked like buckskins stomped up the steps and slugged Glegov in the side of the face. A shouting match started, and the Chief had to stand up and try to calm the woman down, who after a few moments grabbed the hand of the little kid and fairly dragged him away home.

Once the enraged wife/mother was gone, the old

men began to kid Glegov, at which point he became grumpy and marched off down the steps.

Yavit: "Boone, we take you down river soon to Dalnekrasnov."

I glanced back toward the hill: "The sooner the better. I don't want anything bad to happen to the village when they arrive."

"The old men say to Cossacks you give money for boat travel. We not know where you come from. You have money, we need money."

I waited down by Glegov's boat for what seemed an eternity, sure that at any second the sound of thundering hooves would compel me to just steal the boat. As an American, and particularly as a New Yorker, one forgets that everybody else moves at what seems a glacial pace. I'm sure Yavit and his clan had never had occasion to jaywalk, or eat a slice while doing so, or to fight over a cab in the rain while texting – and eating a slice.

That said, my wait was time to think, and I noticed that there were three other boats with motors. To leave them operable would be an invitation for my pursuers to follow. On the porch of the main building, the one on stilts looming over the boats, a knot of young children had gathered to stare at the stranger – yours truly. They watched as I went to the other boats and collected the fuel lines from the outboards to the fuel tanks, and piled them in Glegov's boat.

I heard shouting, and I began to scramble, pushing mightily at the boat to launch her. Yet it was only Glegov's approach, his wife swatting him with a stick and complaining, their little boy in the Falcon's hoodie in their wake, laughing. Yavit appeared from the other side of the boathouse carrying a satchel and a bolt-action rifle of his own.

Glegov's wife continued her harangue as we three heaved and slid the boat into the river, one climbing in after the other. The gunnels were low, and you had to step directly into the middle of what was more canoe than boat.

Drifting into the current, Glegov began to pull the starter for the outboard.

Two-cycle boat engines of this type are notoriously cranky. Once upon a time in New Jersey, such a motor refused to start on a windy evening at the far end of Lake Hopatcong. My date and I were compelled to go ashore and bushwhack through poison ivy to a road, and hike to the marina in the middle of the night. Julie McCluskey never spoke to me again. Then there was the sailboat episode in the middle of Barnegat Bay when the masthead and halyard assembly popped off a rental. We'd just used the outboard to depart the marina not an hour earlier, but when in the clinches, of course, it would not start and we had to call for a tow – as a result, Brenda Willock missed her mother's funeral, and did not return my phone calls. Ah yes, and who could forget the halcyon day I pulled on the start cord of an Evinrude and the entire motor hopped off the stern and B-lined for Davey Jones' locker. I could have sworn I heard it chuckle on the way down, Debra Pakernewsky asking me "Where's the motor?"

So it was perfectly in keeping with this legacy of cantankerous outboards that as Glegov pulled and pulled at the start cord, fiddling with the choke and cursing, we all heard a horse whinny. We had drifted through slush and ice chunks less than four hundred feet.

Past my right ear I heard *spew!* A chunk of ice broke in the water behind me in the same instant, followed by a gunshot. The sound of the bullet passing my ear by inches came before the rifle's report reached me. A glance upriver focused on the silhouette of Katya leaning against a tree on the riverbank pointing an AK-47 in my direction.

"Down!" I shouted. But Yavit and Glegov were already flat to the bottom of the boat.

THUNK. THUNK-THUNK.

Pow! Pow-pow!

Holes were appearing in the boat's hull, and the river happily obliged the opportunity to make use of those holes and join us in the bottom of the boat. The current caught the bow where I was and swung us further to a slip of faster current near shore.

We heard the next shots, and they missed the boat, landing further toward the river center.

Glegov hopped up and pulled on the motor cord. Naturally, it started up as if that's what it always did on the first pull. I peered upriver and could see that we were out of sight from the village and Katya. Clumsily, I put my hands over the bullet holes to try to stem the flow of chilly water, to little avail.

Yavit was up, and he quickly snapped off a low branch.

Glegov swung the boat downstream and we were suddenly slicing down the river through the slush, a spritely 'V' of river shooting up in our wake. Larches, pines and leaf-barren poplars tracked by on both sides, the sun approaching the yardarm in the west. A lovely day, and suddenly nobody shooting at us, how nice.

With a pocketknife, Yavit deftly whittled some plugs for the holes and nudged me out of the way. He hammered them in with the knife flat in his hand. We both began bailing water with our hands before Glegov tossed us two plastic coffee cups next to the gas can.

High and dry, as it were, we ceased bailing, and Yavit smiled at me: "This happen you much?"

I heaved a sigh, bowing my head a moment – that bullet passed within a foot of my head. *Spew!*

I returned a pained smile.

"Yes, it would seem so."

CHAPTER 15

THE RIVER OF SLUSH and ice chunks wound out in front of us, sunlight flickering through the forest. Occasional log shacks appeared on shore, boats similar to ours parked out front. Those at home appeared in a door or window and waved. We waved back. The river got larger the farther we went.

It took two hours and one refueling from a spare gas can before we began to see signs of civilization: power lines, logging roads, logging barges and eventually, the golden onion dome of a Russian Orthodox church twinkling in the distance. Clusters of shacks came and went, along with a dilapidated pier and distant redbrick smokestack. Rounding a bend, the metropolis of Dalnekrasnov hove into view, a sprawling beige and grey town dotted with onion domes and overhung with layers of smoke or smog. A railway trestle crossed the river ahead: that could be my ticket out of there, though I would have preferred something that flew. I had little doubt that Katya was fast on my heels. How close, how far away, was anyone's guess.

Glegov angled the boat toward the nearest pier where many boats like his were parked. Ashore there appeared to be a market area where a string of lights had come on: sunset was about an hour distant.

Without any tall buildings, but with considerable sprawl along the shore and inland, the town resembled many other drab, rustic waystations around the globe, one that catered to river traffic and timbering crews. It was where tribal people obtained supplies and lumberjacks were housed. In essence, a frontier town, complete with equal amounts of hope and desperation.

Yavit scrambled past me to the bow and leapt onto the dock as we drifted near. I tossed him the painter rope and Glegov killed the outboard. With the boat wedged between two similar craft, we clambered up onto the concrete pier, me struggling with my rod cases, satchel and tackle bag. Glegov pointed the way; Yevit and I followed. From the pier we veered from the bustling market to a concrete cottage to one side. A stovepipe from the pitched steel roof belched thick smoke. Working men – both native and Caucasian – stood out in front holding mugs and smoking. We were headed for the local saloon.

Mind you, I was still in my white fur hat and coat, which by that point had become sooty and splattered with fish guts. I was also still in waders that I had been wearing for three days. While under most circumstances I would have been only too happy to dive into the local dive, I most urgently wanted to change clothes – if for no other reason than I stood out like a sore thumb. I had not forgotten about Katya, either. No time for a saloon just then.

"Yavit, I need to find new clothes immediately. Can you help me?"

He nodded and shouted something to Glegov, who waved a hand and trudged onward to the tavern. Between his wife, being shot at, the bear and me, I had to imagine that Glegov was in need of a stiff drink.

Yavit started toward the market, waving me on: "Boone, come."

He took me down a narrow side street of low grey buildings covered in advertisements and with signs indicating what they sold – mostly tobacco and booze. He led me to a corner building with a shabby awning that had barrels of tools and shovels out front – it appeared to be a hardware store. It was, but it also sold work clothes. Piles of dungarees, sweaters, coats and vests lined the walls in back. I showed Yavit the co-pilot's wallet and the money inside – I had no idea how much it was. He bobbed his head and said it was probably enough for a new outfit. So I swapped out my clothes for bib coveralls, a speckled grey woolen sweater, a thick sheepskin vest, and a quilted black winter coat. I chose a woolen black-checked hat – round, flat on top, with brim and fuzzy earflaps pinned up. New socks and underwear were in order, with some extra to go. A pair of fur-lined lace-up boots finished the ensemble. Yukon Linsenbigler, at your service!

Yevit haggled with the shop owner, and offered my discarded clothing in the bargain, which led to shouting, but ultimately led to a sale that used all of my rubles and the wallet.

As we stepped back into the muddy cobbled street, I asked Yevit: "Can you help me buy a train ticket?"

He looked at the sky. "Boone, dark soon. Must to Glegov before much drink, take to boat, go home. I sorry, we go."

I clapped him on the shoulder. "OK, I'll help see you off then."

The saloon was a dreary, world-weary grey affair that smelled of fish, stale beer and body odor. The lights were dim and men played cards on crates by the window so they could see. Glegov was leaning against the plank bar with a line of other poor slobs doing shots and drinking what I think was mead, by the looks of it – milky chardonnay. When we tapped him on the shoulder, the fumes from him suggested that he had made an impressive start on a serious bender, and I believe we got to him just in time and while he could still walk on his own. We set him in the bow. As Yevit prepared to climb in to pilot them home, I handed him a hundred dollar bill and shook his hand. "You saved my life, Yevit, and thank Glegov for me, and the old man."

His eyes goggled at the bill, and he held it up to admire it. "Boone the Bear, do good, our spirits guide you!"

Hopping into the boat, Yevit started the motor on the first pull, pivoted the long wooden boat, and surged up river, waving his entire arm at me as he went.

There I was: alone in a strange Russian frontier town.

Wandering slowly back down the pier toward the market and village, I fished out my cell phone and thumbed it on. I could see a cell tower up on a nearby hill. As happens when a phone finds itself in a foreign country, my device took some time to figure out whether it could latch onto a viable signal nearby. The phone's screen went black, and I figured the long shot fell short.

Then – by God – it lit up with a signal! Then I got a message informing that I was in Russia and that fees for long distance calls would cost extra. How this was occurring when I had not arranged this in advance was anybody's guess. Before I could find Terry's number and hit 'dial,' my phone rang.

Cautiously, I answered. "Hello?"

"Boone, its Hailey."

"How did you know my number?"

She sighed. "I think I mentioned that we know almost everything, and phone numbers are just about the easiest things to know. We activated your provider's overseas connectivity. Been waiting for you to power up – glad you switched it on. You have to keep moving and cannot stay the night in Dalnekrasnov."

"So you know where I am?"

"We've been following your progress."

Indignation began to well inside me. "You knew where I was and could not have come get me?"

"Just because we know where you are does not mean we can launch a rescue mission into sovereign Russian territory and start a war because you wanted to go fishing with Vladimir Putin."

"I didn't plan on fishing with…I suppose you also know about the helicopter?"

"Of course. Did you kill Dax? We couldn't see."

"Hailey, I'd rather not go into details of that horrendous episode. He died, at any rate. Can you get me out of here?"

"We can help. But we have to move you under the radar. Have you changed clothes?"

"Done."

"Good. Head to the train station. There's a first class compartment ticket waiting for you. The train leaves in an hour. Be on it or you're screwed. We have a friend in your compartment to help you move onto the next mode of transportation."

"Can't we charter a plane?"

"Both literally and figuratively, that is not under the radar. They will be expecting that."

"How long will it take to get me to Paris, Hailey?"

"Paris?"

"Well, back to someplace safe."

"What makes you think Paris is safe? Katya was on the Queen Mary, so Katya could also be in Paris or Katya could be in London or Katya could be in New York."

"They would follow me? How does this end?"

"Things don't just stop. You have to make them stop. There needs to be an incentive to let you go."

"What kind of incentive?"

"That's hard to say, we have to see what happens and keep watching and listening. Go catch that train. Don't be doing any Cossack dances in the bar car, keep to your compartment. Don't call anybody, turn off your phone, and remove the battery – if you don't your phone will lead them to you. It acts as a tracking device when near cell towers."

I was a little peeved at being bossed around like a child, as well as feeling – after all I had been through thus far – that I no longer had control of the situation.

"Hailey, I don't suppose that your scopes and probes and what have you were able to tell you that I subdued a bear and saved a child this morning? The villagers said I have the spirit of the bear, and renamed me Boone the Bear."

"Really?"

"And that my trip down river was prefaced by a shot from Katya that missed my head by this much! I camped, I caught my own trout dinner, even had a Siberian Julep and a cigar! I destroyed the helicopter, got my coat and supplies, and liberated the helicopter pilot's watch so I would have a compass! I made my own way here!"

"Really?"

"So while you people are sipping coffee in some sort of situation room linking to satellites I'm actually down here making my escape completely without you thus far. Just a reminder that I'm not an idiot and can fend for myself if I need to."

I heard her laugh quietly. "Linsenbigler, it's like you're made for this."

My phone bleeped and she was gone.

Powering down my phone, I fumbled with the damn thing until the back popped off and the battery fell out, the collected parts finding a home in my tackle kit. I adjusted my rod cases, satchel and pack into hiking position on my back, and marched into the lights of the market. The lure of a hot meal, a flagon of liquor and a soft bed put a spring in my step. A shower and a shave was almost too much to hope for. Whoever this 'friend' was would likely insist upon it if he were bunking with me.

I wandered this way and that through the crooked streets of the town in the general direction of where I had seen the train trestle, and before long began to see the universal signs pointing the way to the train station.

Along the way I dared to reflect on all that had happened, right down to Hailey's comment: *Linsenbigler, it's like you're made for this.* Madness! All but for the thinnest of margins did I survive the Caribbean misadventure. Thus far, the same was true here. Had Katya's aim been ever so slightly more accurate I'd be with half a head at the bottom of the river. My luck would run out sometime. Dax, of course, is one of those people who claims you make your own luck or some such. Oh, yes, Dax *was* one of those people, insufferable bastard, and yet he thought he could take my coat and leave me to freeze, claiming me to be a drunken fool who'd 'wandered off.' Slice it any way you like, but I'd pretty much shown Ol' Vlad that he underestimated Boone Linsenbigler. So keep it coming, Vlad, and you'll get what they got down in Honduras for thinking they could get the best of me!

My dander was up in an uncommon way – surprisingly without the aid or abetment of any cocktails.

The sun had set, and clouds had closed over the sky, a light snow beginning to fall as I tramped into the station. The ticket agent took one look at me and passed the ticket through the portal in the glass – I did not even have to say my name. He flicked his fingers at a train that was already idle in the station. I showed my ticket to an Asian conductor and he led me to the front of the train and to my cabin.

I opened the door and stepped in, eyes darting about the room. The compartment bore little resemblance to the Trans-Siberian cabin. This one was smaller, all white plastic walls, and with blue brocade cushion covers on the bunks to either side, each of which had an upper bunk. The window had an enclosed shade sort of like an airliner but fabric. It was up and I could see the snow falling outside in the lamp light.

Nobody was there, but the lights were on, and on the little table between the beds at the window was what I imagined must be a mirage: a bottle of PennyPacker Bourbon, glasses and rough ice, along with orange slices. It was warm in the cabin, and I realized this was the first time I had been indoors and warm in quite some time. (The hardware store and tavern were heated only marginally.) My face felt hot.

I stripped off my gear and coat and vest, kicked off my shoes, poured myself a cocktail.

Then I stopped, the glass not yet to my lips.

Vlad had served PennyPacker. You didn't suppose…

The doorknob turned.

While I had given my rifle to the Udege Chief as a thank you gift, I retained my pistol, and I fumbled for it.

The weapon was in hand when the door opened.

Under a sable fur hat, in a brown overcoat, was a shortish man with a swarthy complexion. He had large, sleepy eyes and beak-like nose.

He paused, and said: "It is I, sir. Beamish."

CHAPTER 16

THUNDERSTRUCK? More to the point, I was impossibly puzzled, my mind doing backflips: *This means Beamish is with Hailey and therefore a spy. He was sent by her on the Queen Mary to look after me and I did not realize it. He's not really a butler at all.*

As I lowered the pistol, he smiled thinly and removed his hat, hanging it on a peg on the back of the door, which he deftly locked. He ran his hands quickly though his thick shock of black hair and removed his coat. Beneath he wore a pinstriped suit, white shirt and purple tie – the very picture of a traveling businessman.

He waved a hand at my glass: "By all means, sir, indulge, I think you have earned it, and might I say that your travails have been rather remarkable thus far. Dispatching a helicopter in that manner was quite an unexpected development, yet a welcome one." Hiking up his pant legs, he sat gently on the bunk across from mine, tenting his fingers on the edge of the table.

Gun on the table, I leaned forward and extended a

hand, gushing.

"By Jove, Beamish, it is good to see you! Have a drink! But you can stop the butler act now, I obviously know you're a spy."

He blinked slowly, chuckling: "But I am a butler, sir, and not a spy. I'm afraid you have a rather theatrical understanding of how intelligence services work. Entirely understandable. A spy is usually a foreign national in a sensitive position who has been bribed or moved by ideology to turn over secret information within their grasp. I, on the other hand, am an operative, which means I operate afield to facilitate the gathering of information. I do so as a butler. There are others who do so as doctors, nurses, lawyers – what have you."

The bourbon sent a shiver down my spine. "Beamish, how are you facilitating the gathering of information through me? Isn't this a rescue mission?"

He nodded politely. "Yet the two are not mutually exclusive. Intelligence is much more fluid than it used to be in large part due to advanced surveillance techniques. There is much to know, and each piece of information is part of a larger puzzle. For example, everything you have done since I last saw you has created a ripple of communications that we have been able to follow. That ripple, added to other ripples from other occasions, provides a larger picture, a more complete puzzle. It gives us a better understanding of how the opposition reacts to situations, and thus allows us to attempt to manipulate them in the future. Putin could have reacted differently to your escape. He could have sent troops. But he sent Katya."

"Damn this bourbon tastes good. Thanks for this. So why did he send her?"

Beamish grinned. "Yes, why indeed? If Putin were put in the same situation again with someone else, would he do the same? What was his purpose in bringing you here in the first place – to win you over? Or to humiliate you and discredit a United States hero? He may not have made up his mind, but did when he sent Dax to drop you in the wilderness."

My mood darkened. "Dax told me that. He said Vlad decided I was never going into politics because I liked fishing too much. So why not send troops after me? Why Cossacks and Katya on horseback?"

"We surmise he sent Katya to humiliate not only the United States, but also you personally. Isn't that interesting? You see, knowing this lets us better understand him, lets us predict what he will do. Then again, as a former intelligence operative himself, it may be that he did this knowing we would note this behavior, and to corrupt our calculus."

"Why humiliate me personally?"

"Are you familiar with a certain Mr. Kraft who owns the Patriots football franchise? He met Vladimir Putin and after some chitchat about American football, Kraft took off his Superbowl ring to show it to him. Putin put it on, admired its size. He said something to the effect that if you punched somebody with the ring on, you could kill them. Kraft agreed politely and put out his hand for the ring. Putin merely grinned and walked out of the room with the ring, his body guards in tow."

"He really did that? Why?"

He shrugged. "Perhaps it was merely an act of perversity. It is all part of what the Russians call *maskirovka* – the little masquerade. Often, they initiate nonsensical or counterintuitive maneuvers simply to confuse us or distract us from some more directed effort to gain an actual advantage. Taking that ring from Kraft may have been intended throw off our predictions of Putin's behavior patterns. Plying you with Katya, a coiticidalmaniac, could be in the same vein, or it could have a larger purpose, or it could be that Putin's ego is genuinely feels threatened by your persona."

"A what? Coyta…?"

He grinned to himself at my naiveté. "Katya is driven to kill those with whom she has mated. The Russians call her *bogomol*. That translates to *mantis*. The female of that insect species devours their mate after copulation – from the head down. Coiticidalmania is a very curious and rare form of psychosis apparently derived from unaffectionate parents who sexually abuse their children. The emotions and physical pleasure derived from lovemaking are inadequate for Katya, and to elicit a stronger emotional response from her partner, she is not fulfilled until she has put that partner through the fear, terror and eventual agony of premeditated murder. Though some theorize that the psychopath is at least partially acting out latent revenge on the parents that abused her."

"You must be joking!" A chill went up my frame completely independent from the bourbon. "There are such people? How do we get Putin to call her off?"

Beamish stood, stroking his chin. "We don't know yet. But won't that be interesting to find out?"

"Interesting?" I squinted at him. "I'm not sure I like all this. You are using me as a means to gather intelligence on Putin and his operations."

The train car shuddered as the locomotive came to life.

"We've known for a while that he was going to troll you. We also knew that you would likely accept the offer of the trip – based on our dossier on you. Yet we did not lure you out here, you went of your own accord, and you came even after Hailey made your predicament known."

"She didn't say anything about fishing with Putin."

He threw his hands out apologetically. "We were not in a position to fully explain the entire breadth of the situation."

I don't mind telling you I was getting a little hot under the collar – again. "What the devil is that supposed to mean? Not in a position? You were in a position because you knew it and did not tell me."

He took a deep breath. "We are not in the habit of telling people more than they need to know, or relaying information that might result in the opposition knowing what we know, only what we want them to think we know. If you said anything about it, the opposition would know that we are monitoring certain channels and sources."

Whistles blew on the platform.

A gulp of bourbon and now I was on my feet. "Look here. I have an idea. Wouldn't it be *interesting* if you fellows simply sent someone to kill Katya before she kills me? Then what will Putin do? Let's find out!"

Calming hands from Beamish sought to reassure me.

"Sir, I'm quite certain that this ordeal has been trying for you and that you would rather it come to an end immediately. Unfortunately, that's impossible."

I glanced at the window.

In a puddle of light, I saw Katya in her fur hat and camouflage snowsuit. She was standing on the platform, hands on hips, staring at me. Not snarling or anything, just considering me, head cocked. A Cossack in wool turret hat came next to her, and she pointed at me.

I dove back into my bunk. "Gadzooks! It's her! On the platform!"

The train lurched forward.

Beamish slid further from the window's view. "Did she see me?"

"She was standing back on the platform, I don't think so, but she saw me, she pointed me out to one of her Cossacks! What if she boards?"

"She shan't. We're moving, and I guarantee that they would not let her aboard in any case."

"How is it that you simply can't have her killed?"

"There's more at stake than you know, Mr. Linsenbigler, that's all I can say. We have to move you under the radar so that they don't know that we know what they know or where you are."

The train moved faster, the wheels clattering through switches.

"What? They know what…you know that they know that you know that…"

"They can't know that we're here helping you. If they did, they would realize our ulterior motives and behave in a way that is counter to our purpose. We did not compel you to come to Russia, but now that you are here, and have created a bit of an incident, you need our help. Fear not, sir. Have patience and we will prevail."

With a shaky hand I poured another bourbon and pressed my face to the window to see if I could see Katya and her cavalry galloping alongside the train. I did not – in fact, it was just at that moment that the train jolted, and the diagonals of the trussworks knifed across the window like the blades of a gallows. We were crossing a bridge.

How on earth did I get into a situation such as this?

From between his bunk and the window-side table, Beamish lifted a briefcase, and began to rifle the contents, humming lightly to himself and ignoring my simmering panic.

A few minutes passed before the train was pulling into another station, which seemed odd inasmuch as we had just left a station.

"What's this, Beamish?"

He held out a new passport and a card stamped and sealed and scrawled in Asian characters. "A new passport and visa. Your name is Robert Boone, and you're a paleontologist. You'll also find a visa for Kazakhstan in back."

"Bob Boone? I'm a what?"

"Dinosaurs, sir. You seek their fossilized remains."

There was a sharp knock on the door, and Beamish opened it.

A slender Chinese man in a tight green uniform stepped smartly into the room. He wore a green cap with a red band and gold badge with a bright red star. An adjutant without the red stripe on his cap was wearing a gun belt and stood behind him. I guessed by his manner that the one with the red stripe on his cap was an officer, and he exchanged a nod with Beamish as though they had met. Before even examining my credentials, the officer turned to me and said:

"Welcome to the People's Republic of China, Mr. Boone. We've been expecting you."

CHAPTER 17

OUR TRAIN ZIPPED along the rails through dark, snowy farmlands. A food cart had come to our door immediately after we left the border station. Brimming with a mass of rice, my foam container had sides of sticky brown meat strips, a an unfamiliar fried pink vegetable and a steamed translucent green vegetable I had never seen before. It may sound odd, but even while I was running for my life and burning calories at a hectic pace, hunger came and went and had not been debilitating. I suppose that one's metabolism takes a back seat to the necessity of continued exertion to keep from being shot by a coiticidalmaniac.

That's a long way of saying that once actual hot food was put before me, I fairly buried my face in it until it was ingested. The trout had been satisfying and necessary, but this pile of whatever was merely necessary, especially the salt.

My meal dispatched, I suppressed a burp and splashed myself a little more bourbon. Sleep would come hard and suddenly, but not until I knew a little more about what all this dinosaur business was about.

As opposed to the ravenous Boone Beast, Beamish ate lightly – some stack of shaved veggies and a pot of tea. Tea cup in hand, pinkies up, he said:

"It seems the intestines, gourd and wosun met with your approval."

"Intestines?"

"Pork intestines."

"Well, I'm quite sure it's nothing I haven't had in a frankfurter. Needless to say, I was starving. So may I ask precisely why I am now Bob Boone, master of the pterodactyl?"

"Most assuredly. You see, it is our intent to unite you with a team of paleontologists working in the Taklamakan, which is several days west of here."

"Takla…"

"It is a desert west of the Gobi. The name translates to 'those who enter do not leave.' Quite a remarkable place with a very intricate history, with many ancient warrior kings doomed to faded legacies. There's a strong sense that the terrain itself is preordained to swallow up the ambitious. The part of that history in which you will be interested is eighty million years ago during the Cretaceous period. At that time, of course, it was not a desert at all, it was more like the terrain you crossed over the last several days."

"All very interesting, Beamish, but how do a bunch of professors scraping at the desert for bones figure into my return to New York?"

"We have every reason to believe that, although you

are now in the People' Republic of China, you are not insulated from pursuit. If we can operate here, they can operate here. Our mission is not just to return you to safety. As you recall, we need to eliminate Putin's impetus to have you killed and perhaps give him an active reason *not* to want you killed. He does not dissuade easily. You don't want to spend the rest of your life looking over your shoulder, do you? You would not want to wonder if the next woman you met and romanced were not in reality only interested in poisoning you?"

I closed my eyes, summoning patience. "How, precisely, does making me a paleontologist in the Desert of No Return make Putin like me again?"

"The Taklamakan Camp's manager is an operative who can get you to Kazakhstan and then from Almaty by plane to Istanbul and then home."

"Beamish, do you mean to tell me that I am going to have to pretend to be a paleontologist in the presence of other paleontologists?"

He smiled as though his student were finally making grades. "Precisely, sir. And I should think that you would find the subject of your expertise within this discipline fascinating."

"Pterodactyls? Can I be an expert in pterodactyls? I always liked them as a kid."

Beamish smoothed his hair. "We had to provide you with a specialty that was not already accounted for and thus the other academics in attendance will not know your subject that well."

"They already have a pterodactyl expert?"

"Unfortunately so. As such, we have chosen

hadrosaurs."

I sipped my whiskey, becoming so sleepy and modestly toasted that I was ceasing to care what absurd plans Beamish had for me. The entire turn of events was becoming so byzantine as to be unreal. If he had said I was to fasten a spout to my head and pretend to be the teapot at Buckingham Palace I would likely have made a remark such as: "I see."

"Hadrosaur? With big nasty teeth? Dangerous?"

"Hadrosaurs, sir, are duck-billed dinosaurs. Such as the parsaurolophus. They are ornithisian, or bird-hipped dinosaurs."

"So my dinosaur is a giant waddling duck-lizard, is that it? That's what you're giving me to work with here?" I slumped down in my bunk and faced the wall. "Good night, Beamish."

"Slumber well, Mr. Linsenbigler."

And I did. Surprisingly.

The following day we switched trains in Harbin, and at dusk again in Beijing, which required a green and gold taxi to take us through the smoggy, rainy blur of urban bustle to the West Beijing station, a titanic tan building in the shape of an arch with three pagodas spaced on top. That station in London I went through, while impressive, did not hold a candle to this monstrosity.

All the while, Beamish and I read about dinosaurs of the cretaceous period. Periodically, when we had both finished a particular article, Beamish would quiz me on the specifics.

One leg crossed over the other, hands folded on his knees, Beamish would fire questions from memory:

"Hadrosaurids are descendants of the Lower Cretaceous – BLANK –dinosaurs."

I stroked my chin: "Iguanodon?"

He shook his head: "*Iguanodontian.*"

"Oh, come on Beamish, partial credit on that one, wouldn't you say?"

My professor ignored the entreaty: "What are the two subfamilies of hadrosaurids?"

"Lambeosaurines and…saur… *saurolophines.*"

He cleared his throat. "Correct. What differentiates the two?"

"The first had hollow crests, and the second had solid crests."

"Which of the two tended to be heftier?"

"Lambeosaurines."

"Incorrect. Diet?"

"Herbivore."

"Correct."

And on and on in that manner as the third train went through every kind of terrain imaginable. One minute it was like upstate New York, then Iowa, then Utah. I was quickly tiring of the meals. Breakfast was the most curious one. I had never considered what the Chinese ate for breakfast but I never imagined it was what amounted to corn dogs, or salami and hard-boiled egg slices over white rice. I suppose that should have come as no surprise. All I knew about Chinese food was from the stuff they make in the states. Yet the utter preponderance of rice had me pining for good ol' occidental toast. Or just a simple ham sammy.

The bourbon didn't last and I found myself drinking

baijui, which is apparently the most consumed booze on the planet. Imagine I had never heard of it! It's a weak vodka, and I have to admit that it was a little on the tepid side for Ol' Boone, so I took to adding a little strong tea, a pinch of salt, lime and ginger to it just to make a proper cocktail of the thing. I dare say I greatly improved the baijui without sweetening. As they toast in China, *ganbei!* – 'dry your cup!'

Ridiculous as it is to say, I was greatly impressed by the sheer size and infrastructure of the country that passed by the window. I admit to feeling a little foolish for being ignorant of China's vastness and relative modernity. Likely as not, one in a thousand of these people had ever heard of me or knew much of anything of my world except what they bought at KFC.

It was not enough that I had something to do - studying for my final exam in over-sized duck-billed lizards. I also was assigned something *not to do.* Beamish was of the strong opinion that any paleontologist worth his gin had a fuller set of whiskers, top and bottom. As such, I was not to shave. I had not done so since my trans-Atlantic crossing, so I already had a leg up on a bushy spinach chin. Likewise, I was not to tweak my mustache but to let the entire ensemble droop down into my beard in a manner that made me cringe at what I saw in the mirror.

Making matters worse, my trademark rakish locks, which by my estimation were beyond due for a hearty trim, had reached my shirt collar, a wholly unacceptable state.

New attire was also issued. The lumberjack clothing

from Russia was quickly dispensed and replaced with what I can best describe as a winter safari outfit. I was in fleece-lined khaki and olive drab stem to stern, and was assigned a big floppy sun hat like those doctors thrust upon melanoma survivors.

The cherry in this Manhattan, the onion in this Gibson, the candy in this Rock and Rye? Round steel-rimmed specs that hook around the ears.

The horror in the mirror looked nothing like Boone Linsenbigler, though I suppose that was the point. I had no idea that paleontologists were so studiously disheveled.

On the morning of the third calendar day from Beijing, Beamish woke me at sun-up by dropping a long wool coat on my bed.

"Mr. Linsenbigler, our stop is finally at hand within the hour. I suggest you don your warmest clothes." With that, he stepped out of the cabin, leaving me alone.

Rubbing my eyes, I peered out the window at sparse grasslands and hills, the sun casting a strong orange light on the terrain. Griping about the infernal tumbleweed that had taken over my face and head, I splashed water on my face and brushed my teeth. Clothed in my drab paleontologist togs and long wool coat, I shoved my spare clothes into the co-pilot's satchel and collected my fishing tackle.

Beamish returned with tea and a basket of pork buns for breakfast. Setting that down on the table, he cast a disapproving eye on my fly gear. "Sir, I respectfully suggest you part from your fishing tackle. It will only impede you on your travels."

I poured myself some tea. "Not a chance, Beamish. That 'fishing tackle' saved my life, and an angler becomes quite fond of his equipment. I caught my first steelhead with that rod there, and my first Atlantic salmon with that one. The reels have caught innumerable fresh and saltwater fish. These are likely as good and true a friend as a man can have, and I don't plan on parting with them now."

He suppressed a glimmer of disdain for my stupidity, but recognizing my resolve, he straightened his vest and said: "Very well. You'd do well to bring the Russian coveralls for layering, and the warmer checked hat."

The train passed between some hills and emerged on the edge of a desert vista.

On one side were dunes as far as the eye could see in the distance.

On the other, grasslands and yurts with herds of livestock.

The train slowed, shuttered and rolled to a slow stop with a loud squeal of brakes.

A conductor shouted our station stop, and Beamish hustled me down the passageway.

"Say, where's your luggage, Beamish?" I asked.

"I, sir, am to remain on the train."

"What? I'm going alone?"

"Not at all, sir, not at all. You will be in good hands."

I noticed that nobody else seemed to be removing themselves from the train at this particular stop, and when Beamish shooed me down the steps to the wooden platform, I could see why.

Desert was on one side, yurts and cattle on the other,

and in front of me was a grinning man with only two teeth that I could see: his incisors. He looked as if he was bearing fangs. A lopsided fur hat was on his head, and a great shaggy coat hung over his shoulders. He wore leather leggings and fur lined boots. His round Chinese face was mahogany and intricately lined from weather. A cold wind swept from the dunes.

The locomotive emitted a sinister hiss.

"Mr. Linsenbigler, I would like you to meet Ghat. He will usher you to the camp."

I noticed that none of the conductors had even bothered to exit the train, and Beamish himself stood on the steps looking down at me somewhat apologetically. Or possibly he was amused, I couldn't tell which.

Something smelled terrible, and I surmised it was the cattle. I hoped the smell did not come from Ghat.

"Beamish, you have to be kidding me. I'm going to climb into a jeep with this character?"

"Alas, sir…" Beamish now had a handkerchief over his nose. "Jeeps and motorized vehicles are not up to the challenge of the terrain."

"Horses?"

He rolled his eyes far to one side, whereupon I followed his gaze to where a knot of wooly camels stood chewing their cud. When I say wooly, I mean that these were not the sleek models you see in warm desert. These specimens had shaggy manes and humps.

A whistle sounded, and the train lurched forward. "Forget it, Beamish!" I strode toward him, intending to re-board the train.

A hand on my coat yanked me backward – I stumbled

over the rough-hewn boards of the platform and fell. Ghat stood over me, cackling, his yellowed fangs fully bared.

He did smell. Bad.

I struggled to my feet, tripped on one of my rod tubes, clambered to my feet again, and ran toward where Beamish retreated into the train car. As he vanished, a conductor appeared and with a smirk closed the door in my face.

Staggering to a stop on the hewn-log platform, I watched as the clean white train slid away down the tracks, the clickety-clack of the wheels fading.

The train became smaller, and smaller, more and more distant.

I continued to watch the train until I couldn't see it anymore, couldn't hear it anymore.

My ears were filled only with the farts of the nearby cattle, the cold wind, and Ghat's continuing cackle.

CHAPTER 18

DISABUSE YOURSELF of any burgeoning desire to ride camels. I can only assume that Laurence of Arabia was a masochist, at best.

Let's start with the fact that they vomit with regularity and then swallow it. One is not spared the smell of this peculiar habit.

When they are not vomiting, they are farting.

They pee on themselves, shit on themselves and they have fleas. Fleas that bite not just them but anybody so insane as to ride them.

They spit at you when you least expect it; they kick you when you least expect it. The latter they can accomplish with any of their four legs, even to the side.

I think one would be hard pressed to find a more revolting animal than a camel. Even if you were to regularly shampoo one, there's no stemming the stench emitted from either end or the contemptible behavior.

So one might well imagine that anybody who had the desire to make it their livelihood to own and guide camel trains might be a kindred spirit. In the case of Ghat, that would be to imagine correctly.

In the saddle (a blanket between the two shaggy, vermin-ridden humps) you tower over your surroundings. I dare say that it is twice as high as sitting on a horse. The undulations of the beast's gait I also found unpleasant, a gyrating, undulating wobble that seemed to center on my lower back.

Once the fleas began to bite me, I protested to Ghat and demanded to dismount and walk. He of course did not speak a language I understood, so it took some major gesticulations on my part to facilitate the dismount, but eventually Ghat poked and trilled at the animal until it sat down. That part was the only good part about camels – they fold up all the way to the ground. As such, getting on and off was easier than it is with a horse.

Walking was an improvement, and I could keep pace with the camels, which do not move particularly quickly in any case. Admittedly, the dunes were hard on my calves, but if I kept up wind of the camels and Ghat I was spared their foul smell. Dunes gave way to hard, flat scrubby terrain, with foothills in the middle distance and mountains on the horizon.

It was cold. This was a desert purely inasmuch as it was dry and deserted. As we marched toward the foothills, the wind picked up, and it became cold enough that I pulled the fleece-lined safari pants from my bag and wrapped it around my head and neck. Looking through a slit in the wrapped pants also helped stem the sand pelting my face.

With no idea of where precisely we were going or

how long the trip was, I once again reproached myself for the idiotic notion of a fishing trip in Russia in the winter. Yet of more recent decisions, I reproached myself for letting Beamish talk me off that train. Trudging across a desert half-way 'round the globe with the ruffian Ghat and his repulsive herd was a nightmare. I had every confidence that at any moment some horrific turn of events would unfold. Roaming bandits might beset us, or a sandstorm might bury us, or Ghat might decide to cut my throat to amuse his camels.

How on earth did it seem reasonable to me that I should pose as a paleontologist? Was it because I was comfy on a train, and somehow trusted the courtly Beamish? I should have ditched that spook in Beijing and dashed to the U.S. Embassy. Faced with the frigid despair of the Taklamakan, dodging the stench of the camels and my guide, I had to seriously take stock of my mental capacity. Not only was I an idiot to go to Russia in winter, I was also an idiot to let Beamish railroad me into this fiasco – quite literally.

And that's another thing. How did I know he and Hailey were on my side in this? I didn't even know for sure that they worked for the US Government. Fine to say that you work for a super-secret agency, but where's the proof? What possible good could come from tormenting Boone Linsenbigler in this way? How did I even know for sure that the coiticidalmaniac Katya was so intent as to follow me back to the States? Bah, the whole thing was palpably insane.

Dying in this Godforsaken hellhole would serve me right.

I'm an idiot.

Closing my eyes against the grit pricking my cheeks, I longed to be trudging alone across the snowy woods of Russia, camping by streams brimming with wild trout, making myself Siberian Juleps by the fire, and dreaming of Nassau.

Indeed, what would Tanya think of this? She may have admired my steely survival acumen with the helicopter and Dax, as well as my camping and fending for myself, but what would she say to this?

Knowing her adventuresome spirit, she might actually enjoy what I was going through. She liked going under cover and being in danger and tough going. I supposed under the circumstances, I needed to bolster my spirits with the same urgency and resolve that saw me through the helicopter incident. *Here, too, I need to find the tenacity to prevail.*

We marched all day, me with pants wrapped around my head and a long wool coat leaning into the wind like some sort of desert tramp. I was fairly stumbling onward by the time the sun cast our shadows long on the snow-dusted dunes and scrub. Where was this camp? Over the next dune? Over the next rise? Disappointment doused each flickering hope.

Footsteps, one after the other, became a dirge-like drumbeat. My breathing was a baseline to my footsteps, one after the other, my lungs filling and expelling. I idly wondered what it might be like to hear my own breathing stop and know I was effectively dead, that time had run out, that I could endure no more.

What was it that Beamish said? That the desert swallowed up the ambitious as part of their fate or some such? More like the fate of any nincompoop who pretends to be a paleontologist and tramps about with camels in the desert with a thug named Ghat. The Great Boone Linsenbigler's flourishing legend undone by whimsical predestination and buried in the shifting, merciless sands.

A small stone hut appeared in my blurred vision.

Nothing more, just a stone hut with snow drifted on one side.

When we drew near, Ghat dismounted, and led the camels to one side.

He ducked into the dark, open doorway of the hut, and I heard splashing.

On one side of the hut was a stone trench that led through a hole into the hut. Water began to course through the hole and into the trench. The camels loped to the trench and began to slurp.

I understood: this was an oasis.

Scanning the horizon, there was just outback, desiccated twigs and swirling sand, the foothills and snow-capped mountain beyond them seemingly no closer than when we began.

It was late afternoon. How much farther?

Ghat reappeared, and latched onto and untied some of the luggage on one of the camels. He took the pack into the hut.

I walked to the lee side of the hut, out of the wind, wondering what was next, but trying to remain resilient and in survivor mode.

Smoke. I smelled smoke. Turning, I saw smoke coming from the roof of the hut, and when I strode around to the entrance, I could see that Ghat had made a fire from wood and coal in a fire pit to one side of the gloomy stone room. On the other side I could barely make out a stone circle and a bucket that I assumed was the oasis' well. He waved a leathery hand at me to sit on a folding stool next to the fire, and I obliged, greedily warming my hands by the small flames. Above was a simple hole in the hewn log roof through which the smoke more or less escaped.

This hut was a modest improvement over the trek. I had to take what I could get and pray this camp was not more than another day distant.

Ghat brought in more bags, and produced a lantern that he hung from a hook on the low ceiling. He also handed me bottled water, and I thanked him, grateful mostly that I wasn't going to be compelled to drink from the trough with the camels, though I had grimly started to convince myself that I might have to. I was dehydrated.

I drank steadily, but carefully, a sip every thirty seconds or so. I had heard that if you drink water too quickly when dehydrated you bloat.

The little fire began to warm the room, surprisingly – or perhaps just being out of the elements sufficed for warmth. Above, through the hole in the ceiling, I could see the sun was setting.

Before long, Ghat's repeated trips outside began to introduce all kind of improvements to the hut. To one side he laid out a carpet on the dirt floor, onto which he set a teapot, cups and plastic containers. He handed me a thick blanket, which I presumed was to be my bed roll. I was grateful that it smelled not of camels but of soap.

All his bags inside, Ghat finally hung a rug from hooks over the doorway and the burgeoning twilight. Now we were snug.

For the first time since we began our journey, Ghat spoke to me and bared his friendly fangs. If I got his meaning, it was something akin to: "Well, here we are for the night, not too bad, eh?"

He removed his lopsided fur hat and set it aside – twin black braids fell to his shoulders. From a bag next to him, he produced – of all things – a bottle of hand sanitizer, took some, and offered some to me. Again, I thanked him for the unexpected chance to de-grime.

Many fishing trips have guides that particularly enjoy cooking for their guests. This is sometimes to their detriment, as they seem to believe that poor fishing doesn't matter so much if he makes you beef burgundy and fresh Dutch oven bread streamside. Ghat appeared to be one such guide as I watched him open and arrange his plastic containers just so on the carpet and start the teapot.

First, he offered me some visibly unidentifiable brown dried fruit and biscuits, both of which were edible if not actively good. The former I ultimately decided was smoked green apple, and it grew on me.

So there I was with Fang doing his best to treat me to a meal – the least I could do was break out some baijui. His eyes widened when he saw the bottle, and he clapped his hands with pleasure at the sight of it. I poured us each a cup, and we raised our drinks: *ganbei!*

The smoke in the room masked the smell of my chef, and the liquor helped fend off the chill. I was rehydrated and gaining strength from the food calories. My spirits were improving, even if I had no idea whether I would survive yet another ordeal. Perhaps I had a knack for adventure after all as long as there were drinks and appetizer at days end.

Ghat skewered chunks of meat amounting to kabobs, and sprinkled them with some seasoning. I asked to sample the seasoning, and best I could figure it was turmeric, pepper and garlic. Tea was soon ready, and I splashed some into my baijui with a slice of the dried apple. Steeped for a few minutes, I realized we had another sensation on our hands, a Taklamakan Toddy! I made the same for him, and he babbled his wonder at the flavor – it met with his approval.

Meat grilling over the fire, Ghat held out a container of what looked like cottage cheese. I took it, and gave it a sniff and did my best not to make a barf face. It was redolent of gamey rotted milk, and I made an apologetic wag of my head as I handed it back to him. He laughed and waved me off as a fool for not liking it. One might only imagine what animal the milk came from, and I eyed the grilling meat suspiciously. Frankly, it smelled good, though perhaps that was just the spices. Fat dripped into the fire, brightening it.

I poured us another glass as Ghat removed the kabobs from the fire and handed me one.

The meat was not gamey, for which I was thankful. It was not stringy like chicken meat, which is similar in texture to rodent meat, so it was not rabbit or gopher or rat. Personally, I don't have a prejudice against rodent meat. My father was an avid squirrel hunter, and we ate critters regularly. Certainly it was not venison, and it was not goat or mutton – all three of which I dislike. Not pork-like. Beef was the flavor it resembled most, so I guessed it was horse or one of those forlorn cattle back at the train station.

My father, as a history professor and fan of frontier days, was intent on sharing his passion with his kids, thus my familiarity with squirrel meat. A neighbor had to put down a mare so of course dear old Dad had to ply us with horsemeat to honor General George Cook's poorly provisioned expedition to bring the Sioux to task for Little Big Horn. I recall being surprised how close in flavor it was to London broil.

Once again, I found myself ravenous after a rigorous hike, and Ghat was clearly pleased with my gustatory zeal. He made a second set of skewered meat, and I'd guess I ate the better part of a pound of the stuff. This was a camping meal as memorable as my trout, though lacking my sense of accomplishment and thus not on par.

Clean up was largely a matter of tossing the sticks in the fire. I filled our glasses again, and I offered Ghat one of my last cigars. He took the thin cheroot, clearly not sure what it was. With a sniff, his eyes widened and he said "Ahhhh." He snapped it in half and shoved a portion into his mouth and cheek. That got me laughing as I took the other half and lit it up.

Ghat's hosting abilities, under the circumstances, were certainly unexpected thus far. Expectations were then exceeded further still when he brought from his bag a four-foot long wooden spoon that was in two pieces. He assembled the two pieces into one long, thin, spoon-shaped guitar. It had two strings and a headstock at the small end. He twanged the strings to put her in tune, and then set about serenading me. With two strings, the chords were very basic, and it was all strumming, no plucking. What made this musical event more interesting was his voice. He used a technique that I later learned was Mongolian throat singing. There's a croaking sort of quality to the voice that made me think of frogs.

He twanged and croaked away, and I'll be damned if it didn't sound like bluegrass.

Truly a bizarre evening that was to become a touchstone memory for any campfire thereafter.

Hypnotic strains of the music made the end of that evening hazy. I believe at a certain juncture that I spontaneously curled up with my blanket next to the fire and passed out, Ghat still croaking and strumming.

The next moment I was awoken by Ghat moving about the hut making tea and setting out biscuits: morning shone through the hole in the ceiling.

I sat up, scratching my ragged beard, hat still on my head. The temperature in the room was around freezing, but the fire had been restarted and threw off some radiant heat.

Ghat handed me a bottle of water in passing, and as I drank, burgeoning daylight shed new details on the room.

To include a mummified human propped in the far corner behind me.

I blinked.

I stared.

Yes, I was awake. The dried remains were dressed in rags, sitting cross-legged, bone arms casually out to the side. Thoroughly desiccated, the corpse had hollow eye sockets and a face of grey rawhide. Teeth shone from a slit from where the lips used to be. Spindly shoots of grey hair stuck out from under a faded red pointed cap. The deceased had not been tall.

On a flat rock in front of it was a portion of the previous night's meal.

"Ghat?" I pointed. "What in blazes is that?"

He looked at me, then the mummy, then me, and blathered something. His manner was matter of fact, as if to say: "Yes, I know there's a corpse in the corner, thanks for pointing that out."

I was thankful that the corpse was positioned behind me. Of course I had not seen it the night before – could I have slept knowing that was there? My guess was that the departed constituted some sort of good luck shrine. I noted the litter of other meals scattered about in front of the mummy.

Then again, perhaps it was something Ghat and his pals used to freak out their customers, just for giggles.

I assembled my cell phone – I was quite sure there were no cell towers within a hundred miles so that it was safe from Russian tracking. In any case, I was certain that Hailey's ban on cellphone use was relegated to my stint in Dalnekrasnov. Sure enough, my phone lit up, was lost, and had no idea where it was.

While Ghat was loading the camels outside, I snapped a selfie with the carcass, then some other shots of the hut and the camels by sunrise.

Too bad I hadn't taken any photos the night before, much less some video – damn.

CHAPTER 19

AT LONG LAST: YURTS.

Just past noon, we topped a rise as we had topped approximately a million others. Like a miracle, the Taklamakan gave way to orange canyons splayed before us. They were carved as if fingers of a giant hand had been pressed into the base of the foothills. Tucked up next to a butte was a knot of round, white yurts with a corral of horses on one side and a large grey tent on the other. Smoke snaked from the chimneys.

I inspected them with my birding glasses. *Hazzah!*

Ghat grunted, stopped, and peered into the distance.

"*Gai zovlon,*" he growled. He swung his camel to the right, toward a gentle gulley, and the rest of the animals followed in single file. They broke into a trot, as did I.

What the devil is this?

As soon as we were out of sight of camp, Ghat trilled at his animals and got them all to fold up onto the ground. He hopped off his animal, grabbed me by the arm, and led me to the edge of the gulley, putting his fists together to mimic binoculars. I handed them to him.

Lying flat, he took off his hat and glassed the camp. After a moment, he groaned and handed the binoculars to me. "*Bod Gai.*"

I paused. Was that English? "Bad guys?"

His eyes were grave, and he reiterated more succinctly. "Bad Guys."

I glassed the camp. Just what I'd seen before. Then I noted next to the corral a knot of camels, a native dressed like Ghat with a rifle slung over his shoulder.

"Ghat, what do we do?"

He shrugged incredulously and waved a hand back from where we'd come.

"How many of them?" I held up five fingers and shrugged.

Ghat held up three fingers.

I cursed the bad turn of events. Were we to go back, what then? Presumably, I could get on that train if I could flag it down. In doing so, in back tracking, would I walk right in to Katya's waiting arms? I had no idea if she had followed me that far. She saw me in the train to China, so she could pretty well guess I'd be heading west as far as I could go, and as fast as possible. Once they watched the airports and knew I had not traveled by air, they would know I had traveled by either road or train. A train was more likely because it would be faster and more reliable. How much they could find out from the Chinese rail system about who was on what train going where, or if they could interview people who would tell them what westerners were traveling west, I had no idea. Despite my change of clothes and beard, the crisscross scar on my cheek – my dueling scar – was still visible. Surely, she would not be with her gang of Cossacks on horseback – though perhaps she would team up with some Mongol natives.

A familiar chill hit my neck, the hairs standing. Could that be her at the camp, waiting for me? Might Beamish have sold me out? Who knew? That cursed butler could work for anybody, or more than one master.

I slapped Ghat on the shoulder and held up three fingers. Then I held up one, and then with both hands I made the curvy shape of a woman in the air. He scowled, and held up three fingers and grabbed his crotch.

According to him, there were only men out there. Did he see them and I didn't?

I pointed at my eyes, pointed at him, held up three fingers and held my crotch.

He nodded, meaning he had seen them, or somehow knew there were only three.

I prayed he was right.

Having spent a lot of time with fishing guides that do not speak English, I was experienced in communicating in an ad hoc fashion. Yet my next question was harder to gesticulate, made even harder by the fact that I was lying on my side in the dirt.

I held up three fingers, and then shrugged, hands to the side. I had to do it twice, the second time followed by mimicking eating, drinking and money. *What do they want?*

Ghat scratched at his balls, trying to figure what I was trying to say.

He slowly held up three fingers, and I nodded. Then he nodded, shrugged, pointed toward the yurts and drew a thumb under his throat. What I got from that was that they might do some killing as well.

Of all the cursed luck – the paleontologists at that camp would likely be killed. No doubt, the operative that I needed to get home would be one of them. That wasn't a reason to intercede on its own, but nobody likes to turn a back on people in mortal danger. Well, Ghat seemed to be OK with turning tail. Under normal circumstances, I would phone the police. That notion was patently ridiculous in No Man's Land.

Yet if we did not turn back soon, we would not arrive back at the oasis hut until after dark – not desirable. What if there were others already in the hut, perhaps other unsavory characters like the ones in the camp close at hand? That didn't seem likely, but still I hated going back. I wanted to get to Almaty and on that plane and find myself in Istanbul.

On my back in the dirt, the wind blowing sand across my face, I imagined a bar in Istanbul with a view of the old city and Bosporus Sea, the ceiling fans turning slowly and an alert waiter who snapped his heels when I ordered my next Gin Ricky. It would be warm. I would be in a khaki linen suit and white shirt, my Panama hat resting on the table. Below on the street would be the cries of shop keepers, minarets erupting with the call to prayer. Sipping my cool, tangy, tall drink, the view tinted amber by my sunglasses, I would think back to this horrendous situation, smack my lips and say to nobody in particular: "When donuts block your view, look through the holes. Cheers."

Ghat shoved me from my daydream and gestured that

we turn back.

I pulled Dax's automatic from my tackle bag.

Yes, I'd lost it, completely out of my mind. Perhaps it was desert madness, or the ghosts of the Taklamakan directing my fate. Or perhaps I was determined to outwit the fates and manifest my own destiny, chart my own course through stormy seas. Not only had I allowed Beamish to put me in the middle of the desert from which nobody ever escapes, but I was now proposing to intercede on behalf of my supposed comrades in paleontology. Let that be a lesson to anybody who stands between Boone Linsenbigler and a proper barroom.

Ghat stared at me incredulously, at the gun, and then he smiled a sly smile, chuckling.

He pointed at himself, the camp, and then me.

Now he started to really laugh, shaking his head. I couldn't tell whether he was for the idea or against it.

In a flash of steel he held a knife to my throat, his grimacing face inches from mine.

I gulped.

He pushed me away and smiled, holding out the knife – he had only been showing me that he was quick with a knife. The sweat on my brow felt like icicles, and I dare say I peed myself just a little.

Ghat clapped his hands together, his dark eyes flashing, and rolled to his feet. He strode to the camel with the co-pilot's satchel on it, untied it, and zipped it open. From it he pulled the half bottle of the co-pilots brandy, the one I'd drunk only half of in the wilderness. I guess he had inspected the contents of my bags!

Imbibing at that juncture did not seem wise. That

said, and having been one of the two people about to embark on a rescue mission of dubious success, the sheer impracticality of the entire initiative almost demanded that further idiocy be introduced into the proceedings. This was an impulsive, precarious undertaking, so what the hell. Damn the torpedoes and all that.

So it was we left the empty brandy bottle in the gulley, roused the camels, and marched forward to the camp across the arid, wind-swept plain toward the yurts and orange canyons, full sun in our faces.

About halfway there, I heard a croak and a twang, and through the trousers wrapped around my head, I saw Ghat with his two-string guitar, one leg crossed on his beast, belting out a tune.

At first, I imagined this was the result of drunkenness. However, tactically, it made sense to try to alert them to our approach and make them think we had no idea they were there. Better still, as we drew near, the other two bandits emerged from the big tent, wiping their mouths across their forearms, rifles still slung across their backs. They brought with them a Chinese woman with a black eye – I presumed their hostage. The third bandit over by the camels cradled his long gun and joined the other two at the tent entrance. A closer inspection of the weapons suggested that these were single-shot bolt-action rifles, and I did not see any side arms other than knives in their belts. The one cradling his gun would have to be taken out first. I did mention I'd been drinking brandy, right? Lord…

The fur-hatted bandits stood waiting for us, heads cocked: on my side was one in a brown hat, the middle bandit wore a tan hat, and the one on Ghat's side with a black hat.

Ghat continued to strum and croak our way toward them. I heard one of them mutter something, and then others laugh and point at the two approaching idiots.

The Chinese woman seemed motionless but had drifted back closer to the tent, yet I didn't look her over too carefully as I was intent on the one in the brown hat cradling the rifle. I had my fishing sunglasses on so they couldn't see my eyes – and of course to help block the glare from the sun. I needed to see my targets, after all.

Black Hat – on Ghat's side – slung his rifle over into his hands as we drew near and stopped.

Ghat kept playing, and croaking his Mongolian bluegrass. The three bandits gestured at him, laughing, telling him to get down. Black Hat, rifle in one hand, strode next to Ghat's camel and stopped, shouting at the guitar-playing fool to get down.

I drifted forward, closer to Brown Hat, but all eyes were on Ghat. I didn't think they thought the moron with the pants wrapped around his head was any kind of threat at all. My sleeping blanket was draped around my shoulders like a poncho, and under it I held my gun, finger on the trigger.

As if on command – and perhaps it was – Ghat's camel gave Black Hat a mighty kick to the thigh.

Black Hat doubled over, dropping his rifle. Another camel moved forward, blocking my view of Tan Hat.

The woman was off to the left.

Brown Hat was straight ahead. He took a step toward Ghat.

A quick, final glance at Ghat (to make sure I knew where he was so I didn't shoot him) reveled that he had a knife in his teeth. He was crouched between his camel's humps, and launched himself either toward Black Hat or Tan Hat, I couldn't see which. Maybe both?

I leveled my weapon at Brown Hat's chest and fired two quick deafening shots.

BAM-BAM.

He was only ten feet away; I could not have missed.

Yet he still swung his rifle at me, grimacing.

I raised my pistol at his head and fired, hitting him in the jaw. Still, he raised the gun at me and fired a shot from his hip. *CRACK.*

The slug buzzed over my head.

One more shot from me hit him in the eye, and he paused.

Tan Hat ran behind him toward the woman hostage.

Foolishly, I swung the pistol his direction and fired. I took off part of his face, and blood sprayed over the woman as he stumbled and fell at her feet. Were I off a little, I could have shot her in the face. He tried to get up but she began kicking and stomping him brutally.

Brown Hat fell to his knees, and then to his side, a goner, but gasping.

Astonishingly, the camels were completely oblivious to all the noise and gunplay, as though they were used to this kind of thing. I ducked my head under the camel at my side to see what was going on with Black Hat.

Ghat had him on the ground, knife to his neck, but Black Hat was bigger, and had gotten a hand around Ghat's knife hand and throat.

I attempted to take a short cut under the camel; the beast's hind foot kicked me in the side.

My momentum sent me to the far side of the camel, and when I landed on my back, I realized I'd dropped my pistol.

Somewhere.

Yet my head had landed directly next to Black Hat's head.

His bloodshot eye turned toward mine, and I swear he laughed, of all things.

I rolled onto my feet, looking for my pistol, and the camel took another shot at kicking me – he missed and brought his foot directly down on Black Hat's face.

The blow to Black Hat loosened his grip.

Ghat made purchase with the knife across Black Hat's jugular.

An explosion of red erupted.

Yet Ghat – fangs bared – kept pressing even after his opponent released his neck, hands waving in the spray of blood.

Crack – the knife crushed Black Hat's esophagus.

Ghat doubled down, raising his shoulders and pushing the knife down harder with all his weight.

The spray of blood suddenly subsided, and Black Hat's flailing hands flopped to his sides.

Ghat stood, his chest heaving, his eyes wild, his face and chest dripping in gore.

OK, so anybody – video gamers, perchance – who thinks this kind of thing is fun is profoundly deluded. What you take away from such incidents is that when you are trying to kill, people rarely die easily. If you shoot a man in the chest with most rifles or handguns, he doesn't just fall down dead, and if he has a weapon, he can still use it. If you're going to kill you have to keep at it until the person drops unless you want to end up dead yourself. That means you have to be brutal and uncompromising. Keep shooting, kick him, stab him, strangle him, and bludgeon him with a rock. Keep killing until you have achieved certain, pitiless death.

Pure savagery.

And afterward, you have to try going back to not being a savage. That's not easy. There's a part of you that wants to keep killing – a very ugly part of you, and frankly one I wish that I did not know was there. Alas, I do, and unfortunately, I think far more people possess these impulses than is good for our species. Fortunately, the impulse fades soon after you've achieved the desired result. Yet once you've experienced killing, you always know that the knack for it is there. You always know that there's a part of you, however ephemeral and unwanted, *that likes killing.*

Other people, men with beards, burst from the tent and swirled around us. I was a bit light headed, dizzy. I heard a camel honk and excited voices – and shouts. I stepped forward and grasped Ghat by the arm – people were trying to lead him away. He looked back at me, his face a rictus of murderous bloodlust.

I stumbled.

Hands were on me.

Voices.

Flashes of sunlight.

I passed out.

CHAPTER 20

I AWOKE PERHAPS AN HOUR LATER, on my back, with the Chinese woman's face looking down at me. Her shiner had swelled closing her left eye into plum. That was too bad because the rest of her face was quite lovely to my eye – large dark intelligent eyes set wide apart, small nose, slender jaw and rose-kissed lips. Her raven hair was in pigtails framing her face.

There were what I think they call smile wrinkles at the corner of her one good eye, which meant to me she was pushing forty, a few years my junior.

"Linsenbigler?" She spoke without an accent – that is, American. "I'm Lotus Chin, camp manager."

I blinked and cleared my throat. "Pleased to make your acquaintance, Ms. Chin. I suppose that I…"

"Fainted. Call me Lotus."

"Hm." I blinked hard to try to clear the cobwebs from my noggin. "Well, I suppose the excitement got the better of me. Shooting people isn't my racket."

She smirked. "You wouldn't know it. Except for the

fainting part."

"I don't ever hope to go through something like that again."

"Well, we're all glad you did. One of them touched me, I tried to kick him in the balls, and he gave me this shiner. I'm not that good at self-defense, I guess."

"Good Lord. Shouldn't you have guards?"

She sighed. "We had one. They killed him."

"Are there regional police of some sort that will come about this?" I gently swung my legs off the bed and sat up. The bruise in my side from the camel kick stung, and after a little gentle probing I guessed there was no fracture.

"Police? We can't afford the scrutiny."

I inspected my surroundings – the room was round, the walls lined with carpets, and the ceiling was canvass. An iron stove was in the center of the yurt, the crooked chimney poking through the ceiling. I was on a cot surrounded by what looked like stored luggage – guest quarters.

"If you don't mind me saying, Lotus, this seems like a pretty dangerous place for a group of scientists and an attractive woman. I hope that wasn't sexist to say."

She reacted to my compliment by instinctively smoothing her hair and adjusting her pigtails, without smiling. "I'm no wilting flower, Linsenbigler."

"You're the one who will get me to Kazakhstan?"

"Yup." She stood. "I speak Mandarin and Uyghur, so I can communicate with the locals as necessary."

Lotus had a narrow waist; her calves and arms looked athletic. Definitely an outdoors girl, the kind I would think was a rock climber.

"When do we leave?"

"Tomorrow."

"Sooner the better." I stood.

"Steady on your feet?" She held out a hand, but I waved it off.

"I'm OK."

"Perhaps you need a drink – the Managing Director and Associates are waiting in the dining tent."

I laughed mirthlessly. "If you had any idea what I'd been through over the last week you'd know that I need more than a drink. I need a bar."

Lotus waved me to follow her. "This way – but take it easy on the whiskey. We have some serious traveling to do tomorrow."

I scratched my beard and shuffled after her.

Outside there were ethnic Chinese staff darting this way and that with great purpose. As we approached the dining tent – where the killing took place – I averted my eyes from the blood on the ground. While the killing was necessary, I didn't like what I had done to those men, and the thought of it made me a little lightheaded again. Ghat's fountain of blood was a little over the top, too.

Ducking under the tent flap, I found myself across from three men who were the very picture of paleontologists according to Beamish: bearded and decked out in khakis. Light was cast down on them from a plastic skylight in the tent roof. They sat in a row on the opposite side of a long folding dining table, and stood when I came in. Lotus stepped forward to make introductions.

"Linsenbigler, this is our Managing Director John."

The elder Caucasian man in the center reached out his hand across the table He was a tall man with wide shoulders, and sun freckles decorating his thinning grey dome. Blue eyes sat above a ski-slope nose and thin but expressive lips buried in grey fuzz. I shook his large, cold hand.

"…to his right is Associate Joe."

Joe was a slight, middle-aged black gentleman with an open laptop in front of him, and I shook his noticeably warmer hand across the table. Both his short Afro and beard were salt and pepper, and framed small features. A wry smile made him seem impish.

"…on the left is Associate Jay."

Stocky and South American, this gentleman had a wide stern mouth and flat nose flanked by dark eyes under heavy eyebrows. His grip was overly firm.

John gestured at a chair opposite them for me to take a seat. Next to the chair was what looked like a boulder the size of a giant tortoise. He said: "Please, have a seat. Lotus, I'm sure Mr. Linsenbigler could use that drink now."

Linsenbigler? I didn't have to pretend to be Bob? I shifted a little uncomfortably, and John noticed, raising a hand, adding: "Don't worry, none of us are paleontologists. But we all had to assume the pretense to avoid scrutiny and arrive here under the radar."

John, Joe and Jay. Manny, Moe and Mack. Meeny, Miney, Moe.

Managing Director and two 'associates.'

They were paleontologist impostors, with phony

names and odd titles.

I had stumbled into a nest of yet more Haileys and Beamishes.

John affected a kindly, patriarchal smile.

"Mr. Linsenbigler, may I call you Boone?"

"Please."

Lotus placed a tumbler of brown liquid at my elbow and drifted back out of view. A single ice cube was in the tumbler's bottom. The cube and I shared a moment. Both alone sitting in a glass of trouble. A sip indicated that it was a rye whiskey, though it was heavy on the barley and could have been some sort of scotch blend. Didn't matter.

"Well," John began, "first off, we cannot say how impressed we are with your rescue. Top-shelf, and our sincere thanks. You can't fully appreciate what it would have meant if you had not interceded."

I rattled my ice cube, which was already lonely, and Lotus gave me a refill.

"Let's cut to the chase. You gents and Lotus are here for a reason that has nothing to do with dinosaurs, and you brought me here for an ulterior purpose. I don't know exactly how long ago you people planned this charade, whether it was all the way back on New Years' Eve or even before. But now that you've got me here, and there's a coiticidalmaniac on my tail thanks to my little grenade party with Putin, you can go right ahead and tell me what in blazes is going on. Why have you brought me here?

Now it was their turn to squirm uncomfortably. John took another stab at the fatherly smile: "So as you surmise, Boone, we are here on a project. Normally, there would be no paleontologists here in the winter, but we invented the ruse of having to monitor the digs and prevent looting. That has allowed us to be in close proximity to the Kazakhstan border and to prepare our equipment for an event."

I interjected: "Can I assume that you all work for the same organization as Hailey and Beamish?"

"Precisely," he continued. "As I believe has been explained to you by our operatives, our business model is not rigid but fluid. As such, we follow trends, and we follow people who are a part of trends."

"Such as yourself," Joe added. "We have advanced modeling software that affords us quite accurate insights into events, and into people. In your case, you fit a very distinct profile. Perhaps you don't realize it, but your profile, your particular mix of traits, is rather remarkable. You exhibit just the right balance of caution, fear, luck, ill-timed drunkenness and bursts of bravado that make you an excellent subverter."

I had to laugh: "Ah I see, frightened drunkards who enact poor decisions make the best secret agents do they?" I sighed, and sipped, wincing at Joe: "Subverter? I don't even know what that is. Frankly, I don't want to know, because whether or not you think I'm one, I'm not. I'm an "ill-timed drunk" and an angler and a pitchman for Conglomerated Beverages. I'm not trained or qualified for this work, whatever it is. I am not a secret agent."

Every time I said the words 'secret agent' it made them wince.

Jay spoke up, leaning forward on the table and lacing

his hands, his eyes under the dark shadow of his eyebrows: "The way you performed in the tropics last year was extraordinary. We think you must realize that. I know you characterize your escape as just trying to save your skin, but bravery is actually not a good quality for a subverter. Bravery would have just gotten you killed. The balance of qualities that Joe mentioned are a valuable resource. We knew you would make it here from the moment you destroyed the Mi-8. And along the way you worked your luck."

Joe: "The odds were 96.8 percent that you'd make it."

"Really?" I cocked an eyebrow. "So how did the bear figure in there?"

They said in unison: "Bear?"

"Yes, I heard a cry for help and recued a child from a bear that had him cornered on a rock face. Want to know how I did that? The bear was on his hind legs, so I head butted him in the chest, knocked him back. Pretty smart, right?"

They shrugged and nodded, but I wagged my head.

"Not so smart, because after I did that, I didn't draw my weapon when the bear fell and he charged me. If the kid's father hadn't been running up the hill with a rifle at that moment and shot the bear, I wouldn't be here. So your Linsenbigler Algorithm is missing a lot of data that could push it either way. You're just kidding yourselves."

Jay: "Again, that is just an amazing stroke of luck that would not have happened to anybody else."

"Not you too? Dax was blathering about luck, said that I had a knack for taking advantage of opportunities other people don't recognize. Now you're making it seem like I have some sort of super powers. There's a word for this. Bullshit."

Jay grinned. "We have extensive research and algorithmic modeling that luck – as it is conventionally understood – is a myth. Situational awareness, meshed with flaw patterns and timing are no coincidence. Luck is recognizing and capitalizing on chance opportunities, relying on a vivid intuition, creating self-fulfilling prophecies, positive expectations, and embracing a robust and proactive resistance to adversity."

"Malarkey! So if I'm so lucky, why am I here? Not lucky for me, I can tell you that." I jiggled my glass for another refill, and got it. "Gentlemen, if your algorithms and software and models are so smart, did they predict your bandits?"

They exchanged an uncomfortable glance, and Joe spoke up. "It did not. It was an anomaly, like the bear. Your self-fulfilling prophesy and proactivity would not let you turn back to the oasis, with the stinking camels and corpse. Not with Katya out there somewhere as an unknown factor."

Jay: "And we knew that you had a weapon."

Joe hunched over his laptop, looking at the screen through his reading glasses: "Oh, and the forecast predicts you are intent on staying in a nice hotel with a nice bar in Istanbul."

Jay: "One with a nice view."

Joe: "Modeling recommends for you Raoul's Galata Hotel, boutique chic, great rooftop bar."

At that moment, I dearly wished I had turned back, or escaped in Beijing. "Look, you seem like nice people, and

I understand that you have some sort of mission…"

"Project…" they muttered in unison.

I continued: "…OK, 'project'…and need help, but I want no part of your phony names and weird spy titles. No matter what you want me to be, that's not who I want to be, which is really the central point here. Were you really relying on me to swing vine to vine the four thousand miles from Putin's to this Godforsaken dinosaur hut? That was the plan?"

John cleared his throat: "We had someone else to help Lotus on this project. However, last week, he broke his leg in Bucharest. Look, Linsenbigler, this project is critical to the welfare of our nation."

"You mean the United States, right?" They nodded. "OK, just checking, please continue."

John: "There is a sort of war going on in orbit between Russian satellites and our satellites. They have already introduced one interloping satellite, Kosmos 2499, and are set to launch a newer and more dangerous model. Our project is to make sure the second launch fails. Russia's major launch centers – Baikonur Cosmodrome and Sary Shagan – are located and maintained in Kazakhstan. They know we watch those carefully, which is why they have elected to mobilize their more classified launches to random locations where we cannot readily anticipate them. This makes it more difficult for us to determine the exact location of the launch and react to it. We set up here calculating that they would locate the launch somewhere close to China because it is in line with their other tracking stations east of here: Ulan-Ude and Ussuriysk."

Jay flattened his wide hands on the table, eyes still in shadow. "Russia has initiated a cyber-war on the west, which includes the capacity to interfere with or destroy communications satellites."

Joe held up a finger: "Their current satellite, Kosmos 2499, has the capacity to maneuver in close range to our communication and surveillance satellites, and to access the communications satellites to monitor and alter data streams. It is a parasite on our communication systems."

John: "They can read or listen to almost any electronic communications through our satellites just the way we can. That's a problem. The new satellite they are trying to launch is Kosmos 5000. It is more advanced that the previous model and would make their surveillance capabilities total. At least now they are somewhat limited to where Kosmos 2499 can maneuver and in what time frame."

Standing, I turned my chair around and sat on it backward so I could fold my arms over the back and listen. Taking a deep breath, I said: "How on earth – and certainly not in space – am I going to help you with this problem? Can't someone just shoot down this rocket?"

John: "Shooting down the launch vehicle would be an act of war. If we act overtly, they can act overtly. Neither the Russians nor we want an actual war."

"I see." My ice cube was looking high and dry again, but I gave the drinking a rest for the moment and set my glass on the boulder next to me. "So instead of an actual war, you have space wars between machines, wars of stealing information, wars of surveillance."

They exchanged a glance, and John said: "Exactly.

But these wars can cause real damage, even an existential threat to our country, our economy and the welfare of our people."

I hung my head. "Why not send in Special Forces or Delta Force or the A-Team in here to take care of business?"

"Too overt." John leaned in. "If you help us, we will be able to get you home, Boone."

I laughed, nervously: "Now we're getting somewhere. What is it that you want me to do?"

Lotus was at my side, filling my glass as it sat on the boulder: "I will take you across the mountains to Almaty, but I need your help placing an electronic device on a mountain overlooking the launch site. The Russians now have a portable all-terrain launch vehicle – PATLV. They can move the launch vehicle at will to different locations to avoid anyone interfering with the launch electronically or otherwise. Our device needs to be in a sightline with the PATLV. They are positioning the PATLV in a remote valley in Kazakhstan near the border with China, and we can pass that way to Almaty. We just place the device and go. This has the added advantage of eluding anybody trying to track your whereabouts, which we understand is a concern. We will be traveling through remote territory."

I eyed her suspiciously. "Just like that? We don't have to set it off or anything?"

Lotus: "Nope. The PEMP GLONASS Spoofing Transmitter – we call it PEGSPOT – is self-priming and will spoof the rocket's telemetry software remotely."

I raised both eyebrows.

"PEMP? GLONASS? *Spoofing?*"

John cleared his throat. "Launch vehicles rely on several systems to guide them into orbit – a combination of inertial systems supplemented by satellite signals. Inertial guidance systems experience integration drift, which is caused by small errors in the crafts sensors' ability to accurately detect angular velocity in real time in relation to acceleration. These errors are corrected in two ways in this launch vehicle: Kalman algorithms and GLONASS – the Russian global positioning system. Within the PEGSPOT is a Precision Electromagnetic Pulse Emitter that locks onto the electronic signature of the launch vehicle's inertial navigation system in order to hobble the Kalman filtering circuitry that corrects for integration drift. When those filters are compromised, the navigation system is forced to rely on GLONASS to help correct the vehicle's course. The signal from GLONASS is able to be overridden and supplanted with a signal of our own – this is known as spoofing. Once PEGSPOT spoofs the guidance system and links it to our satellites instead of the GLONASS satellites, we can introduce data with false coordinates and relative position to the ground. When the guidance software tries to correct what it thinks is an error it will in the process steer the launch vehicle off course and eventually into the ground. For the launch and tracking crews, interference from us will not be obvious. It will look like a materials or software flaw Others in the government will have their suspicions, and we want them to be uncertain. We want them to think maybe it was us."

With a hard blink, I asked: "So you don't want them to *know* it was you who interfered with their rocket, you want them to think it *might* be you, and as a consequence you will know that they suspect that you know about their plans, so they don't know what to do. Effectively, you want them to know they don't know what you know."

The three of them squinted at me, their lips moving silently as they repeated my words back to themselves.

Joe finally raised that slender finger and said: "Yes. I think."

"So how exactly is all of this going to make Putin leave me alone?"

Lotus: "We're going to let him know you were involved in some subtle way. Once he believes that you're a part of the game and not an outsider, its hands off."

I cocked my head. "Why is it hands off?"

The assembled looked mystified, and John finally croaked: "Putin is ex-KGB. We don't kill each other unless someone foolishly acts against the other overtly in an act of war or direct sabotage. Where would we be if our people killed their people? It would be bedlam."

I paused: "So there are rules, like a game?"

They answered by looking exasperated, and at each other.

At this point, I was stroking my beard trying to take all this in. "So if this device…"

Lotus: "PEGSPOT."

"So, if the PEMP GLONASS Spoofing Transmitter, known as PEGSPOT, is placed in eyeshot of the Portable All Terrain Launch Vehicle, known as PATLV, loaded with the spy satellite Kosmos 5000, won't the crew down below be looking for something like this? Won't they see this device?"

Lotus nodded at the boulder next to me.

I followed her gaze, reached over and thumped the boulder with my knuckle: plastic. "That fake rock is the PEGSPOT?"

They all nodded.

I stared at the plastic boulder a moment. I asked: "One last question."

They leaned in.

"Which one of you got to play the pterodactyl specialist?"

Joe raised that slender finger.

CHAPTER 21

EXHAUSTED FROM THE PHYSICAL STRAIN of crossing part of the Taklamakan Desert, I was also exhausted from the intellectual strain of wrapping my brain around the vagaries of espionage. As such, I requested food and an early retreat to my quarters. They gave me some stew, a hunk of bread and I ate it sitting on my bunk. I think Ghat's meat sticks were better than the stew, to be honest, though perhaps that had something to do with the more exotic surroundings. I mean, where was the desiccated corpse, after all? Where was the Mongolian bluegrass? It didn't matter, as I summarily inhaled the meal and curled into a ball under the blankets. All I wanted was sleep, and it came readily.

Yet I awoke in the dark, uncertain of where I was. The glow of the iron stove cast enough light so that I could take in the basics of my surroundings. Footsteps approached, and it was as if I awoke in anticipation of them.

The wooden door swung open, and I saw the

silhouette of Lotus' curves in the grey pre-dawn light. Before she could say anything, I said: "I'm awake."

"Get dressed, wash up and we'll grab a quick bite."

She let the door swing shut behind her.

Funny, her entrance reminded me of a bazillion fishing trips. Often, one is roused early on these trips, in the dark, and the wake-up alarm is a fishing pal knocking on your door. *Rise and shine!* It was amazing how often I would awake just prior to the arrival of the knock on the door, and how often I spoke before they did: *I'm awake.* So this all seemed very familiar – I was accustomed to what's known as the 30 minute 'O-Dawn-Hundred' drill. This consisted of only the most basic hygiene, the immediate consumption of coffee, a rapid exit and the earliest possible line in the water.

I clicked on a light by the washbasin in the corner and looked at myself in the mirror. Confound it, I looked like a subway vagrant! Sundry toiletries were arrayed before me, so I went to work with the scissors.

In short order, and with the help of a razor, I had Ol' Boone's whiskers back into some semblance of the usual raffish self. My hair was still long, but I could at least shape some decent sideburns and trim my eyebrows. No sense dying looking your worst, aye?

I noted that all the cartons and luggage were missing from the room. As I snored the night away people had been buzzing around the room.

Cold water meant for a splash bath, but I got all the important parts suitably bathed with soap.

I found new clothes laid out for me, and they were comprised of hooded quilted camo coveralls, all-terrain camo knee-high boots, and wind goggles. While the attire made me look like I was heading for a duck blind, it did fit, loosely, and was quite warm. I can't say I was sorry to bid farewell to my paleontologist clothes, which by that juncture were ready for a laundry or fire pit. I slung my rod cases and tackle kit over my shoulder and headed out.

As I made way for the dining tent, I noticed only one or two of the ethnic Chinese staff lounging around. Place seemed deserted.

Lotus sat at the table in the dining tent alone with a thermos of coffee. She wore an outfit similar to mine – except that it was even less flattering. Another thermos for me was next to her. Scattered on the table were pre-packaged breakfast bars, the kind hikers eat. Well, I hadn't exactly expected an English breakfast, but I could have used one. As you might imagine, I had been losing weight, and I did not carry much extra. No doubt I'd lost a notch on my belt.

I sat in front of my coffee and Lotus didn't look up. She seemed lost in thought. I had seen this look on angler's faces at that hour as well, and it was usually the morning of the last day of a trip on which nobody had caught anything. *Might we actually have a great day? Or will it be another stinker?*

My coffee was terrific for no other reason than it was coffee. I had not had any since Paris approximately a century before. The nut fruit bars were the usual dreck, but in keeping with the mood exhibited by Lotus I was no longer in the mood for anything heavy. She was tense.

While my dubious merits as a lucky dipsomaniac eluded me, I did take heart that – as in my career of fishing trips – I am not a slave to food. I prefer to have some, but I can push myself for long periods without much of it and my body does not complain. Rather, I can eat whatever is around and not think much of it, but save my indulgences for when I can enjoy a true feast accompanied by a hearty cocktail, beer or wine. Dining on fresh trout and a cocktail in the wilderness is a testament to my fortitude far beyond stumbling four thousand miles across Asia.

After ten minutes, Lotus capped her coffee and scooped food bars into her coverall pockets. "Ready?"

I stood. "Ever ready!"

She turned and left the tent. I followed. I dare say I was a mite hurt that she had not commented on my vastly improved whiskers.

Burgeoning daylight had rendered the camp in a brighter shade of gray, and by the corral, I spied Ghat fussing with his camels.

I detoured toward him – it wouldn't do not to say farewell to a comrade in arms. Behind me, I heard Lotus huff at the delay of our departure.

Ghat's fangs were in full display as I approached, and we greeted each other with unexpected warmth, grasping each other by the hands. I had almost forgotten how foul smelling he and his animals were. He babbled something. Standing behind me, Lotus translated: "He says that you and he are brothers of the sword, and that he would gladly kill again with you."

How can you top a compliment like that!

I said, and she translated: "And I would gladly eat meat by the fire and listen to your beautiful music."

His eyes actually filled with tears from my words, the murdering bastard! But you know, I suppose his sniffling had something to do with going through a harrowing experience, even with someone you don't know, that it draws you together. I felt genuine affection for Ghat, if not his horrendous stench. There's nary a man you could count on to do what he did with a simple knife.

I bid him a farewell, the camels bellowing, and followed Lotus behind the yurts and over a small rise.

Here was a jeep-like vehicle, the large type with no doors or roof. The back of the jeep was jam-packed with gear covered by camo netting. The PEGSPOT was a noticeable lump on top.

The jeep was on a dirt road.

A dirt road that presumably led to highways and train stations.

"What's this?" I sputtered. "You mean I crossed that confounded frigid wasteland for no reason? I mean, the least that someone could do, under the circumstances, was to pick me up at the station, someone other than Ghat!"

She climbed into the driver's seat, "I didn't make the travel arrangements, Linsenbigler. Get in. Wait, you're not bringing that?" She pointed at my tackle.

"I am indeed." I circled around the vehicle and slung my tackle bag and rod tubes by their shoulder straps into the passenger side.

"Leave it."

"Not a chance. My tackle goes where I go." I swung in under the roll bar into the seat. "Aren't Meenie, Miney and Moe going to at least see us off?"

She cranked the engine alive. "They left last night. We're the last ones to leave." Grinding the gears she backed up the jeep in a three point turn, shifted into first, and then shot me a stern eye: "You shaved."

"Just for you! Almaty or Bust!"

The jeep lurched forward and we tore down the dirt road with abandon.

You might wonder that I could be so jaunty. Perhaps some of what Manny, Moe and Mack had said about me was true – that I create "self-fulfilling prophecies." At that stage, I traveled perhaps ten thousand miles in excess of twenty-three days. I'd been on an ocean liner, planes, trains, sleigh, snowmobiles, helicopters and longboats. I'd been to London, Paris, Moscow, Khabivostok, Dalnekrasnov, and Beijing, to name the towns I could recall. I blew up a helicopter, fought a bear unarmed, had dodged a bullet, and killed five men thus far. I'd also managed to fit a little fishing in there, some of it quite good, and there had been a number of memorable cocktails, if not bars.

In short, I felt as if a lot had happened, which must mean that I was getting closer to the end of this imbroglio. We drop the plastic boulder on the hillside and next stop: Almaty and a jetliner to whisk me to Istanbul and an end to peril. My self-fulfilling prophesy was that I was going to make it to Istanbul, and I was going to make it to that rooftop bar and hotel…ah yes, Raoul's. A long, hot shower and a tall cool drink awaited me. That was destiny if ever there were.

As we drove pell-mell through the arid foothills, snowy mountain peaks ahead, I reflected on my publicist

Terry. Unlike last year in the tropics, he hadn't been able to track me down, which was an accomplishment unto itself. Wouldn't he be thrilled with some of my pictures for the various Boone Linsenbigler social media sites – complete with new nightmares that he could spin into 'adventures?' This 'fishing trip' had certainly put all that hyperactive publicity and Times Square into perspective. Next time I felt oppressed, all I needed to do was reflect on some of these nasty experiences to take a new lease on being a celebrity rather than a normal person. *They may want to make me a Senator, but at least nobody is trying to kill me.*

I would also be spared killing anybody. As I've intimated, there's a lot of baggage that comes with that. Suffice to say, having witnessed death by my own hands, seeing the light of life wink out like a candle is disturbing in and of itself. Jostling along and clinging to the jeep's roll bar, I was indulging in a bit of memory repression, perhaps even denial. It doesn't matter that the killing is necessary. Killing a man is still…murder. Nobody likes to think of himself as a murderer. Ug, what an ugly business.

All I was thinking of was that jet racing down the Almaty runway and that sudden moment of weightlessness – *I'm free! I escaped!*

After several hours' drive, the sun was up over my right shoulder, swinging into and out of view as Lotus guided the jeep over hill and dale, all the while my ears popping as we gained elevation. Ahead of us on the road, the silhouette of us sitting in the packed jeep weaved back and forth across the road. It was still cold and dry, and I was glad for the coveralls, goggles and hood, all of which kept me comfortable even with the wind in my face. The mountains drew nearer.

Around noon, we hit a paved road that pointed towards a pass through the mountains. Lotus pulled over, killed the engine, and got out. I followed suit and stretched my legs. I watched as she struggled to lift a large jerrycan of gasoline from under the camo netting. I stepped up and helped. Together we poured the fuel into the jeeps tank. First one jerrycan, then another jerrycan.

It was startling when she said something for the first time since we left the camp. "Now is the time to go to the bathroom. I'm on this side, you're on that side." And we each peed with our backs to each other and in our respective manner – no cars in sight on the paved highway in either direction.

We climbed back into the jeep and she handed me a food bar. "Lunch?"

I took it. "Don't mind if I do." I peeled the wrapper back and took a bite. Over a mouthful of oats and twigs: "You seem nervous."

She likewise said over her mouthful: "Yup, well..."

"I thought this was what you do?"

She didn't answer or look at me, she just kept chewing and looking at the mountain pass. I continued: "As you say, we just have to sneak up there, place the PEGSPOT in view of the launcher..."

Lotus turned and looked at me, blurting: "I don't like doing this with a novice, OK? So just do what I tell you. No drinking or stupid antics, just do what I tell you when we get there, and if you do, you're home free, off to Istanbul." She resumed looking at the mountain pass.

I swallowed a lump of food bar and considered a number of retorts. Alas, I am a great believer in the efficacy of silence when someone is upset. Often, there are no words that will appease them until they calm down.

Yet it was plain to see that her estimation of yours truly was not simpatico with that of Winken, Blinken and Nod. To her, I was not some sort of espionage savant but just a lucky neophyte. So be it – because I agreed with her. That's exactly what I was, and I had no desire to be doing any of this, if for no other reason than I am not accustomed to attempting skilled work when I am not skilled.

Antics, though? Antics? I suppose she'd forgotten my heroics of the previous day. Perhaps my fainting had colored her appraisal. Perhaps she was just experiencing a case of nerves.

On our way again, she pointed the jeep toward the mountain pass, and we wound up and up and up, the mountain slopes on either side getting steeper and steeper. More snow lined the roads. After several hours of this, we reached a mountain saddle and an alpine lake flanked by pine trees, and a valley on the other side with yet another set of snowy mountains beyond. All of this was strikingly familiar, I felt like I was in parts of Wyoming or Colorado. Snow squalls dusted us in white.

We pitched down toward the valley, winding through orange canyons toward the valley floor, blue skies curtained here and there by veils of flurries.

Once we bottomed out in the valley, the road shot straight across snow-dusted grasslands toward the next set of mountains. We passed the occasional shack with chickens around it and old Chinese peasants standing in their doorways or yards, and they watched with curiosity as we zoomed past.

By midafternoon, we were entering the next set of rocky foothills. Over a rise, a dirt track to one side next to a stream appeared, whereupon Lotus jerked the steering wheel and we made an abrupt left, bounding alongside a stone-strewn stream that looked cold and brimming with trout. Anglers just have a sense about that. We know by sight the kind of clear, cold streams in which trout thrive.

We passed shepherds and their flocks, the jeep winding up along the stream until a grey barn hove into view. It was perched on a hillside next to the stream, and moments later we skidded to a halt broadside to the sagging cowshed.

Lotus switched off the engine, and the relative silence seemed deafening.

I could hear the faint bleat of sheep; the stream gurgled and splashed next to us.

Lotus spoke. "I hope you can ride a horse."

I stepped out of the jeep and stretched.

"I grew up riding – my Mom was into horses. I rode a pack trip into Yellowstone not so long ago."

I refer to my father rather frequently, as he was the progenitor of some of my own quirks, not the least of which is repeating his obtuse sayings and bromides. My mother tolerated him because he tolerated her love of horses. As a youth, my sister Crocket and I were given riding lessons – English, of course. While I learned to ride and post, canter, and jump, I was never much captivated by the horses themselves. Conversely, Mom and Crock just adored them. For me, horses are hard to appreciate on a personal level. What to make of an animal that sleeps standing up? I'm sorry, but I find them more than a little too dim witted to be likeable, and their predilection for shying violently for no perceptible reason is extremely annoying. That said, I don't hate them, I just consider horses a utilitarian form of transport, and have no problem keeping them in line and showing them who's boss. My mother eventually declined to give me further lessons because I chewed bubble gum in the saddle, though I have always suspected that I was dismissed for my lack of enthusiasm for the animals themselves. Equally curious as my father's quotables was my mother's notion that bubble gum was antithetical to horseback riding. In any case, I was better off pursuing other interests. I had another passion – fishing – so did not miss the equines or their giant piles of manure. The fish never minded bubble gum.

As you might have guessed, the barn contained horses, four to be exact. Two were pack horses and two were our steeds. Mine was a grey stallion, and the others were all chestnut or dark brown mares. Breed? Sorry, Mom, I couldn't say, I suppose I was chewing bubble gum too loudly during that lesson. I don't have any clue about how to identify a quarter horse from an Arabian. I can of course identify a Clydesdale. These were not those.

Lotus set about transferring gear to the horses. Our equipage was already packed into large saddlebags so were easily transferred to the animals. I helped hoist them into place and toss Lotus the girth straps under the horse bellies.

Our steeds were already saddled and ready to go, so the entire operation of transferring the luggage to the animals and setting out on our way took less than an hour. Clearly, there had been elves working behind the scenes and preparing the necessary infrastructure for our journey ahead of us, what with the horses ready to go and the jeep left for someone else. Yet I did not see these helping hands. Everything was just there waiting for us.

We left the jeep with the keys in it and hit the streamside trail into the mountains. I took the opportunity to take my grey stallion in hand and turn him in some tight circles to show him I knew how to work the reins and stop him from nibbling at the lead horse's derrière. He yanked his head this way and that in protest, but after a few turns and reminders on the reins, he settled down.

Lotus broke into a trot, and I followed suit, the packhorses following with their ears cocked and unhappy with the pace.

I asked her: "So we're setting out pretty late in the day. Are we placing the PEGSPOT tonight?"

"Tomorrow."

"Ah, so we're camping tonight. You know, I could get us a couple of trout from this stream for dinner."

"We have food bars."

"I can't imagine trout wouldn't be a little more satisfying."

"This is not a fishing trip."

"Indeed it isn't, but that doesn't mean we can't eat

fish."

Lotus did not engage further on the matter, continuing to lead the way around waterfalls, up tricky rockslides, and eventually into a tall, narrow canyon that was deep in shadow. The higher we went, the colder it became, with more snow, and with the stream still on the right side of the trail.

We topped a hillock in the valley floor and to our left and hard up against the soaring canyon wall was a rickety log cabin with a crooked porch and misshapen windows – a very basic hunting or fishing cabin. Lotus aimed for it.

The shack did have a crude rock chimney, and some flame seemed just the ticket even if I were to be relegated to food bars for dinner and no cocktails whatsoever. The brandy Ghat and I drank was the last of my supply, and I didn't think that Lotus in her mood would have brought the slightest dram of distillate.

We moseyed up to the porch, tethered our steeds to the railing and began to unload the packhorses. We'd only been on the trail three hours, so it seemed odd to be unpacking everything again, but you can't leave all that gear on them overnight.

Once our saddles were off the horses, Lotus led them to the stream for water. I went into the cabin and discovered a small iron stove with a considerable pile of kindling and small logs at the ready. The elves thought of everything.

I set about stoking the fire with my cigar lighter, and had it chugging away in a jiffy. Stepping back onto the porch, I found Lotus had unpacked some grain and a small amount of hay for the horses.

"Fire is going," I said.

She looked at me for perhaps the first time all day without annoyance. "Good."

"Anything else I should be doing? Seems you have the horses in hand."

She sighed, and hung her head. "We have some sleeping bags, water and food bars." She seemed suddenly disarmed by exhaustion – we'd pressed on hard all day so it was little wonder.

"Would it really upset you if I caught us some trout for dinner? I mean, the stream is right there. There's no sense eating poorly when we don't have to, especially if we have a big day ahead of us."

She eyed me curiously. "What makes you think there are trout in the stream?"

I smiled gently. "Anglers just know."

Her answer was a shrug. *Knock yourself out.*

I strung up my eight-weight rod, which was more rod than I really needed for a stream thirty feet wide with fish likely not more than a foot long. A five or even three weight would have been appropriate. Yet it was the only operable rod left. I had used the flyline from the ten-weight rod to circle my campsite in the Russian outback. A long, lightly-rippled pool fronted the cabin.

Inasmuch as there was no feeding activity on the surface of the water, fishing subsurface was the way to go. Because it was winter, they would be feeding deep in the pools, and be slow to strike unless my presentation was gentle. As before, I tied on a bead-head wooly bugger. It was a brown, fuzzy fly that was supposed to look like a stonefly nymph, though it also resembled other creepy crawlies from the stream bottom. Behind it, I tied eighteen inches of leader line and a small nymph. True, the Ginger-Tonged Pizzer fly worked last time, but that was a low percentage play. I didn't have any confidence in that lightning striking twice.

As I crunched across the snow and gravel to the stream, I glanced back at Lotus, and she was sitting on the porch eating a food bar, watching me blankly.

Standing on a flat stone next to the stream, I stripped out only a few yards of line and began to roll cast the flies ninety degrees across the stream. I allowed the current to sweep them slowly downstream. Along the way, I threw some slack into the line with gentle flips of my rod tip to help the fly sink deeper. Through the line, I felt the wooly bugger tap on the bottom, and I stripped in a little line to adjust the drift to keep from hooking the stream bottom. I wanted the fly to drift inches above the bottom and right into the path of a trout.

The water was aquamarine and clear; shapes of the rocks on the bottom were a rippling patchwork.

A bump. No, not the bottom, this bump was a fish. How did I know? Tapping bottom with your fly lacks force, lacks pull – a fish bump is a gentle but fast tug.

I leaned in for the next cast, and as the fly swung downstream, I saw the deeper green spot where I thought the bump had happened and threw some slack into the line as the flies drifted into that spot.

This time no bump, but I saw a flash. Could I be sure that it wasn't daylight flickering on the water surface? Yes, I could, because the mercurial flash of a fish taking a swipe at your fly rolls counter to the way the water ripples.

I drew in the fly and changed the wooly bugger from brown to olive, and kept the small tan nymph on a foot of leader behind that. It is astounding how picky trout can be that a simple change from brown to olive can make all the difference.

Gently, I lobbed my flies across the stream, and once again let it drift into that deeper spot, though this time slightly farther upstream.

My ears rang with the trickle of the stream, and I held my breath in anticipation, eyes intent on where my fly was drifting. I'm a big proponent of concentration and anticipation as a key to success in fishing. Use your mind as though through force of will you are making the fish take that fly. I'm probably just fooling myself, but it seems to work, so there's no reason not to believe.

The line ripped the water surface, my rod raised and bent.

A buttery brown fish leapt from the water and splashed down: fish on!

The trout swam to the far side, fighting to dive under the embankment, but I horsed him back into the channel, where he twisted and wriggled furiously, his golden sides flashing. In a minute or two, the fish began to glide, and when I brought him near, he thrashed the surface. In a fluid motion, I reached out and grabbed my line, sliding the trout from the stream and onto the snow and rocks.

He flipped and flopped until I was able to get my hand on him and turn him upside down. It was a foot-long brown trout, with very large spots, brown back, yellow flanks and white belly.

Lotus was suddenly next to me, her eyes bright as she marveled at the fish. "That was amazing. Why are you holding him upside down?"

"If you hold them this way they generally stop struggling."

"Can I see?" She stepped closer, examining the fish. "A very pretty fish. The red spots…and yellow."

"It's called a brown trout. Here, take it, let me see if I can get some more."

Lotus recoiled. "I don't know how to hold it."

"Put your hands out. Like this…that's right…here." I placed the fish into her upturned hands and it sat there politely for precisely one second before jumping from her hands to the ground.

Lotus: "Shitballs!"

I laughed. "It's OK, they're not easy to hold." I snatched it from the ground and promptly smacked its head on a rock three times and tossed it onto the snow. The fish was on route to its maker and onto our plates.

I gathered my line, inspected the flies to make sure they were not tangled, and prepared to cast.

Lotus stepped next to me. "Can I try?"

"Absolutely. First, let me show you how. You toss it across the flow like this….and then you mend the line with these little flips, see? It makes the flies drift a little deeper and so they don't drag. See? And you watch as the flies drift directly downstream into that dark green spot. That's where the trout are holding in the current waiting for snacks to drift into their feeding lane. But I'll strip it back away from that spot and let you catch the next one."

I positioned her and the rod in her hand the correct way, yet predictably her first attempt to lob the flies across the stream met with tangles, and after I had untangled it, she tried to hand the rod back to me.

"Oh, no," I said. "You have to stick with it. Here, let me guide your arms. Now, relax." I reached my arms around her and guided her arms to get the cast out there and then mend the line. This may sound like a come on, but it is a quick way to get a novice's muscle memory enacted correctly. I was close enough to smell her nape: sunshine and a hint of vanilla. I noticed for the first time that she had a dusting of sun freckles across her nose.

The fly drifted into the green spot.

There was a deep flash.

"Now!" I raised her arm, the rod pulsing with the fight of a trout.

She barked a laugh of surprise as I let go of her arms. "What do I do?"

"Lotus, strip the line in to bring the fish toward you...under your fingers...like this."

Moments and a little more coaching later, we had our second fish flopping on the snow. As I fumbled with the second fish, she gushed: "I had no idea that's what fishing was. I thought there was a cork, and you stared at it. Fishing sounded boring."

I smiled, wiping fish-slime off my hands onto a ball of snow. "Fun, isn't it? And this is only one of hundreds of different ways to fish, and for any number of different kinds all over the world."

She glanced down stream. "Do you think there are more?"

I helped her hook another, but it got off, and she was crestfallen that it had gotten away. "SHITBALLS!"

Perseverance resulted in a third fish, at which time the slice of light above us in the canyon was filling with stars at one end.

I cut some green branches from a sapling, cleaned the fish, and skewered them. I noted a tuft of onion grass back by the stream, and some watercress, and I jammed a mixture of the two into the body cavities. Not many people know that onion grass is a wild chive and completely edible. With fish that fresh, you really don't want lemon or any of that rot, completely kills the flavor.

Horses tied loosely to the crooked porch railing, we retired inside the cabin and got the fire roaring again. Furniture in the cabin consisted of two stout upturned logs to sit on around the stove. I managed to wedge the skewers into wall crevices so that the fish were positioned inches from the top of the iron stove. They began to steam almost immediately.

The meal in the oven, as it were, I took a seat on my log, Lotus catty-corner to me rifling through a bag. Voila! She held up the rest of that bottle of whisky from the night before!

"Lotus! I'm astonished! Shame on you."

Her fishing exuberance had faded, but she seemed much more relaxed, and smirked at me, that sun freckled nose wrinkling. "Boone, you're not the only one who needs a drink. It's been a long day, and tomorrow and the next day will be even longer."

Paper cups were next out of the bag, and moments later, I toasted her. "To your first trout!"

"To Almaty."

We sipped.

I asked: "So are you particularly nervous about tomorrow? I promise you I'll do my best to make things go smoothly."

Her pretty round face tightened, the large dark eyes alight by the fire.

"I don't like spiders."

That gave me pause. "Up in the mountains? In winter?"

She closed her eyes and took a sip of whiskey, the fish beginning to sizzle. "Yes. Drones."

"I don't follow, Lotus? Drones?"

She glared at me. "The Russians have flying drones that patrol their launch sites. I was told yesterday they now have drones that crawl. They look like spiders and have infrared vision. I hate even fake spiders; it's the way they move. I know that's really stupid and weak, but I can't help it. I've tried all kinds of therapies and hypnosis, but spiders just make my skin crawl. I'm OK with snakes. Why can't they have snake drones?"

I suppressed a laugh.

"It's not funny," she glowered. "As a kid I got trapped in the basement of an abandoned home overnight with no light and spiders kept on crawling on me. I practically lost my mind."

I sipped, and cleared my throat. "My apologies. I only laughed because I assumed your cross mood all day had something to do with me. I never imagined…"

"My father used to tell me 'If you hate spiders there's a full moon in Detroit.'"

I paused mid-sip. "You're father said that?"

"Yup. He was always saying idiotic stuff like that to make him seem wise. Or me look stupid."

"Well, if your eat ice cream on a Monday, expect the cat to eat grass."

Lotus looked up and winced, clearly confused.

I said: "My father used to say that."

She cleared her throat: "Lederhosen and pancakes make poor bedfellows."

"Nice," I raised an eyebrow. "If corn could talk, parrots could fly."

"Touché," she smirked, her nose wrinkling. "So both our fathers did this? That's insane."

"My advice about the spiders tomorrow, Lotus, is that when donuts block your view, look through the holes."

That got her laughing. "No! He did not say that!"

"Indeed he did," I said laughing with her. "I better turn these fish."

After attending to the fish, I retrieved my tackle bag and rummaged. I then stepped outside to retrieve some snow. I sat back down, took her cup, and filled hers and mine with snow and a piece of spearmint chewing gum. Lotus refilled our cups, and sipped.

"Hey!" She raised the cup, eyes wide. "That tastes like a mint julep!"

"A Linsenbigler Julep. You can chew the gum when you are done. Do you mind if I smoke a cigar?" I had found half of a cheroot in with my leaders.

"Dragons leave marks without a pencil!"

"What?"

"To my dad that meant only if you have one for me."

"OK, there's not much here, but I'll split it with you."

In short order, we were drinking juleps and blowing cigars smoke at the stove, fish sizzling furiously. The scent of cooking chives wafted about the cabin. Lotus was gently smiling, and if I had to guess, she was thinking about her dad.

"Lotus, where did you grow up?"

"California. Bay Area. You?

"New Jersey."

"I guess I knew that."

"Have a full dossier on me, do you?"

"How you became an icon is really remarkable. But you don't like it, do you?"

I thought about that a moment, stroking my whiskers. "I like the money, to be sure, and if I like the money enough I can deal with the fame. Up to a point."

She blew smoke. "You certainly don't seem like a famous person."

"And you don't seem like an 'operative.' How did you get into this?"

"Asian languages. I'm a teacher. They recruit you. Easy assignments at first, lots of travel, great pay, and I was just a translator. Then they train you to do other things because the next project requires you to be more than a translator, you need to be able to ski, or fly a glider, or climb a cliff. And just when you think it is getting too risky and insane, they send you back home for a long break, like a year off before they tap you again. By that time you think, well, that wasn't so bad, and it was kind of exciting. So you go again. It becomes kind of addicting because you like the action and because you have this secret world where you get to be a different person. I'm not that great at the physical part of it, or at any kind of fighting. I can't master the disarming maneuvers, that's how I got this black eye. Not a surprise, I guess, because technically I'm just a language teacher."

"And they give you a name to use that's not your own."

She nodded. "They have to. You can't have anybody know who your family is or they could try to leverage that vulnerability."

"Well, I like Lotus well enough. I won't ask your real name."

"*Lotus* is a little corny if you ask me, you know, as an Asian name. Linsenbigler your real name?"

I nodded. "And my father named me after Daniel Boone – my sister's is named after Davey Crocket. I certainly know what you mean about getting to be a different person, and perhaps being the famous version of me is as addicting as your espionage life."

"Espionage life." Her eyes diverted to the stove's window of flame, orange whorls filling her pupils. "An addiction. Starts out fun and exciting. Then it starts to take over your life. Then..." A tear rolled down her cheek, and I was going to say something but decided the better of it. Either she would say what was on her mind or keep it locked in.

For five minutes I watched her stare at the fire, and I could tell that she had been transported to a different place, a different time. The flames crackled, hissed and popped. One of the horses snorted, and a gust of wind whistled on the roof.

"And then…" her eyes turned to mine. "My last partner died. Was killed. Shot. I had to leave him. That was a first for me. I said that was it, I was done with all this. Now here I am again. It wasn't my fault or anything, this is just dangerous work. You never know what might happen – there's always the unexpected. But I'm not cut out for that, for killing. Or I don't want to be. So why am I here? Do I no longer have control of this 'espionage life?' I suppose some celebrities lose control, as you said."

I tented my fingers, forearms on my knees. "You have no control of the unexpected, Lotus, life throws you a curve ball or two in any walk of life, and sometimes you get beaned. You have two choices. Go home or go back up to bat. I had a fishing guide of mine that was killed. He was a strong, gentle man named Elvis, and they shot him while trying to kill me. I had to watch helplessly as he sank to the bottom of the sea, his hazel eyes looking up into mine. So I'm no stranger to this ugly killing business. My peace was made with that terrible incident, my guilt put to rest, by making sure that the man who shot him met a similar fate. If you ask me, you are taking control by stepping back up to the plate and staring down the pitcher on the mound."

Her eyes met mine. "And what if you get killed? What do I do then? Am I supposed to brush it off, *things happen*? I'm worried that just thinking this way might compromise my decisions and *get* you killed. Get us both killed."

I favored her with a withering smile. "I know I look helpless, but I've survived a scrape or two under difficult circumstance, so I wouldn't count me out. Ol' Boonie is able to look out for himself and then some, so I've got your back."

She wiped away the tear from her cheek. "Do you believe in fate?"

Barking a laugh, I said: "Not a bit of it."

"Neither do I, really, but I worry that it may exist, in which case, I only seem to be in control of what happens, but it's all a sham because fate is running things, meaning you or I have no control over what happens." Her eyes went back to the fire. "You know, I never made the first move."

In my singularly sexist opinion, women have a much greater capacity than men for trains of thought switching tracks without warning. I often wonder if women are more mentally sophisticated than men in as much as they often seem to have many trains of thought all running on parallel tracks. Men, on the other hand, have but two sets of rails on which their trains of thought ride: the matter at hand and sex. Of course, now and again that means there's only one locomotive.

I cleared my throat: "How do you mean?"

"You know, with boys, or with men. They were always in control, I never took control over what happened. I don't know why I've been thinking about that, and why it bothers me."

We were quiet a good ten minutes as I puzzled over this sudden turn in conversation. When I looked up from the fire I found her looking at me curiously, the firelight flickering on her face. "Sorry to unload on you."

"Happy to oblige. Try took look through those donut

holes tomorrow, and look beyond any spiders. What was it your handlers were on about yesterday?" I stood and plucked the fish skewers, the fish suitably blistered and glistening hot. "Oh yes, that rot about self-fulfilling prophesies. Let's fulfill our determination to find ourselves in Istanbul, keep our eye on the prize."

I handed her a skewer, and we ate. The trout was predictably delectable, and after dinner she checked on the horses while I built up the fire.

Our sleeping bags were the cocoon type, and we each stripped out of our coveralls before slipping in our respective bags on either side of the stove. I do believe we both stole a glance of the other in our skivvies, and I don't mind saying that even in form-fitting thermals her gentle curves inspired a pang of desire in yours truly. And I find pigtails fetching for some reason, I have no idea why.

Alas, there's a time and place for everything unless there isn't.

Dad quote?

Nope.

I just came up with that gem on my own.

CHAPTER 22

DUSK THE FOLLOWING DAY found us in far less cozy circumstance. We were on the west side of a breezy, mountain ridge, huddled behind a crag. We were above the tree line surrounded by other crags and snow. The horses slouched behind us, and we crouched next to the plastic boulder that was a sophisticated electronics package known as a PEGSPOT. We were exhausted, and trying to catch our breath. I guessed our altitude at eleven or twelve thousand feet.

The trip from that little cabin had been longer than I think Lotus or Moe, Larry and Curley had realized. We had pushed ourselves and the horses hard all day long. That day easily eclipsed my other death marches – it was one of those where you just have to keep pushing and hope you or the horses don't collapse.

Lotus stood, and stumbled to the packhorses. From a bag she drew two large shaggy objects, stumbled back, and handed one to me.

"What's this, Lotus?"

"It's a camouflage suit. Put it on. It absorbs the cold around us and blocks your body heat from infrared cameras."

I sat on the ground and struggled to put on the loose, shaggy coveralls over the ones I was wearing. It had a hood with a mask that pulled down over my face, which immediately helped warm my cheeks and nose. My view from the eyeholes was through a fuzzy fringe.

Getting to my feet in the half-light, I looked at Lotus in her camouflage suit. "Lotus, you look like a sheep dog."

"We both do. If you see a drone, stop moving and wait for it to go away. When they patrol, they are looking for heat signatures or movement, but they don't stay long in any one place. Let's do this and get out of here."

We grasped either side of the tortoise-like PEGSPOT and rounded the side of the crag. The device wasn't particularly heavy, but I could feel the weight of large batteries in the base.

The crest of the mountain was only a few hundred feet up a steep gravel slope.

Light shone dimly from beyond the ridge, up from the valley on the other side.

Scrambling, we dragged and pushed that confounded plastic boulder up the slope, gravel slipping under us as we gasped for air.

I don't know how long it took us. At a lower elevation, with rest and proper food, it should have only taken minutes. Likely, it took about a half hour.

Gravel gave way at the top of the ridge to a rock outcropping. It was full night.

We paused a few minutes to catch our breath, and then gingerly peered over the edge of the ridge.

On the other side, the view gave way precipitously in a thousand foot drop that made my head swim and testicles ache. Broken boulders were strewn below. They gave way to some scrub and then trees. A thousand feet beyond that, a dark ribbon of water wound out the far side of the valley.

Parked directly in the riverbed below us was a gigantic gantry dotted by flood lamps. It was mounted on a massive reticulated truck with twelve house-high tires. Around it were numerous vehicles, including several tanker trucks that had hoses connected to the gantry. What looked like steam rose from the hoses. I felt transported to childhood stories in which one was spying on a dragon in its lair.

In the center of the steel gantry lattice stood a camouflage rocket over two hundred feet tall. The base of the rocket had four boosters around the base.

If the rocket technicians were making any noise down there, the wind was snatching it.

My stomach gurgled and I had to shove myself back from the edge and look away. I used to be okay with heights. Unfortunately, a terrifying sword fight on a rope bridge over the ocean during my last fiasco had resulted in occasional night terrors about heights. Air travel was not a problem, obviously, it was just being on the edge of a huge drop that made my head swim – and for some reason – my testicles ache. My gonads seem to anticipate the pain associated with a sudden impact. The rest of my body doesn't seem to have this fear, even though it, too, would be severely injured. My brain, conversely, only reacts to heights by making me dizzy. This works counter to the gonads fears – the dizziness makes me much more likely to fall when I would otherwise not. The dizzier I get the more my balls ache. It would be nice if the organs at either end reached some sort of consensual reaction to heights, though the common irony of the brain and testes being at odds did not elude me.

Lotus grabbed my arm.

I froze.

Whirring came from my left, and into view came a four-rotor black drone, the dim glow of an infrared camera pointed right at us. Light from the gantry below glinted off its flickering rotors. Sinister and bat-like, it clicked and buzzed closer.

The drone slowed, pivoted, and hovered, looking to our right.

Then it slid out of view, into the dark.

Lotus released my arm and pointed to our left: a flat spot on the ridge big enough for the PEGSPOT. It was about twenty feet away.

On our stomachs, we slid in that direction over the rock face, shoving the PEGSPOT between us.

When we arrived within arm's reach of the flat spot, we took another peek over the ridge.

No drones, and direct sight lines to the rocket.

I turned to look at Lotus for a nod to continue.

In the dim glow cast from the launch pad below, I saw a twig waving in the air on Lotus' shoulder.

It got longer, and then there was another twig.

My breath caught and I put a hand on Lotus' arm.

I felt her go rigid.

A mechanical spider bot crawled up onto her shoulder, the infrared camera's dull glow turning toward me. All black, the drone was the size of an open, bony hand, with a disc-shaped body. Atop the body was another disc, a turret, with a single 'eye.' On the top of the body was a single antenna that stood straight up like an exclamation point. It moved like a tarantula.

I squeezed her arm: *don't move.*

You can imagine my dilemma. If Lotus knew that thing was on her, she would likely have gone berserk and moved violently to brush it off.

What then? Then the jig would be up, that's what. Not only would the operator of that drone realize somebody was up on the ridge, but he would likely dispatch someone or something to come kill us, to say nothing of disabling the PEGSPOT. We might dash for the horses, but I didn't have any faith that we could elude any helicopters in that open terrain.

The shiny black spider turned from me and looked downhill toward where the horses were behind the crag, out of sight. Did the horses make a sound? Did the drone hear the horses?

While the drone was looking the other way, I lifted my hand from Lotus's arm and placed it over her face. Lord knows what she thought I was up to. At least if she didn't see the spider, maybe she could remain calm. Likely as not, she had some notion of what was going on.

The spider turned back my way, its spindly slick legs crawling down from her shoulder and across her arm.

I felt Lotus tense and tremble – she could feel the

spider.

The bot picked its way down Lotus' shaggy camo suit and climbed atop the PEGSPOT between us, metal legs clicking on the plastic. Could it tell by the sound of its legs on the 'rock' that it was made of plastic?

It stopped and did a three-sixty before moving from the plastic boulder onto my glove and up to my shoulder and over my back.

Tick, tick, tick: I waited, hardly daring to breathe.

After what seemed an eternity, I heard the gentle click of the spider's metal legs on the rocks behind me. They became fainter.

I let go of Lotus' face and put my hand back on her trembling arm.

Gently, I turned toward where the flat spot was.

That blasted spider was standing on that exact place, right where we needed to place the PEGSPOT.

Yet it was looking the other way, down to where the rocket stood in a pillar of light.

Presumably, there was a Russian technician operating the spider bot. Precisely what that technician knew about the drone's surroundings outside the field of vision was an open question. The spider was on a high mountain ledge. It was windy. As they say in New Jersey: *things happen.*

I reached my hand out to the spider's back. With a deft flick of the wrist, I sent the spider bot over the edge.

I wasn't sure whether Lotus had seen what I did, though my guess was she sensed it and was glad. My calculus was that if we did not place the PEGSPOT on the flat rock as soon as possible and make our retreat we risked further visits by spying spiders and bats that might actually see us move. Or might actually see Lotus jump to her feet and scream.

Looking quickly to either side of us, we shoved the PEGSPOT up into place and in full view of the launch vehicle.

After another quick look around us, we slunk mostly crab-like the several hundred feet back down the gravel slide, onto our feet, and around the crag to the horses.

As soon as we were out of sightlines to the ridge, Lotus braced herself on the rock face, lifted her mask, and attempted to vomit. We'd had so little to eat it did not surprise me she had nothing to upchuck.

I patted her on the back, and gave her a reassuring hug, but wasted little time in urging her wordlessly back onto her steed. *Puke if you must but let's get out of here on the double!*

Over the next several hours our horses stumbled through the darkness down a serpentine path until we came to a steep rockslide. Here the horses literally lowered themselves onto their haunches and slid down, me standing full upright in my stirrups. It was inelegant but we made considerable progress quickly in our descent versus the switch backs.

Back into the tree line, we traced a ridge line and wove between sparse spiky conifers. A crescent moon had risen over our shoulders and splashed just enough light to see our way. A warmer breeze in our faces pricked my nose with tangy pine.

All the while, I wondered about that slick black spider drone I'd flicked off the ridge. Had the drone operator sensed something had pushed the drone? Would they assume the wind did it or that the drone made a misstep? Or were the helicopter gunships on their way? There was nowhere to hide, and even with our camo suits, the horses would give us away.

On and on we went, down and down, the trees thickening, complete with tantalizing glimpses of a wide valley below.

"Lotus, are there more mountains after this?" My voice came out as a croak.

"No. The road to Almaty is down there."

"How far?"

"We should be down there by sun-up."

"From the look of it that's twenty miles and an entire day's ride."

"We have a short cut; we're not riding the horses all the way down. Let's stop and eat something, drink water."

We circled the horses, and Lotus dismounted. She cut off the top of a plastic water jug and offered the horses a drink, which they accepted greedily. They snorted and threw their heads, clearly as unhappy as we were about the long trek. I drank the last of my water, and ground through another food bar. I will forever associate food bars with that cold, arduous mountain trek to Kazakhstan, and so loathe them to this day.

While we stood in the puddles of gentle moonlight between the pines, I took the opportunity to light up my cell phone and see what time it was. It was three thirty.

Thunder in the distance.

I turned toward it, back toward the mountains from

where we'd come.

Light flashed over the hills, a rumble echoing down the rocky mountainsides. I could hear cobbles tumbling down the rockslide.

The sky behind us became brighter until a ball of light emerged and rose into the sky.

It was the rocket, and the flames from its four boosters were like a flare that cast shadows of us and our horses on the ground.

My horse shied, skittering to one side, but I reigned him in just in time to pop off a selfie of yours truly with the horse's wild eye in the foreground, the rocket rising behind us in the sky.

The packhorses didn't like the fire in the sky either, and Lotus hushed and calmed them with pats to their necks and words in Mandarin.

Up and over our heads the rocket went, turning due east, the engine flames crackling. It did not look to me like anything at all had gone wrong with it. Perhaps the flicked spider led them to the PEGSPOT and they disabled it?

My phone lit up with a message: "Welcome to Kazakhstan!"

Good Lord, I had a signal, of all things. I never imagined.

We watched as the fireball from the rocket faded into the east, a sonic boom rippling down the valley.

"What went wrong?" I croaked.

Lotus clambered back onto her horse. "I'm not sure anything went wrong."

"I thought it was supposed to crash."

"It is. Just not here."

"You think maybe they found PEGSPOT?"

She swung her reins and turned the horse. "Nothing we can do about that if they did."

An hour later we came to a long precipice. A huge valley was laid out below with a road right up the middle. Small clusters of lighted huts dotted the highway.

The cliff on which we stood extended a mile at least in either direction. As the crow flew, the valley floor and highway were at least twelve miles away. Effectively, we were at a dead end. I stayed back from the edge, my scrotum buzzing with discomfort from the height.

"What in blazes now?" I asked.

Lotus slid off her horse. "We unsaddle the horses. Remove the bridles, too."

I followed suit, but as soon as I took a step I realized that my inner thigh muscles were afire from so much time in the saddle. Gritting my teeth against the pain, I helped dress down the horses and place all the gear under a tight clump of pines. The horses snorted and shook their manes, clearly happy to be rid of their yokes as well as their cargo and passengers.

Lotus patted them each in turn, whispering to them in Mandarin – I do believe she was thanking them. The horses grunted in response and began picking at the snow-dusted ground for food.

"This way," Lotus waved me to follow her to the left along the cliff, me averting my eyes from the view.

I slung my rod tubes and tackle bag over my back and hobbled bow-legged behind her. "Are we just leaving the horses there?"

"Someone will come get them." Lotus turned from the cliff into a large clearing in the pines. In the center, camo netting was draped and pegged over a flat object at least forty feet wide and triangular in shape.

My testicles buzzed. "This isn't what I think it is, Lotus, is it?"

"Let's go, Linsenbigler, help remove the netting. It's a hang glider."

"I can't."

She clamped a hand on her hip. "Can't what?"

"Are we flying…down there? From here? Over the edge?"

"No, we're gliding from here over the edge. Now come on."

"I can't do that."

She shoved her shaggy hood back, exposing her head, and stepped up to me. "You have to. I'm the pilot, you're the passenger, you ride on my back, and I'll be right below you and do all the steering. You just hang on."

I shoved my hood back as well. "Look, you may not be able to deal with spiders, but I cannot and will not jump off the edge of that cliff. I had a terrible experience on the edge of a cliff last year and…"

"Linsenbigler, I may not be able to disarm bandits, not so great at the whole kick 'em in the balls and knee them in the face stuff, but don't make me shoot you." A small black automatic was suddenly in her hand – not pointed at me, but brandished all the same. "I've had about all I can take today what with the spiders and all that crap and I don't need you pulling some sort of tantrum."

"Lotus, you put me in that thing and we jump off a cliff together and I'm likely to panic and get us both killed."

She groaned and stomped a foot. "You know what I'm going to say, don't you?"

"What?"

She moved between me and the sheer drop and held up an open fist with the hand that wasn't waving the gun – that is, you could see through a hole she created with her hand. "What do you see, Boone?"

"I don't understand."

"It's a donut. Come here and look through the hole. What do you see?"

I folded my arms. "It won't work, Lotus."

"I know what I see. I see us down there in fifteen minutes. Ten minutes after that, I see us in a nice warm cabin with food and drink and a night's rest. Now, if you don't look through the hole and only look at my fist, what do you see? You see you hiking or riding by yourself for another entire day to get down there, and when you arrive, I will be gone, I will be in Almaty and on the flight to Istanbul without you."

She stepped up, and went on tiptoe, her narrow jaw and freckled nose just inches from mine: "Yup. That will be me at the rooftop bar at Raoul's bar enjoying a bottle of well-earned Dom Perignon wondering if that dope Boone Linsenbigler ever hitchhiked his way out of Kazakhstan!"

CHAPTER 23

MY LOINS WERE CONFUSED.

On the one hand, my testicles, realizing that I had jumped off a cliff thousands of feet above the valley floor in the distance, retreated to their highest possible position. I would hazard to guess they were cowering somewhere up around my spleen.

On the other hand, I was strung up in the A-frame from a harness in the rather stimulating position behind whereby El Horno was pressed firmly to Lotus's buttocks. Yes, well, it has to have a name, doesn't it? So now you know.

Oh, and yes, we were at some ungodly altitude swooping in low like a drunk swallow over the foothills in pre-dawn Kazakhstan, the fabric of the wings groaning against the metal frame.

You might say it was exhilarating.

Or you might say profoundly terrifying.

The image of us zooming down from the mountain in a pale blue hang glider was – alas – not of flying sheep dogs. We had discarded the camo and donned helmets and goggles as if we were to be shot from a cannon. We might as well have been. This was a stunt and a half.

"LIFT YOUIR LEGS!" she shouted. I lifted them as far as I was able, but the way I was strung up, I had to press my pelvis into her *derriere* to make any significant progress.

Trees at the top of a hillock were a shade taller than we were high. The hang glider wheels ripped through the top branches, a blizzard of leaves in our wake as we soared out over yet another jaw-dropping plunge. We caught a thermal rising from the valley floor and gained height, which was good because the way things looked, we would end up well short of the highway or any cozy cabin.

"WATCH IT!" she shouted.

Ahead: a flock of small, unsuspecting birds. I didn't get a good look at them, but they were small enough that they caromed off our helmets, squawking. A cloud of feathers trailed behind us.

We flew over a flock of ibex – large, pale mountain sheep with great curved horns that looked luminous in the pre-dawn light. They were attached to a sheer cliff and utterly unaware of the daredevils above. Banking right and up again on another thermal, we crested a pinnacle and zoomed over a ravine pointing out over the flat valley plain.

We've made it! I marveled, before reminding myself that we were still flying in excess of one hundred miles an hour and had not yet landed. Landed safely, that is.

In the distance, I could see a truck and its headlights,

seemingly traveling slowly on the highway. On the other side of that, I began to make out the shape of a lone cabin.

Our descent had begun, the truck still approaching our flight path toward the cabin, the windows alight with the orange glow of a hearth.

We approached the highway.

The truck was vectoring right into our flight path.

We were thirty feet up.

We zipped directly over the truck and its roar, a jolting gust of wind rattling the hang glider wheels. We were close enough that I could have counted the rivets on the truck's metal roof.

Lotus made an adjustment tilting slightly upward, and we slowed, the wheels coming on plane with the flat desert beneath us.

"LIFT YOUR LEGS," she shouted.

The last five feet dropped away and the wheels ground into the dirt, dust and sand flying into my face. Lotus dug her toes into the desert to help slow our progress further.

All at once we were stopped in a shroud of dust.

Just the sound of wind, and my heart thumping.

We lay motionless for a moment, reorienting our wits and perhaps saying a brief prayer of thanks, the dust clearing.

"Linsenbigler?"

"Yes, Lotus?"

"Do you have a hard-on?"

"Guilty."

CHAPTER 24

THE REST OF THAT EVENING WAS A BLUR.

We extracted ourselves from that infernal flying machine, pulled some pins on the frame and folded the entire contraption in parts, stowing it under a dirty tarp behind the one-room cabin, which was about a quarter mile from the highway with empty livestock pens.

Inside, the elves had set an iron stove going with a fire. Carpets covered the walls, I suppose for warmth. One large bed was piled high with blankets. One wood chair and one wood table piled with folded clothes.

Devastatingly, the elves had neglected to provide anything more than water and more damned food bars. I admit to having felt cheated. That said, had there been a four-star meal laid out complete with lobster, champagne and strawberries, I don't think either of us had the energy to eat or even pop a cork.

There was only the one bed, and without much ceremony or debate, we stripped down to our skivvies and clambered in side by side. It wasn't as if there was anything sexual in this arrangement. We were beat.

One could easily characterize my little fishing trip to Russia as a series of exceedingly arduous days followed by a total collapse into unconsciousness. Slumber came as quickly as if we'd been blackjacked.

Noon jolted me awake, sunlight blasting from the windows.

Curiously, Lotus was spooning me from behind, and snoring in my ear, her sunshine and vanilla scent wafting. Not an altogether unpleasant sensation after all the cold floors I'd slept on alone for the last week.

Yet it took me a few moments as I lay there, consciousness blossoming, to realize that we were done. No more cold mountains, mechanical spiders, horses, food bars, or being shot from a cannon.

Done.

Gently I extracted myself from Lotus' arms, whereupon she grumbled, flipped over and yanked the blankets over her head.

Even at noon, it was chilly, and I danced about the cabin, re-stoking the fire as fast as possible.

As I shivered next to the burgeoning flames, I heard my phone make a noise. It was the noise signaling that the battery was dying. I had left it on all night.

Digging out my phone, I noted that it was thirty-four degrees in Podunk, Kazakhstan, five percent battery left, and that I had twelve texts from my publicist Terry and two from Tanya. I looked at the two from Tanya.

"*r u ok? ?? there was Mi8 crash. whatz with the hand grenade fishing?*"

"*boone, you cant be dead, i know u r out there somewhere i can feel it*"

I replied: "*On my way home by way of Almaty, more later.*"

I texted Terry: "*Linsenbigler lives, more later.*" I attached the selfie of me with the horse and the rocket soaring overhead. I chuckled to myself – that text would whip Terry into a froth of excitement and angst, to be sure.

Then I powered down my phone. There were no outlets in that rustic cabin. No electricity at all, so no recharging.

As I put the phone back into my tackle bag, I found the pistol with which I had shot Dax and the bandits. I removed it, and just to be on the safe side, I wiped it down before shoving it into the bottom of the woodpile. It wouldn't do to leave my fingerprints on a gun that had been involved in a…well, in any killings. Likewise, to take the pistol to the airport by accident would be just the sort of thing that would throw a wrench in a final escape from my nightmare fishing trip to Russia in winter.

Lotus sat up suddenly. "What time is it?"

"A little after noon, pumpkin."

"Pumpkin?" she mumbled incredulously, rubbing her eyes.

I began to laugh as I could see her wondering if she'd done something last night and could not remember it. Beyond spooning.

"Oh, very funny, Linsenbigler."

I blew into my hands to warm them. "You know, you could call me Boone."

"Yup, well, when you're on a project, you have to keep it impersonal," she said, rubbing her eyes.

"Project is over, isn't it?"

"We're not on that plane yet."

"Look, we've really been through the ringer together, you've had my back and I've had yours. We caught trout together, laughed by the fire, shared a bunk. I'd say that makes us friends."

"There are no friends in this business, Linsenbigler," she snapped. "You seem oblivious to the fact that I might have had to shoot you last night."

I stepped over to the table and lifted a man's sweatshirt, leather jacket, jeans, underwear, socks and biker boots from the pile. The clothes were decidedly the most stylish I had had the occasion to wear in what seemed forever, and diametrically opposed to my Russian lumberjack outfit. "You mean the gun, last night? You don't think I took that seriously, do you?"

Lotus stumbled out of bed, groaning. "I haven't ridden horseback that far in a long time." With a bottle of water, she splashed water on her face and dried it off with a corner of the bed blanket. "Turn around, I'm getting naked."

Ever the gentleman, I turned my back, and used the reflective surface of a window pane darkened by an eave to try and catch a glimpse of her *au natural.* My success was limited, but it is always a man's duty to persevere.

I, on the other hand, dispelled with any pretense of modesty and stripped in full view, though she made a hushed gasp and turned away, mostly.

Funny, isn't it? One minute you're risking your lives and snoozing together, and the next you're saying 'turn around.' I suppose it is a testament to the durability of institutionalized modesty.

Dressed, I turned to behold Lotus offering me a food bar. I snarled at it and headed for the door while downing the last of my water, rod tubes and tackle bag slung across my back.

"What now?" I asked, standing in full sun, the desert terrain stretching flat and far away in both directions. Snowy mountains were aligned in front and back, the highway running straight down the middle. Once again, I was amazed at the likeness of this place to the Mojave Desert and the Owens Valley and likely dozens of other places from Utah to Nevada and beyond.

Lotus didn't respond. She merely turned and walked toward the back of the cabin. Her outfit, like mine, was a vast improvement, going and coming. The motorcycle gear did her justice.

Set apart from the cabin was a dilapidated shed. Kicking open the door, she dove into the resultant cloud of dust and wheeled out a dark green motorcycle. I'm no more an authority on these vehicles than I am on horses, and can only say that it was not a chopper, a racing bike, or a big fat Harley. It was modestly sized, but arranged with a saddle for two people.

I fished my sunglasses from the tackle bag and approached as she straddled the bike.

"You ride?" she asked.

I shook my head. "Not really."

"Didn't think so." It seemed we were back to the stern 'Lotus 1.0' version from before the trout fishing. What could she be worried about at that juncture? Was she afraid of spiders in the wintry desert? By comparison to what we'd just gone through, a long ride on a motorcycle on paved roads was child's play.

"Lotus, can you tell me what's bothering you? Have I done something to upset you?"

She snorted a laugh, and folded her arms across her chest, her legs splayed and holding the bike upright. "Have you ever heard the expression 'loose end?' N-L-E? I was told no lose ends on this trip. Do you know what that means?"

I shrugged as I had no idea where this was coming from or where this was going.

"Well, I'll spell it out for you. No lose ends is nobody stays behind alive. My last partner had been shot and immobilized. So I had to kill my last partner so that he wouldn't be a lose end, and last night you almost made me have to shoot you. There was no leaving you behind alive, and you put me in the position of pulling my weapon and preparing to put you down. I resent the bejesus out of that."

"Well, had you told me that last night, the discussion would have been very short indeed. How was I to know about this 'lose end' business?"

"Everybody knows that. Here's your helmet. Climb on."

She hit a starter button and the machine whirred and then started without protest.

The helmet was a simple black one with a face shield, as was hers. I climbed on behind her and found the footrest pegs. "Ready." I zipped up my jacket all the way to the top of the collar.

In gear, we jolted forward slowly toward the highway. A jeep was passing in either direction, but no other was in sight.

I hollered over the growl of the engine and through my helmet: "Sorry for last night, I had no idea. How far to the airport?"

"Four hours and change."

"Are we there yet?"

CHAPTER 25

AH, THE OPEN ROAD! It was cold as the dickens, and made noisy by the rush of wind and the roar of the motorcycle. Yet it captured my blithe and focused mood perfectly. Sunny and refreshing, the road was straight as the proverbial arrow aimed at the target of an airliner in Almaty.

I know I have come to refer to Almaty as though it were some sort of old stomping ground I could not wait to get back to. Yet I had never heard of it until Beamish spoke of the place on the train across China.

We encountered the occasional rise, curve, foothill and monument, like that of a sitting hawk twenty feet high. I had no idea the significance. Perhaps it was for wayfinding, or a marker that you could say "Meet me at the falcon." Snow dusted the rocks and scrub on all sides.

During the long horseback rides, I had spent considerable time reviewing recent events and evaluating my decision-making at various junctures. On this day, I let all that go. Whatever had befallen me up to this point, whatever my decisions, it had brought me full circle. And who knows, I may have even served my country in some obtuse way in the process, though I didn't necessarily put a lot of stock in the bunk I'd heard from Groucho, Chico and Harpo. Especially inasmuch as they had labeled me as a potential loose end. How bad could my decisions be if I made it this far, if I had survived all that and lived to tell the tale? And, by God, I'd had some not half bad fishing along the way, which all things considered, is really what mattered. Well, to me.

What to make of this 'loose end' business? Would she really have shot me? Gadzooks, it would seem she may have, considering she'd had to kill her former partner. That history certainly put a lot of her moodiness in proper context. Oddly, I didn't so much fret over what may have happened to me the previous night on that cold, windswept cliff. Or that I had put her in that situation – how was I to know? More so, I fretted over the guilt and remorse she'd had to endure from having to finish off her partner. That's hard cheese for sure.

I began to get excited when I saw signs whip past us that were not road signs in Cyrillic but billboards for what seemed to be some sort of tourist attraction. The words were foreign, but the images of a waterfall and some sort of castle and the large golden statue of a warrior were on each. It was as though we were approaching *South of the Border* on I-95 in South Carolina, an amusement-packed fireworks-fueled taco-wielding rest stop advertised roadside by innumerable billboards. Under the circumstances, and compared to whence I had come, this approaching tourist trap sufficed as *civilization*.

While I could not read the billboards, there were kilometer readings indicating how far away this place was. When we reached one kilometer, the final billboard was draped with a banner that was in both Cyrillic and English: *CLOSED*. This amused me – after all the buildup, the place was closed for the season or whatever. Ah, well, no time for it anyway, though the large warrior statue intrigued me.

Soon after that sign, we wound through a hill and over a rise and into a narrow cut: blocking the road was a burning panel truck. Flames funneled black column of smoke in the air. A car was on the other side with people standing in the road.

Nobody could get past.

Lotus downshifted, the engine sputtering.

The entrance to the tourist trap was on the right before the burning truck. It was open, and a little shabby man next to the open gate gestured at us wildly to enter. It was reasonable to assume this was a detour, so Lotus banked the motorcycle past the little man and into the tourist attraction.

Perhaps I'll get to see this giant golden soldier statue after all!

The entrance road curved through a deep cut in the rock, and I glanced back in time to see the little man close the gate behind us.

That, I thought, was odd.

Yet I did not have a chance to alert Lotus before we rounded a blind curve into the modest parking lot of the attraction.

A hundred feet in front of us stood Katya, with a Cossack aiming a Kalashnikov directly at us. Behind them was a line of ticket booths. Peeking above that was the head of that giant warrior statue. I didn't see any castle or waterfall.

Katya held two swords, or *shashkas.*

My first reaction?

This can't be happening. Not now. Wake up, Boone. Just a horrific dream. Get out of bed, go to your rattan bar overlooking the sights of Brooklyn, make yourself a nice drink to settle you back down to some nice dreams about fishing or women.

Yet it was devastatingly, overwhelmingly real.

Lotus brought the bike to a halt and shouted "SHITBALLS!"

My second reaction?

All this way for nothing. I failed.

No plane out of Almaty.

No rooftop bar in Istanbul.

No nothing.

These are difficult emotional whipsaws to overcome and one natural response is panic. Fortunately, I did not panic, I merely dismounted the bike with Lotus and removed my helmet as Katya and her consort approached. Panic was supplanted by instinct – utterly uncalculated, mind you – that had served me and many a coward before me quite well.

Where can I run and hide?

The last time I saw Katya she was on the train platform in Dalnekrasnov pointing a finger at me. She was in a camouflage snowsuit.

Now she was all in tight black leather, her long, glowing red hair in a ponytail. Her eyes were triumphant; her lipstick was as neon as her nipples. Breath from her nostrils came out as steam in the cold. Both swords were in one hand and not brandished, which was good. The Cossack wore a long braided beard, tunic, wool turret hat and steely eyes.

I was encouraged, however briefly, that they had not shot us on sight, which would have been simple enough.

"Who is this, Boone?" Lotus hissed.

"Lotus, this is Katya, she's a coiticidalmaniac bent on killing me. Katya, this is Lotus, my friend."

Katya stepped up and threw a punch at my face – I turned so that the leathered fist landed on the side of my head, likely sparing myself a broken jaw. I stumbled backward and fell. That's what I get for being a smart ass, though in my defense, and as we've seen, being a smart ass is my sorry excuse for a defense mechanism. For those of you who have not had the pleasure of receiving such a blow to the head, yes, you do see stars.

Katya stood over me, her lips twisted into a rapturous grin.

I didn't dare stand or make any sudden moves – I grimaced from the pain, and tried to blink the stars away.

"You know, Boone," Katya began, her Slavic drawl in full bloom. "Sex and murder are very much the same."

Her swords were still not brandished, and the Cossack had his AK-47 trained on Lotus, who grimaced alternately at Katya and me with trepidation.

Unfazed by a smartass comment from me, Katya continued.

"Sex you want to consummate so badly that you rush things. It is also with murder. I almost shot you through the skull on that boat in the river. What a shame that would have been. Like sex, I was in a hurry to consummate. I have had time to consider this, and as soon as the location and direction of your cellphone was detected, I determined that I would not rush your demise but take pleasure in it as I would fucking you. Do you understand?"

The cellphone? I had been told not to turn it on way back in Russia thousands of miles back – but here? I made a bitter resolve that in my next life I would not have a cell phone – probably because karma would bring me back as a trout whose head would get smacked onto a rock by a hungry angler.

Believe it or not, altruism has a place under such circumstances, even in the midst of latent panic, desperation and resignation. Gasping from the blow to the head, I looked up at Katya and said: "I understand. Lotus does not understand. This is between you and me, right?"

Katya laughed piteously. "When you die, she dies, makes it more fun that way as you will suffer for both. I will insert this shashka up her pussy into her neck and twist. Get up, Linsenbigler."

I did so slowly, and away from her and out of reach of another punch or kick.

The empty parking lot was not anything near the magnitude of Disney or Six Flags – it could park maybe five hundred cars. The motorcycle was to one side. Behind us the road wound toward the burning truck. The Cossack with the rifle at the ready meant running or trying to run or hide was fruitless, or worse, pathetic.

"This way." Katya pointed to the empty ticket

booths. Lotus and I marched forward, our captors directly behind us.

As we crunched over chevrons of snow on the pathway and through the vacant booths, I could see ahead the golden statue. I guess it was about forty feet tall and was the depiction of a sturdy, square-jawed man in boots, tunic, belt, scabbard and boxy feathered helmet. He stood feet apart and arms straight down at his side, his gaze directly ahead and over ours toward the horizon.

Behind me, Katya snorted: "You see this statue? He is Golden Man, a statue found here in the sand. He is from third century. You like his mustache, Linsenbigler? He looks like you. Like him, you will be buried here."

There was a resemblance. Not only the whiskers and athletic build, but he was painted of gold, as I was, pure marketing gold. I wondered if The Golden Man, too, was undone by a coiticidalmaniac. Did he cocktail and fish? Unlikely. Battle likely claimed that hero of the steppes. There would be no monuments to me. As I stumbled past the giant statue – one exposed by shifting desert sands – I was reminded of the Shelley poem that I had to memorize in high school about Ozymandias:

I met a traveler from an antique land,
Who said—"Two vast and trunkless legs of stone
Stand in the desert. . . . Near them, on the sand,
Half sunk a shattered visage lies, whose frown,
And wrinkled lip, and sneer of cold command,
Tell that its sculptor well those passions read
Which yet survive, stamped on these lifeless things,
The hand that mocked them, and the heart that fed;

And on the pedestal, these words appear:
My name is Ozymandias, King of Kings;
Look on my Works, ye Mighty, and despair!
Nothing beside remains. Round the decay
Of that colossal Wreck, boundless and bare
The lone and level sands stretch far away."

Funny the things that come to the mind of the condemned. Yet that poem was as apt as they come – this was a faraway land, and my fame was as fleeting as the shifting sands. And it all came down to a winter fishing trip to Russia. Indeed, at that moment I felt kinship with the Golden Man.

I was my very own Ozymandias.

We began to descend a path between two hillocks laced with leafless trees. Lotus and I exchanged a glance that expressed only trepidation.

Above the trees, ramparts came into view – part of a fortification of some kind.

When the hillocks and trees parted, we stood before a fortress with a scenic overview of a forested but leafless and stark valley below. When I say fortress, I mean that it was like the one in the billboards, like the type you would see in movies with the Foreign Legion besieged by Arabs on camels. At the corners were towers that resembled rooks in chess, and between those, high walls topped with the gap-tooth battlements. It was constructed as a giant rectangle – perhaps a little smaller than a football field. In the center was an arched entryway angled toward us – no doors. It was taller than the flanking ramparts and topped with an inverted teardrop shape.

"You see, Linsenbigler?" Katya barked. "They built this fortress for a movie. It is fake. You are an actor; you are fake. You should enjoy dying in your element." She blurted something at the Cossack and he grabbed Lotus by the back of her leather jacket, rifle muzzle in her back. I noticed that the Cossack's hand gripping Lotus' shoulder had a tarantula tattooed on it. Just what she didn't need to see!

Lotus eyed me woefully – I don't think she felt I was any match for Katya. And I didn't think she was any match for the Cossack.

Katya stepped forward and poked me with a sword – the rod cases on my back partially deflecting the blow. "Go, Golden Man, go hide like a coward in your fortress of worthless fame. Katya will follow, and she will consummate your death by fucking you with my sword. Go!"

I returned Lotus' baleful stare with a jaunty eye meant to give her hope even though I didn't have any to give. "You haven't lost this partner yet, missy."

With that, I turned and ran toward the archway and into the fortress.

CHAPTER 26

AS I LAY DOWN TRACKS for that archway, listening intently for her footsteps behind me, I thought how bizarre it was that Katya felt compelled to dramatize killing me with her references to The Golden Man, me being fake, and killing Lotus gruesomely. And 'fucking me' with her sword really made her a prime candidate for Freudian analysis. I recalled what Beamish had said about coiticidalmania. Ramping up the emotion is what she needs – killing me was sort of a secondary way of eliciting the maximum emotional response. She was trying to instill me with as much fear and panic as possible.

So what if I didn't play into that? Could I, in turn, make her angry by denying her what she craved? If she were excessively angry, that could make her act rashly and give me an opportunity? Well, I mean, why the hell not laugh in her face? Even if she did kill me, I dare say I would rather have made it an unsatisfactory affair.

The archway was tall enough to accommodate horses and their riders, and perhaps an elephant and a giraffe –

the opening was thirty feet tall. As I approached, I could see where the brick facing had fallen away to bare plywood. I could see the joints where the wooden arch met the side panels. Indeed, the entire thing was a cheap movie prop but of enormous proportions.

Passing through the high arch, I paused long enough to look back and see Katya striding after me, a sword swinging in both hands. Ahead of me was an open dirt yard, backed by replica Moorish buildings with no doors or windows. To my left was a stair up to a catwalk that traced the battlements and interior circumference. It was where soldiers would stand to fire down on an attacking army. Turrets – those chess rooks – were installed at the four corners. The first one was a pass through. Only those at the back of the fort had spiral stair leading down to the ground. So as I dashed up the steps toward the battlements, I knew that I had a way down on the far side. Perhaps I could merely outrun her and dash back out the archway. Then again, there was the Cossack, and Lotus. I didn't have a lot of faith that she could pull off the one-two kick-knee punch and disarm the Cossack.

As I reached the top step, I raced for the pass-through rook tower in the near corner – maybe there was something in there I could use as a weapon? A mop? A shovel? A machine gun? Bazooka?

Behind me I heard Katya laughing, and shot a glance back at her.

When I passed through the archway, I had neglected to notice two large jerrycans of gasoline. Katya was pouring gasoline on the exposed wood and walls of the arch.

I had determined to remain calm, but this was a serious test of my resolve.

As I stood agape, I watched as she lit the walls of the arch on fire, the flames roaring up to the battlement level in the blink of an eye.

Katya swung a hand up at me and hollered. "There is no escape, Golden Man! You will burn as you die!" With that, she stepped toward the stair and me.

Who knew coiticidalmaniacs had such a flair for the dramatic? Even at her own expense. Of course, this same lunatic that climbed over the open ocean to my stateroom balcony. How exactly did she expect to escape this place? Perhaps her lust for powerful emotions and terrorizing me had clouded her judgment because I did not see another obvious exit from the fortress.

As I backed to the tower, I bumped into the doorframe, my rod tubes jamming into my back.

The rod tubes.

Made of steel and thirty-four inches long, they were covered in dark green fabric. The nylon webbing shoulder straps were fastened to these tubes by brass hasps and steel 'D' rings.

Unslinging them from my back, I held the shoulder strap and began to swing the rod tubes, testing their weight and potential for a weapon. I swung them over my head in a circle – if I was not mistaken, David had used something similar to fell the ogre Goliath. I reckoned swinging the rod tubes over my head could deflect her sword blows, and perhaps even inflict a significant amount of damage if I were lucky enough to make purchase with Katya's head. What remained to be seen was whether I could breach swirling shashkas to accomplish that.

I had a previous occasion to defend myself successfully using Spanish swordplay called *destreza.* The technique – as it was taught to me – incorporates turning constant circles on the opponent to try to outflank them. This would not work on the narrow catwalk with a flimsy railing at the battlements. Likely as not, someone well-versed in *destreza* would have had the necessary techniques, but I was really only a novice. What I could use to my advantage would be the twenty-foot plunge to the fortress yard. I didn't much think I had any hope of her falling through the chest-high battlements to the outside of the fort.

She wanted me to panic, and I had determined not to. She wanted me to be terrified and hide. That I could also not afford to accommodate.

Katya reached the top of the steps, her breath coming hard with excitement, her eyes wild, flames from the gasoline engulfing the wood archway behind her and making her long red ponytail seem itself like a tongue of flame.

If those nipples had been red before they likely were glowing dots of neon about then. Through her leather outfit, I could actually see the outline of her hardened nipples. Were she to summon this level of passion in the sack I would hazard to guess the fate of the unlucky fellow.

Well, I challenge anyone faced with such a vision to remain calm and not give in to shrieks of terror. If the rope bridge incident the previous year gave me night tremors, I could only imagine what howling night sweats this little church picnic would inspire were I to survive.

I tried to summon a saying of my fathers that might help engender courage, but none came. The donuts just weren't cutting it.

As she came toward me, thirty feet out, she began to twirl the swords, Cossack style, twirling and folding together like the blades of a combine.

I glanced at my fly rod tubes. They were the only weapon I had.

I needed them to be my Excalibur, my magic weapon.

I needed to channel Golden Man and stand tall and mighty in the face of my enemies.

I needed the idiotic confidence of Ozymandias that my might was of the ages.

Necessity may be the mother of invention, but survival is the father of resolve.

Katya opened her stance and the breadth of her blade swing.

She lunged.

I had no room to swing the rod tubes with my back to the doorway, so I ducked back into the dark tower behind me, and angled ninety degrees through to the other side, where I stopped and swung the rod tubes over my head.

She came shrieking from the doorway, blades brandished but not slashing. Her one blade struck the rod tubes, sparks flying. My rod tubes came around again and struck her second shashka near the tip. The force of the blow pried the hilt from her hand.

That shashka fell to the catwalk, and spun. She almost

bent to pick it up but lunged back before my rod tubes bashed her in the head.

Wobbling at the edge, the fallen shashka tilted and flipped off the catwalk, down to the dirt below in a puff of dust.

That's one down. And if I could get my hands on the fallen sword by racing down there…

Yet Katya saw what was on my mind and came in fast with a low lunge that put a crease in my pants right at my crotch.

In swordplay, I was taught that you want to limit slashing. Blades in constant motion pose a more formidable defense than offense. The time it takes to haul the blade backward – as in a golf swing – leaves you vulnerable. Less so if you are able to work two swords at once. With one blade, this is achieved through circular and figure eight motions of the blade so that little energy is wasted and the blade is in front of you as much as possible.

So to me, in my limited capacity as a swordsman, slashing was an ineffective way to use a blade, and suggested that Katya was out of her element with just one sword.

It was time to play upon all her weaknesses.

I laughed. "Well, Katya, imagine your embarrassment at the gates of hell when you have to explain that an actor – that idiot Boone Linsenbigler – killed you with a pair of rod tubes."

As I backed away, toward the other tower and stair down to the yard, Katya spat and brought herself up to full height, her single blade working a neat little figure eight as she quickened toward me.

So much for making her lose her cool; so much for her inability to work one sword.

A gust of ash and hot smoke blew across us as I swung the whirring rod tubes toward the blade.

Lost in the black cloud, there was a loud clang, a burst of sparks – my sling was tangled with her blade and I could feel her yanking.

My lungs and eyes stung from the smoke.

I yanked as hard as I could, and felt my sling come free.

Then I heard a rod tube hit the ground below me. *Thump.*

The black cloud cleared. Katya was scrambling to her feet, and I was down to a single rod tube at the end of my sling, the nylon strap frayed. Tears welled in my burning eyes, vision blurred.

I spun the rod tube over my head. My sling was lighter with one tube, and faster. I swung the tube in a fast, whirring arc, and stepped forward, the weapon aimed at her head.

She slashed, deflecting the rod tube, but I brought it around again. The rod tube burst with sparks against the blade again.

Katya lunged up at me from a crouch, blade flying.

I flattened against the battlement, grabbed my rod tube in both hands and intercepted the blow, thrusting her blade away. But she kept coming and I shoved her as she passed by me in the process. Yet the force of my shove pushed her hard to the railing, which cracked. She spun, kicked out her leg for balance and got her footing on the other side of me on the catwalk. A large section of the railing cracked away and fell to the yard where my rod tube was.

Glancing behind me, I had every intent of making for the stairs that I had used to reach the battlements in the first place.

Alas, those stairs were engulfed in flames. Now the only way down was on the other side of Katya. Jumping would only result in a sprained ankle, or worse.

A perfectly good sword was down in the yard where I could see it glinting in the roaring flames.

Katya charged again. Yet instead of trying to pin me to the battlement, she swung the blade to force me toward the railing.

As I leapt back, my foot caught on a warped plank. Tripping, my full weight hit the railing.

I felt it break away, and with my empty hand, I clawed at a railing post.

The rod tube swirled erratically from my other hand as I fell backward – and it caught Katya in the head with a *thonk* as I fell away toward the yard

A cloud of smoke and ash swept over us, and I felt the strap whip tight around my arm. The rod tube had caught on something, likely wrapped around the railing post.

The strap tight, my fall from the catwalk turned into a swing under it.

When I collided into the fort's fake wall, the strap finally broke.

I slid down the wall to the ground under the catwalk, knees bent, falling heavily to my side. Sparks and ash roiled past me and cleared. Scrambling to my feet, I seemed not to have hurt my legs in the fall. The arm that had the strap on it was a little hinky but functional.

The heat of the archway and stair fire was intense, and I coughed from the smoke. Flames danced high above the ramparts. I assumed Katya was still above me, and I scanned the yard for the twinkle of the shashka's blade.

There – off to my right. I dashed to snatch it up.

I felt a thud behind me. When I turned, blade in hand, I saw that Katya had dropped from the gantry, her sword already brandished. Blood trickled from where the rod tube caught her in the forehead, and it made a crimson zig zag down her face.

Anger, ingenuity, calculation and luck had all failed me – she was too good at this, and more than a match for Golden Man.

I dashed for the archway, which had burned so hot and so quickly that it looked as if there might be a way through the flames out of the fortress.

I stopped short – the heat was just too intense.

Footsteps came rapidly toward me and I swung my blade – I had room to maneuver, I could possibly outflank her.

Our blades clashed and she pushed in and up, catching my hilt with hers.

The swords I used with *destreza* had hilts with loop guards that protect your fingers – shashka do not, and the steel of her hilt raked my fingers from the hilt.

My weapon fell to the dirt at my feet with a dull and devastating clang.

Behind me was a wall of fire, and I backed toward it and away from Katya as far as I could without bursting into flame.

I was defenseless.

She pointed her blade at me, a zig zag of blood and a vicious grin on her face.

"Beg! On your knees and beg!" she spat.

It was then that I noticed her ponytail was on fire – apparently, some flying ash had swirled into it. As such, her long hair was like a burning fuse and it was only a matter of moments before it reached her scalp and caused her to try to put it out.

That might give me a chance to grab the sword on the ground between us.

"Why should I beg?" I shouted back above the inferno's roar, my chest heaving from all the smoke and exertion. "If I do, will I survive?"

The arch behind me made a loud groan and there was the drum roll of snapping timbers, embers swirling from the wall and around us in a hellish maelstrom, hairs melting on the back of my neck.

Greedily, she said: "You beg for a swift death for the girl!"

I realized that if I knelt I would be even closer to the shashka on the ground. So I bent my knees and began to kneel, watching as the flames from the burning ponytail finally reached her ear.

Katya screeched and swatted at her flaming hair.

I dove forward for the shashka.

Behind me, from the wall: BANG.

The groan of twisting timbers.

The shriek of splintering wood.

On my stomach in the dirt, my fist on the sword hilt, I reared back – but Katya was stepping forward and about to swing for the fences right at my face.

Behind me: WHOOSH.

The burning archway had snapped free of the walls on either side and fell inward on top of us.

WHAM.

I was positioned within the archway's opening.

Katya was not.

Before she dealt me her *coup de grâce*, the top of the flaming archway and wall landed on her like a manhole cover from a highway overpass landing on a cockroach. A burning manhole cover. OK, so maybe not like a manhole cover at all, but you get the idea.

One second that redheaded harpy hellion nightmare was about to behead me.

The next she was crushed flat by the fiery falling archway – vanished like a demon banished back to Hades by a wizard's timely spell.

I lurched backward away from the fiery wood, a cyclone of sparks swirling around me in a vortex of ash and smoke, and I had to rake the fire from my hair as I staggered back and out of the fortress.

The cool, clean air outside the fortress hit me like a refreshing wave from the ocean, and I took a moment to cough up a bunch of soot from my lungs. Wiping my mouth, I took in my surroundings.

The Cossack still stood behind and a little to the side of Lotus – he was no longer holding her. They both stared at me in wonder, their eyes alight with the burning fortress behind me. I must have been quite the sight. Like Vulcan fresh from the forge, my clothes and hair smoldering, I had emerged from a tornado of embers swirling upward from the fallen archway.

I staggered toward them, panting, sword at my side.

The Cossack seemed a little confused as to what he should do next. With Katya dead, what were his instructions as to how to proceed? She was the one who wanted to kill us. His rifle – cradled in hands that both had tarantula tattoos – was not at the ready.

Alas, you can't be too careful. Or resourceful.

I pointed at his hands and shouted: "SPIDERS!"

Lotus jerked sideways, caught sight of the tattoos, and – with a horrendous shriek – kicked at the shape of offending arachnids.

The Cossack's rifle fell to the ground, and when he bent to grab it, Lotus stepped in and kneed him full-bore in the face, his turret hat sent flying end over end in the air.

His nose broke with a loud snap, and blood shot from his nostrils into his beard.

The eyes rolled back into his head as he collapsed backward onto his heels in an awkward heap.

Lotus took a step back as though she had done something wrong, but then took a step forward and looked down at the unconscious Cossack.

Her big eyes met mine: "I did it!"

Look on my Works, ye Mighty, and despair!

CHAPTER 27

IT HAD NOT OCCURRED TO ME what Istanbul would be like in late January. It was not the semi-tropical paradise I had imagined. Just the same, Lotus and I each booked a room at Raoul's, and at my earliest opportunity I made my way to the rooftop bar. Corduroys, quarter zip and a windbreaker comprised the outfit – not the tropic-weight suit of which I had dreamed. And a tweed snap-brim cap on my head had replaced the Panama hat. They had gas-fueled fire pits on the veranda so that outdoor cocktailing was possible. The waiter came to attention next to me, and I ordered a cognac. He didn't click his heels or anything, he just went to fetch my drink. The Bosporus Sea was out there somewhere – I could hear foghorns, not a call to prayers from the local mosque. Well, if nothing else, I had the terrace all to myself, and by thunder, I'd made it. Though I'd lost both fly rods, and there had been a few last minute hurdles to overcome.

At the Almaty airport barbershop, I had to have my mane shorn short to remove all the fried hair. Likewise, my whiskers suffered mightily from the fire and had to be trimmed to what amounted to a pencil mustache. My clothes were a wreck, but I bought a tracksuit and a Golden Man T-shirt in the gift ship. In the restroom, I washed what the barber had not. In effect, I had been whittled down to a shadow of my former self and into the track-suited New Jersey native that I was. *I'll have a cawfee and hot dawg.* At least I didn't think anybody would recognize me.

As we waited in queue for the flight, a ceiling-mounted TV flashed news footage of the fire that we'd escaped. We'd taken the motorcycle cross-country on trails and intercepted the road down in the valley, avoiding any police or fire trucks.

There was a tense moment while attempting to board the plane. I had changed my appearance so much that they were not sure I was the same Bob Boone in the passport. The phony visa noted that I was a paleontologist. So to prove who I was, I launched into a detailed description of *Arstanosaurus*, a genus of the Upper Cretaceous Bostobinskaya Formation, considered both a hadrosaurid and a ceratopsid, or both at the same time, though accepted as subfamily Lambeosaurinae on the basis of the form of the caudodorsal margin of the maxilla. I offered to continue but they insisted I board.

Once aboard, I wedged myself into a corner of my economy window seat, pulled the shade and covered myself in blankets. I was sore from the horseback riding, and had bruises from the camel kick to my side, Katya's punch to my face, and my collision and fall from the fortress catwalk. I also appeared to have a sunburn, my face smeared with aloe. There were numerous times during the ordeal at which I thought I would collapse. I finally did.

The overnight flight put us at the hotel in the morning, and thankfully, we were allowed to check in straightaway, and not in the afternoon. I'd slept again until midafternoon before asking the concierge where I might buy some clothes. I was anxious to shed my Jersey togs, the ones that made me look like a Bendix Diner regular.

The result was that I had myself put together in time for cocktail hour and sought out my rooftop respite.

My reward.

My bar in the sky.

Alas, there is no rest for the weary, as they say.

No sooner did I put the snifter of cognac to my lips than I spied a gentleman approach – he was decked out in a bowler, trench coat and umbrella dangling from his arm. The swarthy complexion, sleepy eyes, and beak-like nose…

It was Beamish.

He stopped in front of me with a wry, courteous grin, the one I once trusted, but had come to distrust.

I cocked an eyebrow at him. "Sorry, Beamish, Linsenbigler is officially off duty once and for all, so there is no more subterfuge for me, I am a free man."

With a bow at the waist, he said: "Indeed, sir, and might I say how well things turned out, and largely due to your diligence and perseverance, quite remarkable."

He lowered himself into the chair catty corner to mine, the fire pit to one side, and propped his gloved hands on the handle of his umbrella.

"Spare me the compliments, Beamish; whatever you're selling this time, I'm not buying."

"You misunderstand my purpose, sir. I bring you interesting news." From his coat, he pulled a thin stack of eight-by-ten photographs and handed them to me. "Do you know what that is in the photos?"

I leaned in to the light of the fire and examined them. They were reconnaissance or aerial photos. All I could make of them was a river on one side, some forest, and then some sort of crater. It looked like some of those pictures you see from war zones. I handed them back. "I don't know what that is, no."

He raised his chin, eyes twinkling. "Did you ever wonder where that rocket just happened to come down?"

I paused. "Frankly, I had not. I've been rather busy with other matters, like escaping with my life from a series of predicaments largely precipitated by your employer."

He completely ignored that comment and handed me a close up photo of the crater. "Does that not look familiar?"

"Look, what is it you want, Beamish? I mean it, I am done with all this."

"What you see there is the dacha where you went fishing."

"That looks nothing like…"

"That is where the rocket crashed and exploded, into Putin's dacha."

I almost choked on my cognac, and broke into a heavy cough. I sputtered: "You did what?"

"Indeed, we sent it to his dacha, to let him know that we know he knows..."

"Shut up, Beamish! They told me that they were going to do something subtle to let him know I'm involved. Dropping a two-hundred foot tall rocket on his fishing lodge is not exactly subtle. You realize what you've done? Now he'll really want to kill me, he'll never leave me alone! Why are you people so set to ruin my life? Is it not enough that I'm run ragged through deserts and mountains and burning fortresses..."

"Sir, please calm yourself and try to understand. These things don't work the way you think they do."

"I know damned well that if someone blew up my fishing lodge while at the same time destroying my satellite I would be majorly miffed!"

"Mr. Linsenbigler, in our world, this is practically the only thing that would compel him to leave you alone. You see, you are now part of the great game, not just a bystander."

"Boone Linsenbigler dying in the wilderness of the Far East is not a game!"

"Sir, the 'great game' has come to be a general term to mean the game of espionage, of tit for tat, of balancing suspicions and calculated intrigue. We don't wreak vengeance on each other, only outsiders and spies die. You're now an insider."

"Oh, that's fine then, as long as we insiders survive, never mind that poor slob harpooned on the street." I stood. "If you think this means I'm now an operative like yourself or Lotus, think again."

He tossed the photos into the fire pit and they flared

and shriveled to black. Standing, he said: "Not a bit of it, unless you so choose. But let me just say that your aptitude for this work likely goes beyond your timing and other attributes."

I laughed bitterly. "I'll say. Katya had me. She was better than me – that hellion outfought me, and was a second away from sending me to my maker when the fort archway collapsed on top of her, but not me. Now come on, that's dumb luck, there's no denying that, I couldn't have timed that or made it happen."

"Indeed, that may be so." He briefly inspected his umbrella handle, lips pursed, thinking. Then he squinted at me. "Yet it could also be that you are living out a destiny — kismet, Mr. Linsenbigler. Intrigue may not be something you can avoid." He held out a hand. "I know it has not been so for you, but it has been a pleasure. *Adieu.*"

Mentally drained once again, I shook his hand and watched him vanish into the mist.

The waiter was at my side, and I handed him my empty glass. "Another, sir?"

"Eight ball says… yes! But with a lemon peel this time."

Glancing after him, I did a double take. Through the glass doors, on the television over the bar, was some news footage picturing the "Atatürk Airport" sign mounted on the main terminal overlooking the tarmac. In the foreground, Putin and the Turkish president Erdoğan were shaking hands at the foot of an airliner stair.

I followed the waiter inside, transfixed by the image

on the screen. Sunlight and lack of fog meant that this meeting took place earlier in the day. Putin was in town. He was in Istanbul that very minute. What if by some freak chance he knew I was here as well? My blood turned to ice. I didn't care what Beamish thought, or about his great game, I wanted to keep as much distance between Vlad and myself as possible. It occurred to me that I likely should not even be seen in public until he was gone – not that there was anybody else sitting in the fog on Raoul's terrace. Or likely to be.

I took the drink from the waiter and headed for the elevator. Sequestering myself suddenly seemed like the perfect plan.

When the elevator doors opened, they revealed Vladimir Putin and his five goons inside.

I drifted backward and blinked as hard as I could to make the image go away, to wake up in the plane from Almaty, but it didn't happen. How on earth did they find me? The concierge? Was he an operative? Or was it the waiter or the cab driver or maybe when I swiped my credit card at the front desk?

Goons jammed the doors of the elevator open as Putin swaggered out of the elevators dressed in a blue serge suit and matching tie that made his blue eyes pop.

His thin smile could have meant he aimed to kill me where I stood.

Or it could have meant he was ready to share some perch angling tips.

Vlad stopped in front of me, his little blue eyes fixed on mine. He put a hand on my shoulder, and tilted his head to inspect the bruise Katya had left on the side of my head, nodding with apparent approval.

Eyes back on mine, he said in a confidential tone: "You know dancing bears, yes? Spiridon Ivanovich, my grandfather, he say bear dancing on two feet is foolish, is clown, and simple for man to push to ground. But bear pushed down from two feet to four feet is no longer clown, yes? Is now bear again and quick to avenge. Yes?" He patted my shoulder, and I dare say his eyes glowed with something that looked like merry surprise. "Linsenbigler is dancing bear!"

With that, he strode back into the elevator crammed with his goons, and as the doors closed, I could see him laughing in his chest.

The cognac snifter fell from my grasp and shattered on the floor.

The waiter and bartender were at my feet in a trice with a mop and broom, and I stepped past the shards to the bar and leaned on it, head bowed. My brain was spinning in my skull.

What in blazes was that all about? When would this stop? Was that it? *Can I go home now?*

"Boone!" Lotus trotted from the other elevator and up to me. She was no longer in pigtails. Framing her face were bangs and shoulder-length black hair streaked lightly with grey. She wore a black cocktail dress, and I daresay I hardly would have recognized her if it weren't for the waning black eye. "Your publicist Terry! He's in the lobby!"

It always comes in threes, doesn't it? Lotus had heard all about Terry on our way to Istanbul, as I was afraid he might corner me and drag me kicking and screaming back into the limelight and make me relive my recent travails.

I shot an eye out at the fog bank sitting engulfing the veranda: *Well, it wasn't really that great a bar experience anyway.*

"Boone, let's use the stairs, come on!"

She led me around the corner and through a door into the stairwell. We scrambled several floors down before I asked: "Where are we going?"

Lotus stopped at a fire door to the third floor and put her ear to the door. "Shhh!"

I whispered: "We're not going to 302, my room, are we? That's the first place he'll look."

"SHHH!" She cracked open the door and peered down the hall. Rolling a hand in the air, she signaled for me to follow her, and I did. We stopped short of 302 and ducked into room 300, Lotus quietly closing the door behind us. It was much like my room next door. The brick walls hung with colorful impressionist paintings, with a large wood frame bed with white linens against one wall, and a butterscotch fabric couch opposite that. At the far end was a balcony.

"Is this your room?" I removed my tweed cap.

She let out a sigh of relief, smoothing her dress. "Yup, this is it."

I stepped cautiously further in and closer to the bed, my eyes on the balcony. "Is that an ice bucket, Dom Perignon and two flutes out on the patio table?"

Lotus started to fold her arms across her chest, but self-consciously locked her hands behind her back. "Yup, it is."

I took a step back to the door. "Well if you're expecting someone I can..."

She averted her eyes, but they finally met mine. "Shitballs. Why is this so hard?"

I waved my hat at the balcony. "Is that for us?"

"My name is Ginger. I know, it's really not much different than Lotus, really, kind of corny…but that's my real name."

"A lovely name!"

"This job…I'm not breezy like you, Boone. You're two people, the famous mustache guy on the commercials, and then you're the cocktailing angler guy who confronts adversity with amazing ease. You're comfortable switching back and forth. Me? Not so much."

I laughed softly, and she scowled at me. "Ginger, who was it that rescued you from the bandits? Who was it that helped you with the spider bot? Who was it that helped you vomit atop the mountain?"

"…who was it that pressed his hard-on into my backside on a hang glider for twenty minutes…"

"Yes, well, that was incidental, of course…and who was it that was your side-sleeper pillow? Who has a father like yours that spouts crazy sayings? Who helped you knee a Cossack in the face? I know married couples that don't have that much in common!"

"I know one thing: when you told Katya I was your friend, I felt that was true. Thanks for not getting killed. Thanks for looking through the donut so I didn't have to kill you." She waved a hand at the balcony and champagne. "Anyway, I thought a little celebration was in order now that our self-fulfilling prophesy is fulfilled."

I took her hand in mine. "Ginger, now that the bad

stuff is behind us, let's spend some time together doing good stuff and having fun while we're in Istanbul. I don't expect anything more than that – oh, perhaps a little trust. I think I've earned that."

"Did you have sex with Katya?"

By Jupiter, women have the most uncanny minds! That train switched tracks again! Fortunately, I count myself as being particularly agile when the conversation suddenly switches to my proclivities.

I said: "If I had, would she be trying to kill me?"

"But I thought…"

"Your superiors can verify that Katya came to my balcony on the Queen Mary II by crawling on the outside of the ship wearing just tennis shoes and a white fur coat. I kicked her out. You don't think I would then hop in the sack with her later, do you? As you could see – and what I saw immediately – is that she was bonkers."

Ginger laughed, her moist eyes meeting mine. 'Really? She climbed on the outside of the ship in the middle of the ocean?"

I laughed. "You doubt me after what we just saw at that fort?"

Call me an unconscionable liar if you must, but I'm a firm believer that much personal information is strictly 'need to know.' She didn't need to know. More importantly, she didn't *want* to know.

I guided her toward the champagne.

She eyed me sideways. "Boone, I have a confession."

We stopped in the doorway to the balcony. The fog had lifted, and the lights of ships twinkled in the harbor, the city on both sides like a bed of cool white embers.

The evening call to prayer warbled in the distance.

"I think I know your confession. Terry isn't in the lobby, is he? You just said that to…"

I was interrupted by a sudden thumping in the hallway – on the door of Room 302. "Boone, its Terry, open up! We've got damage control front and center on this whole hand grenade fishing thing. Boone? I know you're in there! You can't hide from this, we need to buckle down, full court press, rally the troops, run up the flag, get face time with the right people…I've got the pass key and I'm coming in!"

We listened as he keyed the lock and burst into my room. There was a pause, before his footsteps stomped back into the hall, my door slamming shut. The elevator dinged, the doors opened, and they shut.

The hallway was silent again.

I cleared my throat and blinked at Ginger. "OK, so what's your confession?"

She turned to face me, went on tiptoe, and pressed her rosebud lips to mine, one hand gently on my cheek. It wasn't a long kiss, but she meant it.

Parting, she pulled back, smiling awkwardly, that sun-flecked nose wrinkling.

"I confess that I wanted to make the first move."

'HAIL, LINSENBIGLER!'
COMING SPRING 2018

ABOUT THE AUTHOR

Brian M. Wiprud's previous novels have earned starred reviews from Kirkus, Publisher's Weekly and Library Journal. Winner of the 2003 Lefty Award, he has been nominated for Barry, Shamus and Choice awards, and been an Independent Bookseller's and regional bestseller. His books are available variously in large print, audiobook and Russian and Japanese translations, and have been optioned for film. He has also been widely published in fly fishing magazines to include American Angler, Fly Fisherman, Fly Tyer, Massachusetts Wildlife and Saltwater Fly Fishing.

<u>Previous Novels</u>

10. Linsenbigler
9. The Clause
8. Ringer
7. Buy Back
6. Feelers
5. Tailed
4. Crooked
3. Sleep with the Fishes
2. Stuffed
1. Pipsqueak

Made in the USA
Middletown, DE
13 December 2018